D1016551

Other Fresh-Baked Mysteries by Livia J. Washburn

The Pumpkin Muffin Murder

Killer Crab Cakes

The Christmas Cookie Killer

Murder by the Slice

A Peach of a Murder

The Gingerbread Bump-off

Wedding Cake Killer

The Fatal Funnel Cake

A Fresh-Baked Mystery

LIVIA J. WASHBURN

AN OBSIDIAN MYSTERY

OBSIDIAN
Published by the Penguin Group
Penguin Group (USA) LLC, 375 Hudson Street,
New York, New York 10014

USA | Canada | UK | Ireland | Australia | New Zealand | India | South Africa | China
penguin.com
A Penguin Random House Company

First published by Obsidian, an imprint of New American Library,
a division of Penguin Group (USA) LLC

First Printing, November 2013

LIBRARY OF CONGRESS CATALOGING-IN-PUBLICATION DATA:
Washburn, L. J.
The Fatal funnel cake: a fresh-baked mystery/Livia J. Washburn.
p. cm.—(Fresh-baked mystery)
ISBN 978-0-451-41661-2 (pbk.)
1. Newsom, Phyllis (Fictitious character)—Fiction. 2. Baking—Fiction.
3. Weatherford (Tex.)—Fiction. 4. Murder—Investigation—Fiction. I. Title.
PS2573.A787F38 2013
813'.54—dc23   2013020028

Printed in the United States of America
1   3   5   7   9   10   8   6   4   2

Set in New Caledonia   •   Designed by Elke Sigal

*Dedicated to the State Fair of Texas
and to Big Tex for all the joy you
gave to adults and kids alike.*

The Fatal Funnel Cake

Chapter 1

$\mathcal{S}$ am Fletcher came into the living room, sat down on the sofa, looked at the television, and said, "I just don't get cookin' shows."

From the other end of the sofa, Phyllis Newsom glanced over at him. "That's because you're not a cook," she said. "I've never understood the appeal of fishing shows."

"Me neither," Sam said. "Now, I like to fish, mind you, but the idea of sittin' there and watching some other fella sit in a boat and fish—well, that's just not something I want to spend a lot of time doing."

Carolyn Wilbarger, who was sitting in one of the recliners—but not reclining—had her knitting in her lap. Without looking up from her needles and yarn, she said, "At least it's not NASCAR. Why in the world anyone would sit there and watch a bunch of cars drive around and around all day is just totally beyond me."

From the other recliner, Eve Turner added, "Anything is

better than those awful reality shows where people sit around and yell at each other all the time."

"They should make a reality show about us," Sam said.

The three women all turned their heads to look skeptically at him, even Carolyn. She said, "A reality show about a bunch of retired schoolteachers living in a house in Weatherford, Texas? I don't think that's what TV producers consider dramatic, Sam."

"We've got plenty of drama," Sam said. "Why, you could make a whole show just about Phyllis and the way she—"

He stopped in midsentence, and Phyllis was glad he had understood the warning look she was giving him.

For more than six months now, ever since the tragic events following Eve's wedding and honeymoon, there had been an unspoken agreement in this big two-story house on a shady side street in Weatherford: No one talked about murder.

Of course, it was hard to forget how that ugly subject had come up on a number of occasions in recent years. More than once, a member of this very household had fallen under suspicion, and it was thanks to Phyllis's efforts that the actual killers had been uncovered. Sam was probably right, she thought. Some sensationalistic television network probably could make a series about the murder cases in which they had all been involved. But the chances were that everything would be changed for TV and the results would be dreadful. Not only that; it would draw way more attention than any of them wanted. From what Phyllis had seen, becoming a celebrity often ruined a person's life.

So it would be just fine with her if no one ever mentioned the word *murder* around her again.

Sam, bless his heart, knew that, even though he had forgotten for a moment. So now he changed the subject by saying, "What show is this, anyway? I know I've seen that gal before."

"Of course you have," Phyllis said. "I don't see how anyone could have missed seeing her in the past few years. This is *The Joye of Cooking*, and that's Joye Jameson."

"Nice-lookin' young woman," Sam said.

Carolyn said, "Hmph. Trust a man to reduce everything to physical appearance."

Phyllis felt like she ought to come to Sam's defense, so she said, "Well, you can't deny that she *is* attractive."

That was true. Joye Jameson, who was in her midthirties, Phyllis estimated, had a wealth of thick, wavy auburn hair that framed a heart-shaped face with a dazzling smile. At the moment she wore an apron over a green silk blouse that went well with her hair and coloring and matched her eyes. The apron had a sunburst design embroidered on it.

With the camera on her, Joye stood at a counter covered with mixing bowls, spoons, a rolling pin, and the other utensils and accoutrements of the project she'd been working on during today's show. Smiling that unshakable trademark smile directly into the camera lens, she said, "That buttermilk pie we put in the oven a while ago ought to be just about ready. Let's have a look at it, shall we?"

She turned and went along the counter, and the camera angle changed to show her opening an oven. Using pot holders, she reached in and took out a glass pie plate that she placed on a cooling rack on top of the counter.

"I think it looks beautiful," Joye said as yet another camera took an overhead close-up of the pie, which did indeed look good with its lightly browned crust and filling. The shot went back to Joye as she continued, "Of course, we'll have to let it cool before we cut it, but we have another one just like it that I baked earlier today. A couple of tips about serving this heavenly pie. If you want to avoid a messy, crumbly pie, let it cool to room temperature before slicing. I know what you're thinking— you like your pie warm with ice cream. If that's the case, you can either have a messy slice, or put that slice in the microwave and warm it up a little before putting the ice cream on top. And the last but not least important tip about serving: Don't lick your fingers between each served piece."

She turned, revealing that while the camera had been pointed elsewhere, someone had placed a second pie on the counter. It was already cut into pieces. Joye took one of them out with a pie server and put it on a fine white china plate decorated with flowers around its edge. She picked up a fork, cut off a bite, put it in her mouth, chewed, and closed her eyes for a second in obvious pleasure before she said, "Oh, my, that's good."

There was a close-up of the piece of pie with a bite missing, then another shot of the whole pie that had just come out of the oven. "Now, remember, if you'd like a copy of the recipe, it's on the website," Joye went on. "And if you'd like tickets for the show here in Hollywood, you can request them through the website as well."

Applause came from the previously unseen studio audience as a camera panned over them, then went back to Joye.

"Now I have a special announcement," she said. "In two weeks the show will be going on location to Dallas, Texas, for the big State Fair of Texas. For those of you unfamiliar with it, it's a spectacular fair held every fall with cooking and arts and crafts competitions galore! We'll be showcasing some of the winners, and I'm very excited about sampling some of the best cooking in the great state of Texas."

Carolyn had lost all interest in her knitting for the moment. "Did you hear that?" she asked Phyllis.

"I heard," Phyllis replied. She couldn't stop herself from leaning forward a little on the sofa. Joye Jameson's announcement definitely had caught her attention.

Joye went on, "One thing we're going to be doing . . . Do you know what a funnel cake is? Do you know, Hank?"

The camera that had been on Joye swiveled around so that it showed another of the huge, bulky TV cameras, along with the burly, shirt-sleeved man running it. He grinned and shook his head. Phyllis couldn't tell if he really hadn't heard of funnel cakes before or if he was just playing along with Joye.

"How about you, Reed?" she asked, and the camera moved to another man, this one wearing a suit and a headset. He didn't look particularly happy about being on television, but he forced a smile and shook his head.

"A funnel cake is a delicious deep-fried treat that's poured from a funnel into hot oil," Joye continued as the shot returned to her. "I'm sure a lot of you have had them. They're a legendary snack at state and county fairs all over the country, along with corn dogs and cotton candy and lemonade. The ones at the State Fair of Texas are supposed to be some of the best, so we're going to find out. I plan to try the winning recipe from this year's funnel cake competition. Won't that be fun?"

More applause from the audience indicated that they agreed with her. Either that or the APPLAUSE sign was flashing, Phyllis thought, then scolded herself for being a little cynical.

"So if you're in Dallas in a couple of weeks, or anywhere in the vicinity, I hope you'll drop by and see us. We'll be broadcasting live from the fair every day!" Joye's smile threatened to overwhelm the screen. "In the meantime, I'll see *you* tomorrow, and remember . . . always find the joy in life every day!"

More applause, more shots of the happy audience. One of the cameras pulled back to reveal the set with cameras, boom microphones, and crew members arrayed around it. Joye picked up her fork and resumed eating the piece of pie she had taken a bite of earlier. Credits began to scroll up the screen as a young woman with long brown hair, wearing jeans and a sweater, came out from the wings to talk with Joye. The shot switched to a graphic of the show's website address and some fine print that Phyllis didn't bother trying to read.

"Isn't there a cookbook called *The Joy of Cooking*?" Sam asked.

"Yes, there is," Phyllis said as she used the remote to mute the sound on the TV.

"But she calls her show *The Joye*—with an *e*—*of Cooking*?"

"That's right."

"And she can get away with that?"

Carolyn said, "Joye is her name. How could anyone complain about that?"

"I'm not complainin'. Just strikes me as a little strange, that's all."

"Cooking shows strike you as strange," Carolyn said with a dismissive note in her voice. "You said so yourself." She turned to Phyllis, pointed a finger, and went on, "You heard what she said."

"I did," Phyllis said.

"You know what that means. We have to go."

Sam said, "To see that show?"

"No, to the state fair," Carolyn said. "Why don't we make a week of it? We can enter some competitions, check out all the exhibits—"

"Maybe ride some of the rides on the midway," Eve suggested.

"I think we're all too old for roller coasters," Carolyn said.

Eve smiled. "Speak for yourself."

Phyllis was glad to see that. It had taken quite a while for Eve to start getting over everything that had happened, but she was beginning to get some of her usual feisty nature back. If Eve wanted to ride a roller coaster, that was just fine.

But she might have to ride it by herself. There was no way Phyllis was getting on one of those things.

She said, "I have to admit I'm intrigued by that funnel cake competition. I've never made any before. I think it would be fun to give it a try."

"I think I'll stick to the more traditional baking contests," Carolyn said. "I've got a new cookie recipe I'd like to try out."

Something occurred to Phyllis to temper her enthusiasm. She said, "There's just one problem. The fair is in Dallas. That's a pretty long drive to be making every day, and think of the traffic."

"My cousin lives in Highland Park," Carolyn said. "That's just right up the freeway. She's been asking me to come visit her. Her husband passed away last year, you know, and her children are all grown and gone, so she has that big empty house. I'm sure she wouldn't mind."

"You don't think we'd be imposing?" Phyllis asked.

"No, I don't. It certainly won't hurt to ask."

"That would make it a lot easier," Phyllis admitted.

Sam had gotten up and gone over to the computer desk in the corner, evidently having lost interest in the conversation about the state fair. Now he turned the desk chair around to face his housemates again and said, "You know what? They have other kinds of cookin' contests besides the ones for pies and cookies and funnel cakes and stuff."

"Like what?" Phyllis said.

A grin stretched across Sam's craggy face. "Like the notorious Spam cook-off."

"Why in the world would we be interested in a Spam cook-off?" Carolyn wanted to know.

"Well, I wasn't necessarily thinkin' about you ladies . . ."

Carolyn's eyes widened. "You?" she said. "You're going to enter a cooking contest?"

"I was thinkin' about it. I've fried up many a panful of Spam in my time. And you and Phyllis seem to get so much fun out of these competitions, I figured why not give it a try?"

"Why not indeed," Phyllis said. "I think it's a fine idea, Sam."

"I still think it's odd," Carolyn said, "but you can do what you want, I suppose. Then it's settled. If my cousin agrees to let us stay with her, we're going to the state fair."

Phyllis nodded and said, "We're going to the state fair."

Chapter 2

Carolyn's cousin Peggy Stockton was more than happy to have Carolyn visit . . . and her three friends, too. So two weeks later the four of them packed up, loaded their luggage in the big trunk of Phyllis's Lincoln, and set off for Dallas.

Under normal conditions the trip would take between an hour and a half and two hours, Phyllis knew. The thing was, you never could tell what sort of traffic you'd encounter along the way. It usually wasn't too bad in Fort Worth—although it could be if there was a wreck or construction—but in Dallas it was almost a given that there would be a traffic jam somewhere. Because of that, Phyllis had asked Sam if he would mind driving. Her nerves weren't meant for sitting at the wheel of an unmoving car stuck in traffic.

"Sure," he'd said. "I don't much like that bumper-to-bumper stuff, either, but I can handle it."

At least they didn't have to be at Peggy's house at any particular time, so they didn't have to worry about that. Carolyn had told her cousin they would be there sometime around noon but insisted that Peggy not go to any fuss over them.

"I don't think she will," Carolyn had told the others. "Peggy's not really the type to make a fuss over anything. She's very levelheaded. Salt of the earth, you know."

"Then how did she wind up in Highland Park?" Eve had wanted to know. "That's where all the snooty upper crust live, isn't it?"

Earlier in the year, the others had discovered that Eve was much more well-to-do than they had believed she was, but no one could ever call her *snooty*. She had continued teaching for years, despite her wealth, simply because she enjoyed it and thought she was doing something worthwhile.

"Not everybody in Highland Park is a millionaire," Carolyn had said. "It just so happens that Peggy's late husband was a pretty successful businessman, but he certainly didn't start out that way. Starting out, he had just one little furniture store in a bad neighborhood, and they struggled for years to build the operation into a chain. When they finally had some money, he wanted to give Peggy a nicer place to live, so they moved."

Phyllis was looking forward to meeting Peggy. If she was anything like Carolyn, Phyllis knew they would get along . . . although Carolyn could be a little prickly at times.

Phyllis was glad that she and Carolyn wouldn't be competing directly against each other at the fair. Over the years since their retirement from teaching, they had entered many of the same cooking and baking contests, and although the competition had remained friendly, a rivalry between the two of them definitely existed.

They had looked over the list of state fair contests online, and Carolyn had settled on the cookie contest. Since contestants didn't have to preregister or send in recipes ahead of time, just show up with the cookies they wanted to enter on the day of the contest, she was going to enter in three different classes: drop cookies, icebox sliced cookies, and bar cookies.

The funnel cake competition Phyllis entered was different. It was a special contest in which the entries would be prepared at the state fair, during the competition. With funnel cakes there was really no other way to do it, since they were best eaten fresh, as soon as they had cooled slightly from the boiling oil in which they were fried.

Phyllis made the first batch using a funnel cake pitcher but didn't like pouring the batter that way. It felt like cheating. She wanted to learn to make them using a funnel, so she bought a good funnel and spent a week experimenting with recipes, to the point that her housemates were probably sick of funnel cakes . . . except maybe for Sam, who had a prodigious appetite and had been blessed with a metabolism that allowed him to eat as much as he wanted and never add an ounce of fat to his lanky frame.

Since funnel cakes were all made basically the same way, the differences came in things that could be added to the recipe and the cake maker's skill at manipulating the funnel and drizzling the batter into the hot oil. Phyllis had watched videos of people who were able to create dazzling patterns within the traditional roughly circular shape of a funnel cake. She didn't think that she could manage to compete on that level without years of practice . . . but she was confident that she could come up with a funnel cake that looked acceptable and tasted great.

So she had experimented with pumpkin funnel cakes, strawberry funnel cakes, French vanilla funnel cakes, chocolate funnel cakes, and several other varieties. She had dusted them with regular powdered sugar, with powdered sugar and cinnamon, and with powdered sugar and nutmeg. She had made funnel cakes from biscuit mix and pancake batter, frosting the latter with maple syrup.

As Carolyn had commented at one point during the week, "Good grief, it's a wonder we're not all in diabetic comas already!"

Phyllis hadn't quite settled on the recipe she wanted to use yet, but she still had a few days to prepare and planned to get in some more practice while they were staying with Peggy. Ultimately she thought it would be fun just to go to the fair and see everything, as well as compete, and if they got a chance to attend one of Joye Jameson's live cooking shows, so much the better.

The drive from Weatherford to Fort Worth and on past downtown went smoothly. It wasn't until they reached the stretch of interstate highway between Fort Worth and Dallas that traffic began to slow down. This was a busy area and a big tourist destination at certain times of the year, with the amusement park Six Flags Over Texas and the stadiums of the Texas Rangers and the Dallas Cowboys all within about a mile of one another on the south side of the highway. Six Flags was closed during the week now, open only on weekends since school began, the football games were on the weekend as well, and the baseball games were at night. Even so, there were lots of people going about their everyday business and lots of cars. Sam wasn't ruffled as he navigated the traffic, though.

It got worse as they passed Arlington and the Dallas skyline came into view up ahead. The traffic wasn't particularly slow, but it was heavy, and Phyllis wasn't sure but what that was worse. Being completely surrounded by cars, pickups, vans, SUVs, and eighteen-wheelers, all of them going sixty-five to seventy miles an hour only a few feet away, was nothing if not nerve-racking.

"I still don't know why people watch NASCAR," Carolyn said. "They could just watch Dallas traffic cameras instead."

"What would drive me crazy," Eve said, "is all the roads that come in from all directions all the time. How can you ever be sure you're in the right lane?"

"Oh, it's not too bad," Sam said. "All you have to do is be able to look in six different directions at once."

Eventually they reached downtown Dallas and negotiated the exit that put them on North Central Expressway, which would take them to Highland Park, the exclusive neighborhood adjacent to Southern Methodist University. Phyllis was glad when they finally got off the freeways and were back on residential streets.

Peggy's house was a two-story brick structure behind a green lawn. A circular drive bordered by shrubs and flower beds ran in front of the entrance. In a lot of neighborhoods the place would have been considered a mansion, but in Highland Park it was just a normal house—if anything, perhaps a little smaller and less fancy than most. Of course, Phyllis thought as Sam pulled the Lincoln into the driveway, with the rise of those so-called McMansions, big, fancy houses weren't as uncommon as they once had been.

The front door opened as Sam stopped in front of it. Out

came a short, stocky woman with silvery hair and glasses, wearing blue jeans and a man's shirt with the sleeves rolled up a couple of turns. She must have been watching for them, Phyllis thought.

Carolyn got out of the car and hugged the woman as the others were getting out. "Everyone, this is my cousin Peggy," she said. She introduced Phyllis, Eve, and Sam in turn.

"I'm glad you were all able to come," Peggy Stockton said. "Let me help you with your bags."

"I can get 'em," Sam said. "You ladies go on inside and get acquainted."

"Nonsense. I insist. Now, open the trunk, Stretch."

"His name's Sam," Carolyn said.

Sam grinned and said, "I know what she means." He opened the trunk.

Everyone pitched in carrying the bags inside, and Peggy showed them their rooms on the second floor. When they were back downstairs in the living room after freshening up, Phyllis told their hostess, "You have a lovely house here, Peggy."

"It's too much house for one old lady—that's for sure," Peggy said. "But Lloyd liked it and I can't imagine getting rid of it. I'll have to, one of these days, when it gets to be too much for me to keep up with, but for now . . ." She shrugged. "I'm just glad not to be rattling around in it by myself for a while."

"I know that exact feeling," Phyllis said.

"That's why we all moved in with her," Carolyn added.

"You can tell me all about it over lunch," Peggy said. "Hope you're not expecting anything fancy. I've got a lady who comes in and helps me keep the place clean, but I do all my own cooking and I have simple tastes. I've got tuna fish sand-wiches in the refrigerator."

"Sounds good to me," Sam said.

She eyed him up and down and said, "You've got a hollow leg where all the food goes, don't you?"

"I have been blessed in that manner, yes," Sam said, still smiling.

Peggy jerked a thumb over her shoulder toward the dining room. "Come on, we'll see if we can fill you up. I like a chal-lenge."

As they were going into the dining room, Carolyn whis-pered to Phyllis, "See? I told you she was very down-to-earth."

Phyllis certainly couldn't argue with that.

Over lunch, which included an excellent fruit salad as well as the sandwiches, Peggy said, "So all of you used to be teachers, eh?"

"That's right," Phyllis said. "I taught American history in junior high, Eve was a high school English teacher, and Sam taught math and coached."

"Basketball, right, Stretch?"

"Yep," Sam said. "And volleyball and baseball and the line-backers and defensive backs on the football team. It was a small school."

"That's the best kind. Some of these schools now, my God, they're as big as shopping malls! About as warm and wel-coming, too. Of course, I'm on the outside looking in, but it seems to be that education's just become a big business, when it's not being used as a political football."

"Some places it's like that, I suppose," Phyllis said. "When we were teaching we tried to make it more than that."

"Oh, I don't doubt it. It's not the teachers' fault. It's those bozos in Austin and Washington. How can anybody do a good job running something when they've never actually done it themselves?" Peggy lifted both hands in the air, as if surrendering. "But they don't ask our opinion, do they? They just do things to suit themselves, like always. So all of you are widowed, right?"

Carolyn looked slightly uncomfortable, and Peggy's sudden change of subject made her wince. But Phyllis said calmly, "That's right. We've all lost our spouses. And when I said that I knew what you meant about rattling around in a big house, I meant it. That's why I decided to rent out some of the rooms in the place to other retired teachers." She smiled. "Although it's not really like they're boarders. We're all more like family now."

"Well, it's good you had friends. That's a hard thing to get through when you don't have anybody else close." Peggy sounded like she knew that from experience. She looked at Phyllis and went on, "You're the one who solves murders, like some detective on TV."

"No, nothing at all like that," Phyllis said. "I've just helped the police figure out a few things—"

"Are you psychic?"

"What?" Phyllis shook her head. "No, not at all."

"Got some sort of mental condition that makes you brilliant but wacky in the head?"

"Uh . . . no. I don't think so."

Sam burst out laughing.

"Well, how can you solve crimes, then?" Peggy wanted to know. "It's got to be one of those two things. Or forensics."

Phyllis said, "I just . . . sort of figure things out . . ." She turned to Sam, who had restrained his laughter but was still shaking. "You're not helping."

Peggy suddenly grinned and said, "Aw, I'm just messin' with you, honey. I want you folks to feel at home while you're here, and we don't tiptoe around things in this house. We just come right out and say whatever we're thinking."

"I'll keep that in mind," Phyllis said.

"This is gonna be a good trip," Sam said as he picked up his glass of iced tea and lifted it as if he were toasting Peggy across the table.

Phyllis could only hope that he was right.

Chapter 3

Peggy had said that she wanted them to feel at home here, so Phyllis took her at her word. That afternoon she and Carolyn familiarized themselves with Peggy's kitchen, which was spacious and furnished with every kind of gadget anyone could think of.

"I told Lloyd this was more kitchen than I needed," Peggy said as she sat at the big butcher-block table sipping a cup of coffee. "He insisted, though, bless his heart, and I didn't want to disappoint him."

"He sounds like a wonderful man," Phyllis said.

"He had his moments. And he was a heck of a kisser."

That brought a smile to Phyllis's face. She already liked the plainspoken Peggy quite a bit.

"No kidding, I'd like to hear more about that murder stuff," Peggy went on. "I never knew anybody who caught killers before."

"I don't actually catch them . . . ," Phyllis said, although there had been a few times Sam had physically corralled one of the criminals whose schemes Phyllis had uncovered.

Carolyn said, "It's not nearly as exciting as it sounds. She just talks to people and thinks about what they tell her. It's just a matter of paying attention, the way we always told our students. Isn't that right, Phyllis?"

There was a little more to it than that, Phyllis thought, but she didn't really want to have this conversation and she certainly didn't want to sound like she was bragging about her abilities as a detective. So she said, "That's pretty much what it amounts to, all right."

"You must be one of those gals people open up to," Peggy said. "I never was like that myself. Folks seem to clam up around me. Darned if I know why."

"We've been trying not to talk about the whole crime-solving business around Eve," Carolyn said. "She suffered quite a loss last winter and we don't want to remind her of it."

"Mum's the word when she's around—got it. Say, what about that tall drink of water Sam? Pretty good-lookin' for a skinny old man, isn't he? I'm surprised one of you ladies doesn't have your hooks in him yet." Peggy raised her eyebrows. "Or maybe one of you does. Maybe more than one. A man living in a houseful of women like that, he might just consider it his own private harem—"

"Peggy!" Carolyn said. "That's enough of that kind of talk!" Instantly, she was apologetic. "Of course, it's your house and you're being kind enough to let us stay here, and you can say anything you want—"

"Take it easy, Carolyn. I'm not offended. I just wondered what the story was."

"Oh. Well, I suppose you could say that Phyllis and Sam have a sort of understanding."

Phyllis would have just as soon that Carolyn hadn't said that, but she wasn't going to deny the affection she and Sam felt for each other. She didn't see anything wrong with down-playing it a little, though.

"We just enjoy each other's company," she said. "It's nothing serious."

"Well, there's two ways of looking at that," Peggy said. "At our age, who needs serious, right? I mean, we've likely had our share of drama in our lives already."

"Exactly."

"But on the other hand," Peggy continued, "none of us are getting any younger, so if there's still something out there that's important to us, we'd better not waste any time going after it, you know what I mean?" She took a sip of coffee. "We're all probably going to need somebody with medical power of attorney sooner rather than later."

Carolyn said, "Oh, goodness gracious, I don't want to think about that."

"You better think about it, dearie," Peggy said. "None of us know how long we're going to be here, or be in any shape to make important decisions."

"The only important decisions *I* have to make are what kind of cookies to enter in those contests."

"I hope that's true for you for a long time yet."

That sort of put a damper on the conversation for a while. After half an hour or so, Sam wandered into the kitchen while Phyllis and Carolyn were sitting at the table, too, talking about recipes.

Peggy perked up immediately and said, "Honey, we were just talking about you."

"Thought I felt my ears burnin'," Sam said with a smile. "Should I say thank you or just deny everything?"

"Oh, it was nothing bad. I was just telling these ladies that they're lucky to have a man around the house. You know, to handle the heavy lifting and get things down from high shelves."

"That's about all I'm good for, all right. That and my sparklin' wit and dashin' good looks."

"Yes, there's that," Phyllis said. "I notice that it's almost time for Joye Jameson's show. You don't mind if we watch it, do you, Peggy?"

"Help yourself. There's a fifty-two-inch plasma TV in the den. Another of Lloyd's ideas. And the cable system's got every channel under the sun, including some that completely baffle me as to why anybody would ever watch them."

Carolyn said, "I know exactly what you mean."

The four of them moved to the den. Eve had gone up to her room to lie down after lunch, something that she did most days, and Phyllis didn't want to disturb her. Eve wasn't a particular fan of *The Joye of Cooking*, although she would watch it if she happened to be in the room. She was more interested in the other lifestyle features that Joye Jameson did, rather than the cooking.

After they had watched for a few minutes, Carolyn said, "This episode is a rerun. I remember seeing it before. She's going to cook tamales."

"That sounds good," Peggy said. "Probably more complicated than I could ever manage, but I wouldn't mind watching."

"Oh, I wasn't saying we shouldn't watch. That's fine with me."

During the next commercial break, Peggy said, "Seems like I used to watch a show like this several years ago, but it didn't have this girl on it. I think the woman who did it was named Gloria or something like that."

"Exactly like that," Carolyn said. "You're thinking of *Gloria's Kitchen*. The host was named Gloria Kimball."

"Yeah, that's her. Whatever happened to her?"

"She retired from *Gloria's Kitchen*," Phyllis said, "but she's still on TV. Here in Dallas, in fact. She does cooking and lifestyle segments on *Good Morning 44*."

"What's that, the morning show on Channel 44?" Peggy said. "That explains it. I'm never up that early. I'm not one of those people who get up with the sun. I like my sleep."

"She's all right," Carolyn said, "but she's no Joye Jameson. I guess she just couldn't keep up with the pace of a successful network show anymore."

The show went to a commercial again, and during that break there was an announcement that *The Joye of Cooking* would air live the next day from the pavilion of the State Fair of Texas.

"That's why they're showin' a rerun today, I'll bet," Sam said. "They're busy gettin' all set up for tomorrow."

"More than likely," Phyllis agreed.

Carolyn said, "We should go to the fair tomorrow and watch. The cookie contest is the day after tomorrow, so I'll be busy then."

"I think that's a good idea," Phyllis said. "The funnel cake contest is the next day, too."

"Not at the same time, I hope."

Phyllis shook her head. She had checked the schedule for conflicts. "No, the cookie judging is in the morning, and they won't be doing the funnel cakes until that afternoon."

"And the Spam cook-off is a couple of days after that," Sam put in.

Phyllis frowned slightly in concern. "Are you going to be ready so soon?" she asked him.

"Sure. It's just a matter of decidin' which recipe I'm gonna use. I hope you folks like Spam, because I'm gonna need some guinea pigs between now and then."

"Just what are you going to fix?" Carolyn asked with a wary look on her face.

"Well, I was thinkin' about making Spam enchiladas."

Phyllis said, "That's unusual, but it doesn't sound bad."

"Then there's the Spam tamale pie."

Carolyn said, "I'm sensing a Mexican food theme here."

"And the south-of-the-border Spam cups with biscuits, cornmeal, cheese, and black beans."

"That actually sounds good," Phyllis said.

"But I'm leanin' toward Texas-style Spam sushi," Sam went on. "It's sort of like Mexican food, too, since it has jalapeño peppers in it. It's a Texas twist on Hawaii's Spam *musubi* recipe."

Carolyn didn't look too enthusiastic about that one, but Phyllis said, "I'm looking forward to trying whatever you come up with, Sam."

Peggy said, "You know, you can make just about any sentence dirty by adding the words *in bed* after it."

Carolyn frowned. "What in the world made you think about that?"

"Oh, just the way Phyllis said she was looking forward to trying anything Sam came up with."

"Oh, good grief! Grow up and get a grip on yourself."

Peggy let out a cackle. "In bed!"

Phyllis felt herself blushing, but at the same time she wanted to laugh. It was terribly juvenile humor, the sort of thing her eighth graders would have come up with back when she was teaching, but she had to admit that Peggy made it funny.

Sam looked a little embarrassed, too. He pointed at the TV and said, "Uh, the show's back on."

"Yeah, but it's not as good as the show here, Stretch," Peggy said. She laughed again and went on, "Don't worry, I'll behave myself."

Eve came downstairs a few minutes later and asked, "What was so funny? I heard laughing while I was upstairs."

"Nothing," Carolyn said. "It was just something on the TV. You had to be here."

She obviously didn't want the subject raised again, so Phyllis and Sam didn't say anything. Neither did Peggy, although Phyllis saw a smile lurking around her lips and could tell that Peggy was having trouble restraining herself. For Carolyn's sake, though, she did it.

"We're going to the fair tomorrow to see Joye Jameson's show," Phyllis said, thinking it best that they move on, too. She turned to their hostess and went on, "You'll come with us, too, won't you, Peggy?"

"I don't know," Peggy said. "I don't want to intrude on your outing."

Carolyn said, "Nonsense. How could you possibly intrude?"

"Well, it might be fun at that. You know, I've lived in Dallas my whole life, and yet I've never been to the state fair."

"That's not unusual," Sam said. "A lot of folks never take in the sights that are right in their own backyard. When they want to do something special, they go farther off."

"It's settled, then," Phyllis said. "We'll all go, and we'll have a fine time."

Of course, that last part wasn't settled yet, she reminded herself . . . but one could always hope.

Chapter 4

$\mathcal{S}$aying that Fair Park, where the State Fair of Texas was held and where the Cotton Bowl was located, was just down the road from Peggy's house didn't necessarily mean that the drive was easy, not when the roads involved were North Central Expressway and Interstate 30, also known as the R. L. Thornton Freeway. Traffic bound for the fair was already backed up on both highways by the time Phyllis and her friends approached their destination the next morning. Sam was at the wheel of the Lincoln again, with Phyllis in the front seat and Eve, Carolyn, and Peggy in the back. All of them were dressed casually and comfortably. It was going to be a warm autumn day, and since they expected to do quite a bit of walking, they had all opted for sensible shoes as well.

Eventually they reached the exit that took them to the parking area and the main entrance to Fair Park. As a rule Phyllis didn't like crowds, but as they joined the throng of people entering the fairgrounds and strolling along the esplanade, she couldn't help but feel a little excitement. Everyone was here for a good time.

"There's Big Tex," Sam said, nodding toward the giant animatronic figure of a cowboy that had replaced the rebuilt Santa that had welcomed visitors to the fair for decades. It was located not far inside the fairgrounds in a circle where several roads came together. A deep voice boomed out, "Howdy, folks!" over loudspeakers as people posed in front of the figure for photographs taken by friends and family members.

"Huh," Peggy said. "I thought he'd be bigger. You know, after that fire that destroyed the one they had for so long, I thought they were going to make the new one a lot bigger. But he's still pretty impressive, I guess."

"He's plenty big enough for me," Carolyn said. Then she pointed a finger at her cousin and warned, "Don't you say it."

"Me?" Peggy asked in broadly feigned innocence. "What could I possibly say that would embarrass you, Carolyn?"

"Just remember," Carolyn said sternly.

Sam chuckled and Phyllis tried not to smile, while Eve said, "It seems like I never know what's going on anymore."

"Don't worry, dear," Carolyn told her. "Some people are going through their fourth or fifth childhood, or else they never grew up to start with."

"Should we all stay together?" Phyllis asked as they began walking around the fairgrounds. "With this many people, if we got separated I don't know if we could ever find each other again."

"Well, we all have cell phones," Sam pointed out. "So I reckon if anybody got lost we could get in touch that way. But I don't have any problem with staying together."

"You don't mind looking at quilts and crafts?"

"As long as you ladies don't mind lookin' at cars and trucks later on," Sam said with a smile.

There were so many things to see, Phyllis hardly knew where to begin. So they just started walking and took things as they came to them, which meant strolling through pavilion after pavilion filled with arts, crafts, industrial exhibits, historical displays, and museums. Endless food vendors lined the roads and walkways. Corn dogs, cotton candy, frozen lemonade, and dozens of other treats ranging from the mundane to the bizarre vied for fairgoers' attention. After a while Phyllis began to wonder if there was any kind of food that *couldn't* be dipped in batter, dropped in boiling oil, and deep-fried. Of course, anything that couldn't be fried could have bacon wrapped around it. Or chocolate. Or both. If anyone came to the fair looking for healthy, nutritious snacks, they were likely going to be disappointed. She had to admit, though, everything looked and smelled absolutely delicious.

They passed the cattle, swine, and horse barns, which added a definite, distinctive aroma to the air in that area of the fairgrounds. They walked through the midway with its Texas Star Ferris wheel towering more than two hundred feet, roller coasters, and games of chance, then looked up at the elevated skyway cars, running back and forth on thick cables, which gave riders an aerial view of the fair.

Looming over everything was the aging grandeur of the Cotton Bowl, which had been filled with screaming fans for some of the most epic college and professional football games ever played. Phyllis knew that Sam, a die-hard Dallas Cowboys fan, still had bitter memories of his team's loss to the Green

Bay Packers in the championship game played in the Cotton Bowl nearly fifty years earlier. Of course, as Sam had been known to point out, the Cowboys' loss in the infamous Ice Bowl a year later had been even worse. Phyllis had vague memories of both games herself, since her late husband, Kenny, had usually watched the Cowboys play.

There was so much to see and do, Phyllis didn't realize she was getting tired until early in the afternoon, when the group paused for lunch. But then it all caught up to her, and she said, "I'm glad we're going to see Joye's show next. I'll be glad to sit down in a nice, air-conditioned building for a while."

The others chimed in, agreeing with her, and when they had finished with a definitely unhealthy meal of deep-fried jambalaya, chicken-fried cactus bites, fried bacon-cinnamon rolls, and iced tea, they started toward the Creative Arts Building, where the cooking contests would take place and where *The Joye of Cooking* would be broadcast all week.

They probably should have gotten here earlier, Phyllis thought as she saw the lines of people filing onto some temporary bleachers that had been set up. The seating faced a low stage set made to look like a kitchen. It was surrounded by cameras, boom microphones, and other pieces of broadcasting apparatus that Phyllis didn't recognize. Wires and cables ran everywhere. She didn't see how anyone could ever keep them all straight.

A man and a woman, each wearing a headset and carrying a clipboard, ushered the audience onto the bleachers, which weren't at all fancy. They looked like something that would be found in a small high school's gymnasium.

As Phyllis and the others got in line, Sam said, "I don't

know if we're gonna get a seat or not. Looks like lots of folks want to see this Joye Jameson."

"Of course they do," Carolyn said. "This is one of the most popular shows on cable in the whole country. Her cookbooks are best-sellers, too. She has millions of fans."

A man standing near them turned and nodded. "She sure does," he said. "And I'm one of 'em."

He wasn't in line to watch the show. Instead he wore the uniform of a security guard, with a name tag pinned to his shirt that read CHET MURDOCK. He was short and broad, muscular rather than fat, had close-cropped brown hair, and wore glasses.

"I can't believe I was lucky enough to get assigned here this week," he went on. "I could have been stuck on the midway or in one of the livestock barns, but instead I get to watch one of my favorite shows being broadcast live."

"And get paid for it at the same time," Sam pointed out.

"Yeah," Chet Murdock said. "That sure doesn't hurt."

"Do you think they're going to run out of seats before they get to us?" Phyllis asked.

Chet studied the line of potential audience members and the rapidly filling seats for several seconds before he said, "I dunno. They might. But you can always come back tomorrow and get here earlier. Joye's going to be broadcasting from here all week."

Carolyn said, "We know. But we're going to be entering some of the cooking contests tomorrow."

"Really? Which ones?"

Phyllis didn't see anything wrong with passing the time by chatting with the friendly guard. She said, "My friend is in several of the cookie contests, and I'm going to be entering the funnel cake contest."

That put a grin on Chet's face. "I love me some funnel cakes," he said, patting his belly as he added, "As you can probably tell. I also love to cook. I probably would have been a chef if I hadn't gotten into the security business."

He walked along beside them as the line slowly advanced. Carolyn said, "You must get to see a lot of behind-the-scenes things in your job."

"Oh, yeah. I've worked all sorts of concerts and celebrity appearances. I could tell you stories about some of those folks . . . Let's just say that for every celebrity who's more nice and down-to-earth than you'd expect them to be, there are a dozen who are just as obnoxious as they can be. It's not just the stars, either. Take that guy."

Chet nodded discreetly toward a man in a suit who had come out onto the kitchen set. He had a Bluetooth unit tucked in his ear and was talking animatedly even though there was no one around him. A pair of headphones hung around his neck, even though he wasn't wearing them at the moment. Wires ran from the various devices down to battery packs on his belt that were visible under the open suit coat he wore. Slender, sandy haired, and handsome, he had a familiar look about him, but it took Phyllis a moment to realize where she had seen him before. He had appeared briefly on camera during the episode they had been watching the week before, when Joye Jameson had asked one of her cameramen and then this fellow if they knew what funnel cakes were.

"His name's Reed Hayes," Murdock went on. "He's the

producer of the show. I don't see how they put up with him. He's always complaining about something."

"Well, that's a producer's job, I suppose," Phyllis said. "It's up to him to make sure that everything goes smoothly."

"Maybe so, but he talks awful sharp to everybody. Except Ms. Jameson, of course. Everybody sort of tiptoes around her, even Hayes."

Carolyn asked, "Is she one of those obnoxious celebrities?"

"Not really," the guard said with a shrug of his beefy shoulders. "Oh, she's got a temper, I guess. I've seen her get mad a couple of times since they've all been here. But mostly she's sweet and smiling."

"A man may smile and smile and be a villain," Eve said. "That's Shakespeare. A paraphrase of the Bard, anyway."

"Yeah, but Ms. Jameson's not a villain," Chet said, looking shocked that anyone might think so.

"No, dear, of course not. But I used to teach high school English, so quotes like that spring to my mind."

"What I really don't get," Chet continued, "is how Ms. Broderick puts up with Hayes."

"Who's that?"

"Bailey Broderick." Chet pointed discreetly at the woman with the headset and clipboard who was waving people onto the bleachers. "She's Ms. Jameson's assistant, but Hayes keeps her loaded down with work, too, since she's also the assistant producer."

Phyllis looked at the young woman and recognized her from occasional appearances on the TV show, as well. Bailey Broderick was the person who checked on things cooking in the oven and took them out while Joye was on camera so they would be ready for the star whenever Joye was ready to show off her latest culinary creation.

"And the worst part about it is, Hayes is supposed to be her boyfriend," Chet went on. "Like I said, I don't know how she puts up with it."

"You know an awful lot about what goes on here, considering that these people just got here yesterday," Carolyn said.

Chet shrugged. "I pay attention to everything. That's what they pay me for, after all."

The line had moved closer to the bleachers, which weren't quite full yet. Phyllis began to hope that they would get seats after all, although from the look of things they would have to climb almost all the way to the top row. She supposed they could manage that. It would be good exercise, she told herself.

They had almost reached Bailey Broderick. The young woman was really very pretty, Phyllis thought, although the jeans and sweatshirt she wore didn't do anything for her, and neither did the way she had her long chestnut hair pulled back into a plain, functional ponytail. She wore a harassed expression, which was understandable considering the things Chet Murdock had said about her demanding job.

She was about to wave Phyllis and the others into the bleachers with the clipboard in her hand, when loud, angry voices suddenly cut through the hubbub of conversation in the big hall. Bailey glanced in the direction of the commotion, muttered, "Oh, no, not her!" and hurried off, leaving Phyllis and her companions unsure what to do next.

The man who was working with Bailey stood at the other end of the bleachers. He called, "Keep moving down there!" and made a curt gesture with his clipboard. Phyllis could tell he was talking to her, so she started climbing the steps that led to the top rows. Sam and the others followed.

"Looks like there's some sort of trouble," Carolyn said. "Why am I not surprised?"

Phyllis wanted to tell her not to start that. Carolyn's implication was that trouble followed her, and that just wasn't true. A few months earlier they had all gone to the annual Peach Festival in Weatherford, and nothing out of the ordinary had happened. Certainly no murders.

But as they reached the top row, where the only empty seats were located, Phyllis turned and looked down at the kitchen set. Several people stood there, stiff with anger and tension, and Phyllis couldn't help but wonder what was going on.

Chapter 5

$\mathcal{D}$own on the set, Reed Hayes was apparently being lectured by an attractive, well-dressed woman with sleek blond hair. A few feet behind her stood a man carrying a handheld video camera. He wore jeans and an open flannel shirt over a T-shirt, and with his shaggy dark hair and short beard he bore a strong resemblance to Maynard G. Krebs, the beatnik character from the old *Dobie Gillis* TV show, Phyllis thought, only he was stocky while Maynard had been slender. At the moment the camera the young man carried was pointed toward the floor.

Hayes tried to interrupt the blonde, but she wasn't having any of it. She kept up her finger-waving tirade. Bailey Broderick stood over to one side, looking like she wanted to intervene but wasn't sure what to do.

The spectators in the bleachers had begun to notice the confrontation, and more and more of them fell silent as they tried to see and hear what was going on. Phyllis could hear the blond woman talking, but she couldn't make out the words.

Peggy said, "Hey, I know her. That's Gloria Kimball."

Peggy was right, Phyllis thought. She knew the blonde looked familiar, but she hadn't recognized her until Peggy's comment. Gloria Kimball, the former host of *Gloria's Kitchen*, was now a feature reporter on a local Dallas TV station. It made sense that she would be here for Joye Jameson's show, thought Phyllis. In the cooking, home, and lifestyle areas, Joye was a star, and her visit to the State Fair of Texas was certainly newsworthy. The fact that Gloria's formerly nationally syndicated program had been transformed into the even more successful *Joye of Cooking* just added to the story.

Carolyn commented, "Gloria doesn't appear to have aged much."

"Celebrities never do," Sam said. "It's probably all that plastic surgery."

Eve said, "Either that or they have portraits of themselves in the attic."

Peggy smiled, clenched her fists, and moved them around a little in front of her. "Maybe Joye Jameson will come out and they'll have a fistfight." She nudged Sam with an elbow. "Bet you'd like that."

Sam just cleared his throat and didn't say anything. He was saved from having to respond to Peggy's gibe by a sudden eruption of applause from the audience. They had spotted a familiar figure coming through a door at the back of the set.

Joye Jameson wore tan slacks and a bright green blouse and looked beautiful and wholesomely sexy, as always. As she approached the group at the front of the set, the bearded young man with Gloria Kimball started to swing up his camera. Reed Hayes took a quick step to block him and put a hand on the camera, forcing it back down. The young man jerked back and looked like he was about to throw a punch at Hayes, but a large, burly figure loomed up behind him. Phyllis recognized the cameraman called Hank who worked on *The Joye of Cooking*. Joye often joked with him about various things. One of his hands came down on the shoulder of the younger, smaller cameraman, who appeared to think twice about starting a fight.

The audience continued to applaud for Joye, who waved and bestowed one of her dazzling smiles on them. "Thank you, thank you, everyone," she said, her voice carrying clearly despite the fact that she wasn't wearing a microphone. "My, what a wonderful welcome to Texas!"

Gloria Kimball said something to her. As Joye turned toward the blonde, she was still smiling. Nothing seemed to shake that. Instead of joining in the argument, Joye put her arms around Gloria and gave her a friendly hug. Gloria was stiff at first, but she seemed to relax after a moment.

Keeping an arm around Gloria, Joye looked at the audience in the bleachers and said, "Let's hear it for Gloria Kimball, people! Without her I wouldn't be here today!"

More applause welled up, punctuated by occasional cheers. Gloria actually smiled a little. She glanced over and said something to Reed Hayes, who shrugged, nodded, and motioned to the bearded cameraman, who, it was now obvious, had arrived with Gloria and probably worked for Channel 44. He brought his camera to his shoulder and started recording the reunion of the two cooking show stars.

"Isn't that sweet?" Peggy said dryly.

"It looks like Joye put a stop to that argument, whatever it was about," Carolyn said. "I'm not surprised. Who could stay angry with her?"

Gloria had been holding a small microphone. She lifted it now and launched into an impromptu interview with Joye that lasted a couple of minutes. Phyllis couldn't make out any of it except that Joye was glad to be here in Texas and looked forward to getting together with Gloria and trading new recipes and tips. While that was going on, Hayes kept checking his watch, and the producer finally said something to Joye, who nodded. She hugged Gloria again and moved toward the door through which she had come a few minutes earlier. While the camera was still on her, Gloria turned and said a few more words into the microphone, then lowered it at the same time the cameraman lowered his equipment. Phyllis assumed they had been recording a segment for the local channel's newscast or morning show. Hayes hadn't wanted to allow it at first, but Joye had overruled him. Now things could get back on schedule.

"Well, that was exciting," Peggy said as Gloria and her cameraman left the set and moved off into the crowd. "Even if nobody threw a punch."

Carolyn said, "Joye Jameson would never stoop to brawling."

Maybe not, Phyllis thought, but only the presence of the burly cameraman, Hank, had stopped a fight from breaking out between Hayes and Gloria's cameraman.

She noticed the security guard, Chet Murdock, standing near the set. He had probably been ready to break up any struggle that had started.

With Gloria Kimball gone, the danger of that was past now. The time for the broadcast to start was rapidly drawing closer. Technicians scurried around the set. Hank and the other cameramen took their positions. Reed Hayes consulted something on his smartphone, swiping a fingertip across the display in swift, curt motions. He put on a headset, probably to allow him to communicate with the director outside in the network's satellite truck. After talking to someone for a moment, Hayes pointed to Bailey Broderick and nodded.

Bailey set her clipboard aside, removed her headset, and picked up a wireless microphone. She went to the front of the kitchen set, smiled up at the audience, and said into the microphone, "Hello, everyone!"

That greeting quieted the crowd. Still smiling, the young woman went on, "Hi, I'm Bailey, Joye's assistant, and I want to welcome all of you to our first live broadcast from the State Fair of Texas!"

Whooping and clapping surged from the audience.

"We're very glad to be here for the world's biggest and best state fair!" Bailey continued, and that drew an even more enthusiastic response. Phyllis didn't know if that "biggest" claim was true, and "best" was certainly a subjective judgment, but clearly the audience was in full agreement on both counts and that was really all that mattered right now.

"The show will be starting in a few minutes," Bailey said, "and there are a few things you need to know. We don't insist on absolute silence, but you'll need to be quiet while the broadcast is going on, except when the applause signs are lit up." She pointed to portable signs on both sides of the stage, out of view of the cameras. "I want you to understand, no matter what you might think, the purpose of those signs is *not* to order you to applaud. They're just there to let you know that it's all right to clap, that it won't interfere with what we're doing during the broadcast. But Joye wants me to make it clear that these are just general guidelines. If she or one of the guests says something, or if something happens that makes you want to applaud, you go right ahead, whether those signs are lit up or not. *You're* the reason we're all here, and the real purpose of this is for all of *you* to have *fun*!"

She was good at warming up the crowd, Phyllis thought as more applause followed Bailey's words, even though she had sort of contradicted herself about the applause signs. Phyllis took it to mean that the people involved with the show wanted the audience to be spontaneous, but they wanted it to be a controlled spontaneity.

"Now, if you'll just sit back, it'll only be a few more minutes before we get started," Bailey concluded. "And don't forget to have a great time!"

Smiling, she waved to the crowd as she moved back through the set and disappeared through the door at the rear. Reed Hayes followed her. The members of the crew stood around the set waiting, and the feeling of anticipation in the air grew stronger.

Sam leaned over to her and whispered, "This is where somebody screams because they've just found a dead body backstage."

"You hush!" Phyllis told him in an emphatic whisper. "Nothing of the sort is going to happen."

But she had to admit, that worrisome thought had crossed her mind, prompted by Carolyn's comment earlier. Sometimes it really did seem like trouble followed her around. And not just run-of-the-mill trouble, either.

Murder.

From the Peach Festival to an elementary school carnival to Christmas and Thanksgiving celebrations, over the past few years Phyllis had been involved with enough murder cases to make her wonder if she was an out-and-out jinx. She had seen her friends accused of being killers, and once she had even wound up behind bars herself. It certainly hadn't been the peaceful life she'd envisioned for herself when she retired. How was it possible that she'd been able to live for almost seven decades with very few encounters with crime, even of the most trivial sort, only to find herself stumbling over bodies and chasing murderers at her advanced age?

She had no answer for that other than sheer happenstance, but there was no denying that the events of recent years had had an effect on her. She was more alert than ever for potential trouble, and she paid close attention to everything that went on around her. There was no telling when some little thing that someone said or did might turn out to be the last, vital piece of the puzzle that would reveal a killer's identity to her. She didn't necessarily want to be that way. It had become a matter of habit.

Or maybe she was just paranoid, she told herself sternly as she sat with her friends and waited for *The Joye of Cooking* to get under way. After all, it was crazy to think that something terrible was going to happen right here in the middle of the state fair, in front of hundreds of people . . .

The door at the rear of the set opened.

Phyllis held her breath.

And Joye Jameson came onto the set with a smile on her pretty face and a spring in her step as her recorded theme music welled up. A red light glowed on the camera Hank pointed at her as she said, "Howdy, Texas and the rest of the country! Welcome to the show!"

Chapter 6

"Admit it," Carolyn said later that evening at Peggy's house. "You expected something to happen, didn't you?"

"Where?" Phyllis said, although she had a pretty good idea she knew what her friend meant.

"At the fair this afternoon, when there was that trouble at Joye Jameson's show."

The two of them were in the kitchen, where Carolyn had a batch of cashew butterscotch shortbreads for the next day's contest in the oven. She took out the second log of cookie dough and removed the parchment paper. While the first batch was baking, she sliced the second log, putting the chilled cookie slices on the baking sheet. She filled the baking sheet just as the first batch was ready to be taken out of the oven. Carolyn looked around for an oven mitt to pull out the hot cookies. Phyllis commented, "Those sure do smell good."

Carolyn found the oven mitt and took out the cookies, putting the second pan in to cook. She set the timer and asked, "Is there anything I can do to help you while these bake?"

Phyllis was doing some last-minute experimentation with her maple pecan funnel cake recipe. The others were all in the living room.

"I didn't see any real trouble," Phyllis said. "Just a slight misunderstanding. I'll bet Gloria Kimball showed up to tape a segment for Channel 44 and didn't clear it ahead of time with Joye's producer. He tried to stop her, and she gave him an earful."

"Yes, but what about the hard feelings between Gloria and Joye?"

"What hard feelings?" Phyllis asked. "They looked like the best of friends to me when they were hugging each other."

Carolyn opened the oven door slightly and bent down to look in and check on the baking cookies. As she straightened, she said, "Hmph. What were they going to do, start pulling hair and trying to claw each other's eyes out in front of all those people? You know how phony celebrities are. They just pretended to be friends so the crowd wouldn't know how much they hate each other."

"I don't recall ever reading anything about how they're supposed to hate each other. Didn't Joye used to work for Gloria?"

"See, you've proven my point," Carolyn said. "It's *All About Eve* all over again. The ambitious assistant stabs her boss in the back and winds up with the top job."

Phyllis shook her head. "I just don't see it."

"But for a second there, you wondered if there might not be a murder backstage."

Phyllis didn't like to admit it, even to herself, but she knew that Carolyn was right: For a second, even before Sam had made his none-too-humorous joke, she had expected *something* bad to happen. When it hadn't, she had been relieved.

"I'm just glad there wasn't any trouble, that's all," she said now. "We've all had more than our share."

"No one's going to argue with that," Carolyn said.

She continued working on the cookies while Phyllis fried funnel cakes. Sam came into the kitchen a while later and said, "You ladies have got this house filled with the most irresistible smells." His gaze fell on a sheet of cookies that were cooling, and he took a step toward them.

"Touch one of those cookies and I'll break your arm," Carolyn warned. She sounded like she meant it, too.

Sam held up both hands in surrender and backed away from the counter where the cookies were sitting. "You *are* makin' some extra besides the ones you have to enter in the contest, aren't you?"

"We'll see," Carolyn said. "For now, keep those meat hooks of yours off of them."

"Yes, ma'am," Sam said with a grin. He looked over at Phyllis, who was smiling, too. "I hope you're not gonna be as stingy about those funnel cakes."

"Help yourself," Phyllis told him. "Although how you can be hungry after that supper you put away is beyond me."

"It's a gift," Sam said as he scooped up one of the maple pecan funnel cakes covered in maple syrup and pecans.

Carolyn said, "We were just talking about what happened at the fair today."

"You mean when I almost got sick from eatin' too much cotton candy?"

"No, and you know good and well what I mean. Joye Jameson's show."

"Yeah, Phyllis got a little annoyed when I said something about how they were liable to find a body backstage."

"It's nothing to joke about," Phyllis said. "After all the tragedy we've seen, we should all know that murder is no laughing matter."

"I agree," Carolyn said. "It's not funny. But it *is* bizarre sometimes, the way you seem to be attracted to it."

"Or vice versa," Sam added.

Phyllis rolled her eyes, shook her head, and said, "You're both crazy. Anyway, nothing happened at Joye's show, and since we've already seen an episode, we probably won't be going back. I don't particularly want to get in that mob again, and the three of us all have contests to enter the next two days."

"That's true," Sam said. "I have to decide which Spam recipe I'm gonna use. They've all been pretty good so far."

Phyllis had to agree with that. Sam had surprised her with his abilities in the kitchen. He had made a breakfast casserole, south-of-the-border Spam cups, enchiladas, tamale pie, and the Texas-style sushi, all with Spam, and Phyllis had enjoyed each and every one of them. If it had been up to her, she would have been leaning toward the tamale pie, but it was Sam's decision, of course.

Carolyn said to him, "Actually, I didn't know you could even cook. I assumed that like most men, even microwaving something was a challenge to you."

"Well, I guess I've picked up a few pointers from watchin' you ladies," he said. "I just needed to practice some."

Phyllis smiled and said, "You may regret this, Sam. Now that we know you can cook, we may be expecting you to prepare meals more often."

"You mean, never let folks know you're good at something, because then they'll figure you can do it again."

"Exactly."

"Like solvin' murders."

Phyllis narrowed her eyes, and Sam took that as his cue to grab one of the plates with a funnel cake on it and beat a hasty retreat, still grinning as he left the kitchen.

The five of them left earlier the next morning, knowing that the traffic would be bad, and arrived at Fair Park not long after the gates opened. Carolyn had three plastic containers with her, each containing two dozen cookies. She also had the three recipes printed out neatly, and an entry form for each class of cookies in the contest.

Phyllis could tell that her friend was nervous as they walked toward the Creative Arts Building. Carolyn had competed in dozens of cooking contests over the years, but now she was going up against bakers from all over the state and possibly even out of state. Of course, it wouldn't be the end of the world if she didn't win or at least finish among the top ranks, but it would be quite an accomplishment if she did.

"I'm sure you're going to do fine," Phyllis said, hoping to reassure Carolyn. "Those are excellent cookies."

"They sure are," Sam said, adding, "I appreciate you lettin' me sample them last night."

"Well, you *are* a reliable judge of cookies, I suppose," Carolyn said. "You've done pretty good about predicting the outcome of contests in the past." She smiled. "Of course, that's probably because you always tell Phyllis and me that we're going to win, even when we're competing against each other."

Phyllis said, "You didn't know that we knew that, did you?"

Sam chuckled. "If I said one of you was gonna lose, you might not let me sample the entry next time. Anyway, you're both always in the top two or three, so I just hedge my bets. If Eve entered the contests, I'd have a trifecta to put my money on."

"Don't hold your breath waiting for that to happen," Eve said. "You don't really bet money on cooking contests, do you, Sam?"

Sam just smiled.

"Good grief," Carolyn said. "Where would you even find a bookie to take a bet on something like that?"

"There are fellas who'll bet on just about anything," Sam told her. "Of course, they're sick in the head. They're gambling addicts. I'm not like that, mind you, although I do like a good wager now and then."

"Well, I hope you haven't lost too much money betting on us," Phyllis said.

"Oh, I'm ahead of the game. You can count on that."

They had reached their destination, and Phyllis was grateful to Sam for helping to take Carolyn's mind off the upcoming contest for a few minutes. She was convinced that was what he'd been doing. She didn't think he had actually bet on any of their contests . . . although she couldn't rule it out entirely.

The main hall of the big building was filled with dozens of tables where the judging for the various contests would be held. Phyllis and her friends looked around until they found the spot where the entrants in the cookie contest were checking in. A lot of women and more than a few men had lined up to turn their samples over for judging, which would take place between ten and eleven o'clock, with the ribbons awarded after that.

"Wonder how a fella would go about gettin' to be a judge in these contests," Sam mused.

"I have no idea," Phyllis told him. "I'm sure you could find out if you really wanted to, though."

He smiled and shook his head. "Nah. I'd hate to have to come to Dallas every year. Besides, if I had to pick somebody's pie or cake or cookies as the best, that means I'd be disappointin' all the other people in the contest, and if there's one thing I hate, it's disappointin' lovely ladies such as yourselves."

"Hmph," Carolyn said. "I've never been disappointed by a man. In order to be disappointed, you have to expect something in the first place."

Peggy laughed and said, "That's telling him, honey."

Phyllis enjoyed listening to their banter, but at the same time, her eyes were roaming over the inside of the hall, not looking for anything in particular, just checking out all the people and seeing what was going on.

That was how she came to spot a familiar figure acting rather furtively. Hank, the big cameraman, was moving through the crowd with his shoulders slumped and his head bent forward as if he were trying to make himself less noticeable, something that was going to be difficult for a man of his size. He was nowhere near the part of the building where the kitchen set for the TV show was located.

Whatever Hank was doing, it was none of her business,

Phyllis told herself. But she watched him anyway, until he disappeared into what looked like some sort of service corridor. Phyllis was about to turn her attention back to her friends when something else caught her eye.

Another person she recognized ducked into that same corridor, acting almost as suspicious as Hank had, and Phyllis had to ask herself a question.

Was Bailey Broderick following the cameraman . . . or having a rendezvous with him?

Chapter 7

It was none of her business, of course. Phyllis knew that in the past she had been accused of being a nosy old busybody, poking into affairs that weren't her concern. She didn't see it that way, but she supposed she could understand why some people would have that attitude toward her. What they failed to realize was that she had just been trying to get to the truth in order to help her friends. She wasn't going to turn her back on that responsibility.

In this case, though, there was nothing for her to investigate, and even if there had been, she wasn't personally acquainted with any of the people involved. No matter what Bailey and Hank were doing—if, in fact, they were doing anything at all—Phyllis had no stake in it whatsoever.

So she gave a little shrug, mental as much as physical, and turned back to the table to watch as Carolyn officially entered her cookies in the contest.

Sam said to the woman in charge of the entries, "Might as

well save time and give this lady three blue ribbons right now. Nobody's cookies are gonna beat hers this year."

"That's all right, Sam," Carolyn said. "You shouldn't be trying to influence the judges."

"Our judges are above reproach," said the woman sitting at the table. "I'm sure you feel that way about your wife's cookies, sir, but we'll have the contest anyway."

"Wife!" Carolyn repeated. "You think this man is my husband?"

"That's all right, honey," Sam said. "You don't have to claim me if you don't want to."

Phyllis stepped between them, took hold of Sam's left arm and Carolyn's right one, and said, "Come on, you two. Let's let these people go on about their business."

That was good advice for everybody, she thought.

It would be more than an hour before they learned the results of the contest, so in the meantime Phyllis led the little group away from the cookie contest tables, saying, "Let's take a look at some of the entries in the other contests."

They strolled past tables full of pies and cakes, and it was just sheer happenstance that they headed toward the entrance of the service corridor where Phyllis had seen Hank and Bailey a short time earlier. If it wasn't happenstance, it was her subconscious that led them there, she told herself when she realized where they were going. It certainly hadn't been a conscious decision on her part.

But since they were right there, she couldn't help but notice when Hank emerged from the corridor, still acting rather furtive. The others were looking at a table where half a dozen lovely chocolate cakes were displayed. Phyllis didn't hurry them along. She kept an eye on the corridor, and sure enough, Bailey appeared a couple of minutes later, eyes downcast and hurrying through the crowd.

Phyllis was about to ask herself once again what that meant, when she noticed a sign above the corridor entrance with the universal symbols for restrooms, phones, and water fountains on it. That was the answer right there, she thought. Hank and Bailey both had to use the restroom. Nothing sinister or mysterious about it. The idea that they'd been, well, skulking was just a figment of her imagination.

Bailey's route through the hall took her past where Phyllis was standing. Without thinking about what she was doing, Phyllis nodded and said, "Hello, Miss Broderick."

Bailey stopped short and actually flinched. It was a guilty reaction if Phyllis had ever seen one. The young woman stared at her and demanded, "Do I know you?"

"No, no," Phyllis said quickly. "I'm just a fan of *The Joye of Cooking*. I was at the broadcast yesterday, and I've seen you on the show many times before that."

"So you think that just because you've seen me on TV, you know me? You consider us friends? Is that it?" Bailey looked and sounded angry now, which was completely at odds with the way she seemed to be on television. "What is it you want from me?"

"Why, nothing," Phyllis said, somewhat flabbergasted by Bailey's reaction. Or overreaction, rather, she thought, and once again she was reminded of the way a person who felt guilty about something might act. "I just recognized you and said hello."

Bailey's eyes widened, and now she looked stricken. "Oh,

my God," she said. "Did I actually just do that? I nearly bit your head off just because you said hello to me. I can't believe it. I'm so, so sorry. I just . . . I . . ."

"It's all right," Phyllis said, sensing how genuinely upset Bailey was. "I imagine you're under a lot of pressure. It's got to be a tremendous amount of work putting on a TV show from somewhere like this."

"You don't know the half of it, Ms. . . . ?"

"Newsom. Mrs. Phyllis Newsom."

Bailey summoned up a weak smile and put out her hand. "And you know who I am, obviously. I'm glad to meet you, Mrs. Newsom, and again, I'm sorry for the way I acted."

"That's quite all right, dear," Phyllis said as she shook hands with the young woman.

"Not really. I had no right to act like some prima donna celebrity when I'm pretty much a nobody."

"I taught school for many years," Phyllis said, "and one thing I made sure my students knew was that they weren't nobodies. Everyone has value."

Bailey smiled and canted her head slightly to one side, as if to say that was a nice ideal but not something that was necessarily true in real life.

"Anyway, I'd like to make it up to you," she went on. "You say you're a fan of the show?"

"Yes, and so are my friends." Phyllis glanced over her shoulder, expecting to see Carolyn, Sam, Eve, and Peggy standing there, but to her surprise the four of them had wandered off and were several tables away, looking at more contest entries and having no idea Phyllis was talking to Joye Jameson's assistant.

"Well, here's what I want you to do," Bailey said. "Come by after today's broadcast and I'll see if I can introduce you and your friends to Joye. It'll just be for a minute, mind you—"

"Oh, a minute would be fine," Phyllis told her. "I'm sure they'd all be thrilled, and so would I. That's very nice of you, Miss Broderick."

"Bailey. And without fans like you, well, we wouldn't have a show, would we?" She reached into the pocket of her jeans and took out a business card. As she handed it to Phyllis, she went on, "If anybody tries to stop you or gives you any trouble, you show that to them and tell them I said you were welcome. And if they have any questions, they can come and ask me."

Phyllis took the card and nodded. "All right. Thank you."

"We'll see you later, okay?" Bailey smiled again and turned away, and it wasn't until she had disappeared in the crowd that Phyllis remembered the funnel cake competition was this afternoon. She might not be able to visit the broadcast set after all. It would all depend on how long the contest lasted.

They might be able to meet Joye later in the week, but for now maybe she would be better off if she didn't say anything to the others, Phyllis decided. She was turning back toward them when Peggy said, "Hey, weren't you just talking to that girl from the TV show? What was that all about?"

So someone had noticed her talking to Bailey after all, Phyllis thought. And since the others had come up to her in time to hear what Peggy said, now they all knew about it. Well, it wasn't that big a deal, Phyllis told herself. She smiled and nodded.

"Yes, I was talking to Bailey Broderick," she said. "You

know, Joye's assistant. We just sort of bumped into each other and got acquainted. She, uh, told me to come by the set after the broadcast this afternoon and she would try to introduce us to Joye."

"Really?" Carolyn said. She looked impressed, and Phyllis knew from experience that it wasn't easy to impress Carolyn Wilbarger. Carolyn frowned and went on, "But won't that conflict with the funnel cake contest?"

"I don't really know. The contest might be over by then." Phyllis paused, then added, "And you know, I don't actually have to enter that contest . . ."

"Nonsense," Carolyn said without hesitation. "I've seen how hard you've worked trying to come up with a winning entry. You're not going to just walk away from the chance."

Sam said, "Carolyn's right. Meetin' some TV personality doesn't stack up to that."

"Celebrity is pretty shallow, anyway," Eve put in. "Some people are famous just for being famous. Like that girl whose family owns all the hotels."

"Or Snoopy," said Peggy. "No, wait a minute. That's the dog from the comic strip. Who am I trying to think of?"

Phyllis wasn't sure and didn't really care. She said, "Let's just wait and see what happens. If the funnel cake contest is over in time, we'll go right over to the broadcast set and see if Miss Broderick can introduce us."

"And if it's not, it won't be the end of the world," Carolyn said. "That sounds like the sensible approach to me."

Before they could talk about it anymore, an announcement came over the loudspeakers that the ribbons for the cookie contest were about to be awarded. Carolyn's eyes got wide with excitement and anticipation. She turned and led the way back to the part of the hall where the awards presentation would take place.

The ceremony was low-key, not really a ceremony at all. All it amounted to was several members of the judging committee going around to the tables placing ribbons beside the winning entries. A woman wearing a name tag announcing her status as a judge stopped in front of the table where Carolyn's butterscotch sandies were displayed along with several others in the icebox sliced cookie class. Phyllis held her breath as the woman's hand reached out with a blue ribbon in it.

The blue ribbon went down next to someone else's plate of cookies. That brought a cheer from the winner and her supporters, but Phyllis heard a sigh come from Carolyn.

"There's still second or third place," Eve said. Carolyn shrugged.

The other two ribbons didn't find their way to Carolyn's entry, either. Sam said, "Well, those folks just don't know what they're doin'. Those were some of the best cookies I ever ate."

"Don't coddle me, Sam," Carolyn said. "I can stand being defeated."

The judges moved on to the next class. Carolyn didn't have an entry in that one, but then the suspense level rose again as they reached the table where her pumpkin oatmeal bar cookies were on display. Again Phyllis held her breath as the judges placed the first-, second-, and third-place ribbons on the table next to those entries.

"That's all right," Carolyn said when none of those ribbons wound up next to her cookies. "They may have considered that cookie too cakelike. I never really expected to win, you know."

Peggy said, "I don't much care for contests that have to be judged. It's too damn subjective. Give me a race anytime, where you can see who wins with your own eyes, or a game with a scoreboard where you can see every point go up."

"There's an old sayin' about how the scoreboard doesn't lie," Sam agreed.

"Well, it's not that way in cooking," Carolyn said, "and if you're trying to cheer me up, there's no need. I'm fine."

That might be what she wanted them to believe, but Phyllis knew better. She and Carolyn had been friends for too long and competed against each other too many times. She knew how the competitive fire burned inside Carolyn.

But there was still a third contest, and Phyllis thought that Carolyn's dark and nutty Nutella drop cookies were the best of the three she had entered. She watched eagerly as the judges moved on to the tables where those entries were set out on plates with their recipes above them.

The woman with the blue ribbon headed straight for the plate with Carolyn's cookies on it. Phyllis was afraid she would go past it or turn aside, but as the judge neared the plate her steps slowed, and she reached out and almost delicately placed the blue ribbon next to Carolyn's cookies.

Beside Phyllis, Carolyn let out a long sigh. When Phyllis glanced over, smiling in happiness—and a little relief—for her friend, she saw that Carolyn's eyes were closed.

"Are you all right?" Phyllis asked.

"Yes. Just enjoying the moment." Carolyn sighed again and opened her eyes. "A state fair blue ribbon winner! Can you believe it?"

"If you were a fella, I'd give you a big ol' slap on the back,"

Sam said. He settled for patting Carolyn on the shoulder instead. "Good job, pal."

"Thank you." Carolyn accepted hugs of congratulations from Phyllis, Eve, and Peggy. "I was trying not to let it bother me, but I have to admit . . . I'm so glad I won!"

"So are we," Phyllis said. "You deserved it."

"I predicted it all along," Sam said. "Just like I'm predictin' that Phyllis will win that funnel cake contest this afternoon."

"Well," Phyllis said, "we'll have to wait and see about that."

Chapter 8

The funnel cake competition was scheduled for one o'clock that afternoon. *The Joye of Cooking* broadcast was at two. There was a chance she and her friends would be able to attend both events, Phyllis thought, or at least get to the broadcast before it was over. Bailey had said she would introduce them to Joye Jameson after the show.

Phyllis had brought along some of the ingredients she would need and left them in the car along with the pan, funnel, and cooking oil she would use. The fair furnished the perishable ingredients and the stoves. This competition required advance registration, and Phyllis had worried that she wouldn't be able to get a spot. There must have been a cancellation, though, because when she went online to sign up, there was one opening and she'd been able to grab it.

Maybe that was a good omen, she had thought at the time, although she really wasn't a big believer in luck. Preparation, hard work, and a spark of creativity were much more important in cooking contests, as well as in life in general.

But a bit of good luck never hurt anything, either.

With the competition at one o'clock, the group ate an early lunch; then Phyllis and Sam went out to the car to fetch the things Phyllis would need for the contest. It was a beautiful autumn day, with a definite nip in the air that was balanced by the warmth of the sun. Phyllis barely noticed the weather, though. Her attention was focused on the task in front of her.

She had decided to make the maple pecan funnel cake topped with maple syrup and pecans. It was a departure from the traditional recipe, but not so offbeat that the judges would consider it bizarre, she hoped. She had practiced pouring out the batter until she was confident she could form the cakes in the usual shape. Fancy designs were still beyond her abilities, but there was something to be said for a well-executed classic funnel cake shape.

"Is there a special prize for winnin' this contest?" Sam asked as they entered the hall, each carrying a cardboard box containing the things Phyllis would need.

She shook her head and said, "Not that I know of, other than the recognition. And all the winning recipes are published each year in a new edition of the state fair cookbook. That's true of all the cooking contests."

"Well, that'd be good, you and Carolyn both bein' in the same cookbook. Although that's probably happened before, hasn't it, what with all the different contests the two of you have been in?"

"As a matter of fact, it has," Phyllis said. "But they were all locally produced cookbooks. People all over the state, and probably all over the country, buy the State Fair of Texas cookbook."

"You'll be in it. I'm sure of it."

"Like Carolyn said, you don't have to give me a pep talk, Sam. Although I do appreciate the support."

"That's just the ol' coach in me talkin', I guess," he said, smiling. "Confidence is a big part of winnin'."

Phyllis was confident that she would do her very best. Beyond that, it was out of her hands.

Carolyn, Eve, and Peggy were waiting for them at the row of stoves set up along one wall. Other contestants were already there getting ready. An official wearing a state fair name badge consulted a list on a clipboard and told Phyllis which stove she was supposed to use. It was at the end of the row, so she would have a competitor to her right but not to her left.

"And good luck to you," the official added.

"Thank you," Phyllis said. She had decided that she would take all the luck she could get. Some of the other competitors looked very serious about what they were doing.

At the stove next to hers, a short, slender Hispanic man with a neatly trimmed gray mustache was setting up. He looked over at her and said, "I don't think I recognize you. How long have you been coming to the fair?"

"This is my first time in years," Phyllis said.

"Oh. You're one of the amateurs."

Phyllis wasn't quite sure what he meant by that, and he must have noticed her confusion, because he went on, "This contest used to be open just to the food concessionaires. It wasn't really an official state fair contest. But it was always good publicity for whoever won." He smiled. "Modesty forbids me from mentioning that I took top honors a few times myself."

"That's wonderful. Congratulations."

The man shrugged. "This year, though, they decided to throw it open to anybody. I don't think any of the amateurs will win—no offense, but we do this for a living, you know."

Phyllis laughed. "Well, now I'm more intimidated than ever. I never made funnel cakes before last week. I just thought it would be fun."

"Oh, it's serious business. A big chunk of our yearly income comes from the state fair. Some of the concessionaires weren't happy about the contest being open to the public." He shrugged. "It didn't bother me, of course. Competition never does. By the way, I'm Ramón Silva." He held out his hand.

Phyllis shook hands with him and introduced herself. He didn't seem to recognize her name, which came as no surprise. Outside Weatherford, not many people knew about her cooking skills. And she certainly didn't want to draw attention to her skills as a detective. The less said about that, the better, as far as she was concerned.

Silva looked with interest at the ingredients Phyllis was taking out of the boxes. "What are you going to make?" he asked.

Normally she wouldn't give that sort of information to a rival, not even Carolyn. But with the contest about to begin at any minute, Silva couldn't really steal her recipe. He already had to have his own plans in place.

Phyllis told him about the maple pecan funnel cakes she had decided to make. Silva nodded and said, "That sounds interesting. If you can pull it off, it might be enough to get a little attention from the judges. Not enough to win, of course, but still, it might turn out nicely."

His confidence—which bordered on arrogance, Phyllis thought—was starting to get on her nerves. She repeated what she had told Sam earlier. "I guess we'll have to wait and see."

"That's right," Silva said, but he still managed to sound like he thought she had no chance at all of beating him.

She could understand why people whose livelihoods depended on the food they cooked and sold at the state fair might not be too fond of the idea of competing against amateurs who really had nothing to lose. But that was the way things were set up this year and she didn't think she was doing anything wrong. So she wasn't going to worry about the possibility of hurting Ramón Silva's feelings if she happened to finish ahead of him in this contest, no matter how far-fetched he apparently considered that possibility.

In fact, she realized, the idea held some definite appeal for her, if she was being honest with herself.

Phyllis looked over her shoulder at the spectators, who were standing back behind a taped line on the floor to watch the competition. Sam smiled and gave her a little salute. Carolyn, Eve, and Peggy waved. Phyllis smiled back at them. It felt good to know they were there to root for her.

The starting times for the contestants were staggered, so that the judges could sample each funnel cake when it was still fresh and warm. Since Phyllis was at the end of the line, she had to wait, but the judges moved quickly in her direction, increasing the tension she felt that much more.

"All right, get ready," one of the contest workers told her. "Your time begins . . . now!"

Phyllis put oil in the iron skillet and started it heating while she mixed her ingredients. She paid no attention to what

Ramón Silva and the other contestants and the judges were doing but focused all her attention on her own efforts.

When the batter was ready and the oil was hot enough, she set the metal ring into the hot oil and began pouring the batter inside the ring, using a traditional funnel. It took a steady hand to keep the line of batter from coming apart as it lay down in the hot oil, and there could be no stopping and starting if she wanted a smooth, unbroken design. More time to practice that skill might have come in handy, but this was all for fun, Phyllis told herself, so she didn't take any of it too seriously. She supposed that experienced funnel cake makers like Ramón Silva could do this automatically, without even thinking too much about what they were doing.

She tried not to let herself get too tense. Her movements needed to be smooth and flowing. As the oil sizzled, the funnel cake began to take shape in the pan. The loops and strands intersected and overlapped within the metal ring, giving them the strength required for them to hold together.

It seemed like the rest of the world had gone away, receding from around her until the only things she was aware of were the funnel, the batter, and the pan. She had to rely on instinct to know when the cake was ready to be turned over, and she hadn't had long to develop that instinct. Phyllis had always prided herself on being a quick learner, though, all the way back to the days when she was a student. She set the funnel inside a small bowl to keep the drips contained, and when she felt like the time was right, she picked up the tongs she had sitting there close at hand, ready for action, and used them to first remove the metal ring, setting it aside, and then take hold of the cake. A deft flick of the wrist, and the funnel cake came up and over and settled back down into the oil. The side that was now turned up was a rich golden brown. Despite hoping that she would do a good job, Phyllis was a little surprised at just how perfect it looked.

A few minutes later she used the tongs again, this time to remove the cake from the pan and place it on a plate with a paper towel on it. As soon as she thought the cake had drained enough, she moved it to another plate and picked up the high-quality maple syrup and the pecans she had chopped in Peggy's kitchen the night before. She drizzled the syrup on the hot funnel cake, being careful not to use too much or too little. Just like Goldilocks, she thought. She wanted it to be *just* right.

As she set the syrup down and sprinkled the pecans on top, she reminded herself that she wasn't finished. She had to make two more cakes, three in all for the judges, and there was no time to waste. It was a delicate balance, keeping the oil at just the right temperature.

Even though she knew better than to check on the competition, Phyllis flicked a glance over at Ramón Silva. He was just taking his first cake out of the pan. His design was a lot more elaborate than hers, so it had taken longer.

Of course, this wasn't a race, Phyllis thought. The contestants would be allowed all the time they needed, within reason. If they weren't satisfied with the way a cake turned out, they could discard it and start over, as long as they didn't go over that time limit.

She began working on her second one, trying to make it exactly the same as the first one. Uniformity was important, as was appearance, but the cakes were judged primarily on taste.

"Looks good," Silva said. "Not as spectacular as mine, of course, but not bad for a newbie."

"Thank you," Phyllis said without taking her eyes off what she was doing. She wasn't going to allow him to distract her as she began to pour again, and she certainly wasn't going to engage in trash talk with him.

"Better be careful. You know how easy that batter breaks."

She started to get angry, knowing that he was trying to get her goat. But that was exactly the response he wanted to provoke, she told herself, so she called on the almost Zen-like calm that every good teacher developed in order to stay sane in the classroom. She was even able to summon up a tranquil smile.

That ought to infuriate Ramón Silva, she thought.

Her second cake looked just as good as the first. When she took it out of the skillet, Silva was just flipping his second cake. It was totally irrational to feel that way since speed didn't matter, but Phyllis was pleased that she was pulling ahead of him.

Silva wasn't happy about it, though. She could tell that from the hooded glances he kept shooting in her direction. Phyllis did her best to ignore the man and concentrate on her own efforts.

"No funnel cake can match up to mine," Silva muttered. Phyllis heard him but pretended that she hadn't.

Her movements weren't quite as smooth as she poured the third cake. Tension was taking its toll on her muscles, she supposed. But the strands didn't break and the cake formed the way it was supposed to. There were minor variations, of course—like snowflakes, no two funnel cakes were exactly alike—but it was obvious that all three were poured by the same hand. Phyllis adjusted the temperature on the stove's burner, bumping it down a little to keep the oil from getting too hot. She picked up the tongs and turned the cake.

This was the home stretch, she told herself. As soon as this side finished browning, she would be almost done. Again relying on instinct, she waited as the seconds ticked by and turned into minutes. Then, holding her breath, she reached out with the tongs and grasped the cake.

When she lifted it from the pan, she heard a murmur of approval from the spectators. She supposed that like any other activity, there were funnel cake aficionados who knew all the ins and outs of the game and recognized good work. She began soaking up the oil from her third and final funnel cake.

Ramón Silva wore a dark scowl now. He had his third cake cooking. Phyllis didn't take a good look at the first two he had cooked until she was finished pouring the maple syrup and sprinkling the pecans over her third cake. Silva's cakes were beautiful; there was no denying that. And she was sure they were light and fluffy inside and would taste wonderful. There would be no shame in losing to an old pro like him.

Phyllis hoped her cakes would at least be competitive. She thought they would taste good. There was no reason they shouldn't.

She stepped back, looked at the three funnel cakes on the counter next to her stove, and heaved a sigh of relief. She was finished, anyway. She had done her best. Now it was up to the judges.

She turned to look at her friends. They all smiled broadly at her, and Sam gave her a thumbs-up. Phyllis returned the gesture, feeling a little foolish as she did so, but Sam's enthusiasm was infectious.

Ramón Silva stepped back, beamed at his cakes with obvious pride, and said, "Those are the winners, right there." He looked over at Phyllis. "They'll see they never should have opened the contest to amateurs."

"Oh, I don't know; it adds some excitement to the proceedings, don't you think?" she said.

Silva snorted. "This isn't a game. It isn't about excitement. This is business. If I can claim I make the fair's best funnel cakes, I'll sell more of them."

Phyllis could understand that, and she didn't have any desire to hurt anyone's business. But she hadn't made the rules, and as far as she could see the contest had been fair for everyone involved, concessionaires and amateurs alike.

The judging got under way. Phyllis glanced at the clock on the wall. Nearly an hour remained until Joye Jameson's broadcast would be over. She hoped that she and the others would be able to see part of the show and meet Joye afterward.

Now that the cooking was finished, the spectators were allowed to mingle with the contestants. Sam, Carolyn, Eve, and Peggy came over to Phyllis and congratulated her.

"It's a little early for that," she told them. "The judges haven't even tried my cakes yet."

"Yeah, but you got through it," Sam said, "and I could tell it was a little nerve-rackin'."

"Phyllis has always handled pressure without any trouble," Carolyn said. "When you're a teacher you learn how to do that, or you don't last long in the job."

"That's certainly true," Eve agreed. "And she's never broken under the pressure of all those murder investigations, either, even when she got thrown in jail because she was trying to help me."

The others looked at her in surprise.

"Oh, for goodness' sake," Eve went on. "Do you think I don't know you've been avoiding talking about anything like that in front of me? I appreciate the consideration for my feelings, but it's time we all moved on, don't you think? From now on, you don't have to watch what you say around me. Just be yourselves." She smiled at Carolyn. "I know it must have been terribly difficult for you, dear."

"What does that mean?" Carolyn demanded. "Do you think I'm just naturally tactless or something?"

The arrival of the judges saved Eve from having to answer.

Phyllis introduced herself, showed the judges—two women and a man—the printed recipe she had used, and watched in tense anticipation as each judge sampled one of the funnel cakes, cutting off a couple of bites and chewing them slowly as if savoring everything about the experience.

Then they thanked her and moved on. Phyllis hadn't been able to tell a thing from their expressions about whether or not they had liked her entries.

"Is that it?" Carolyn asked. "Just two bites?"

"I reckon they can't eat the whole thing every time," Sam said, "or else they'd have such a sugar rush they'd be bouncin' off the walls for the next two days."

"I couldn't even eat that much," Peggy said. "My blood sugar would go sky-high if I did."

The judges were just as expressionless as they sampled

Ramón Silva's cakes. He tried to chat familiarly with them, but they didn't seem to pay much attention to what he said.

It was a few minutes past two o'clock when the judges finished sampling all the entries and drew off to the side to confer among themselves. The discussion seemed to take forever, even though it was really only a couple of minutes. Finally, they all nodded as if they had reached a consensus, and when they turned around and approached the contestants again, the male judge had a big blue ribbon in his hand.

His course led him straight toward the stoves where Phyllis and Silva had prepared their funnel cakes. Phyllis couldn't tell which of them was the judge's destination. Silva thought he knew, though. A smug, self-satisfied smile appeared on his face.

Then the judge veered slightly, just enough to take him to Phyllis, who stood there too stunned to move as the man held out the blue ribbon, smiled, and said, "Congratulations, Mrs. Newsom."

Chapter 9

"**N**oooo!"

The shout of anger and disbelief came from Ramón Silva. He lunged toward the judge, getting in the man's face and continuing, "You can't give the blue ribbon to an amateur! You just can't! It's not right!"

"Please, Mr. Silva—" the startled judge began.

Silva made a grab for the ribbon. "Gimme that!" he demanded. "It's mine!"

Phyllis was just as shocked as anyone else at the man's outburst. She saw one of the female judges saying something into a walkie-talkie and figured the woman was calling security.

The male judge backed away hurriedly. He was taller than Silva and held the blue ribbon over his head, out of Silva's reach, but that didn't stop the outraged concessionaire from trying to get it. Silva jumped and grabbed at the ribbon several times, and Phyllis thought the scene would have been comical if it hadn't been so sad.

"Mr. Silva, you have to stop this," the judge said. "If you keep it up, you'll be banned from the fair!"

"It won't matter!" Silva said. "When word gets around that a little old lady's funnel cake beat mine, my business will be ruined!"

Phyllis thought that had to be an exaggeration, and she didn't much care for that "little old lady" comment, either.

Sam moved up beside Silva and said, "You'd better take it easy there, buddy." He put a hand on Silva's shoulder.

Barking a curse, Silva turned and swung a punch at Sam's head. Phyllis gasped in alarm, thinking that Sam was going to be hurt.

Not seeming to move fast at all, Sam leaned aside so that the blow missed him. Silva lost his balance and stumbled. Before he could right himself and try to attack anyone else, a couple of uniformed security guards pounded up and grabbed him. Silva thrashed back and forth, but since he probably didn't weigh much more than 130 pounds, he was no match for the two guards.

"What's going on here?" one of them asked. Phyllis was a little surprised that she recognized him. After a moment she remembered his name: Chet Murdock. He had been working near the set of Joye Jameson's show the day before.

"Mr. Silva is upset about the results of the funnel cake contest," the male judge said.

"Didn't win, eh?" Chet stepped back as the other guard pulled both of Silva's arms behind his back and looped a plastic restraint around his wrists. Being bound like that seemed to take all the fight out of Silva. His shoulders slumped.

"I'm sorry, sir," the judge said to Sam. "If you want to press charges—"

Sam stopped the man by shaking his head. "No need for that. The fella was just shook up. No harm done."

"You're sure?" The judge seemed quite nervous, and Phyllis had a pretty good idea why. In this day and age, everybody who dealt with the public was scared to death of lawsuits.

"Positive," Sam said.

Chet Murdock asked the judge, "Do you want us to call the cops, Mr. Thaxter?"

The judge sighed and shook his head. "I suppose not. Mr. Silva has been coming to the fair for a long time. I guess we can give him a break . . . this time."

"Okay." Chet nodded to the other guard, who was still hanging on to Silva. "Take him somewhere and let him cool off."

As the second guard led Silva away, the crowd parted to give them plenty of room. Silva had acted like a crazy man, and nobody wanted to get close to him.

The judge turned back to Phyllis and managed a weak smile. "Well, after all the excitement, this might be a little anticlimactic," he said, "but congratulations again, Mrs. Newsom."

He held out the blue ribbon. Phyllis took it and said, "Are you sure this isn't some sort of mistake?"

"No mistake. Your funnel cakes were the best we tasted today. You are definitely our winner."

"Thank you. I can hardly believe it. I never even made any funnel cakes until recently."

"You picked it up quickly, then," the judge told her. "Those were some of the best funnel cakes we've had here." The two female judges had come closer now that the trouble was over, and they nodded in agreement. "We'll send over a photographer in a few minutes to take your picture with the winning entry, if that's all right."

Phyllis looked at the clock again. "If it's not too long," she said. Across the hall, Joye Jameson's broadcast soon would be drawing to a close.

"We'll see to it right away," the man promised.

Carolyn, Eve, and Peggy gave Phyllis congratulatory hugs, as did Sam. She shook her head as she looked at the blue ribbon and said, "I still can't believe it."

"I'm not a bit surprised," Sam said. "I told you all along you were gonna win, didn't I?"

"You're a funnel cake Nostradamus," Carolyn said dryly.

Sam looked thoughtful for a moment, then said, "You know, Funnel Cake Nostradamus would be a good name for a rock band."

Chet Murdock hung around that side of the hall for a few minutes, until the fair's photographer showed up to take Phyllis's picture. He explained that he'd been covering temporarily for another guard but didn't have to get back to the set of *The Joye of Cooking* right away.

While they were waiting, she told him about meeting Bailey Broderick earlier and how Bailey had invited her and her friends to visit the broadcast set.

"Really?" Chet said. "That's pretty cool. I'll go with you, just to make sure nobody gives you any trouble." He grinned. "And if I, uh, happen to get a chance to meet Ms. Jameson, too . . ."

"You haven't met her yet?" Carolyn asked.

"No. She's not exactly standoffish, but she doesn't really mingle with the staff, if you know what I mean. Hollywood types, they sort of stick together, even the nice ones."

Phyllis thought about asking him whether he had noticed any odd behavior on the part of Bailey and the cameraman Hank, but she stopped herself. That really would be sticking her nose in where it didn't belong. She didn't want to take behavior that was probably totally innocent and make something suspicious out of it.

Besides, that might just get the others talking about her being a detective again, and she could do without that.

The photographer arrived and took several pictures of Phyllis and the fourth funnel cake she had made for the photo after winning the blue ribbon, then moved on to photograph the second- and third-place finishers. Phyllis and her friends, accompanied by Chet Murdock, headed across the hall toward the broadcast area. Today's show would just be coming to an end.

The audience was leaving the bleachers when they got there. Phyllis's eyes scanned the kitchen set, and she felt a little disappointed when she didn't see Joye Jameson anywhere. But then she spotted Bailey Broderick standing in the open door at the rear of the set, talking to someone on the other side of it. Bailey glanced around, perhaps feeling Phyllis's gaze on her, and smiled in recognition. She raised a hand and motioned for Phyllis to join her.

Phyllis gestured toward her companions. Bailey nodded and waved for all of them to come on.

"You come along, too, Mr. Murdock," Phyllis told Chet. "That way we'll have an escort."

He chuckled. "Don't think I don't know what you're doing . . . but thanks."

Phyllis took the lead, stepping up onto the kitchen set and crossing it. The bulky cameras were still sitting in their positions around the outside of the set, although their operators were nowhere in sight, and the boom microphones were still in place, too. Phyllis felt a little like an intruder, as if she shouldn't be here. But Bailey was waiting for her and still smiling.

The others followed her, so at least Phyllis wasn't as nervous as she would have been if she had been alone. Just having them around made her feel better.

Bailey said, "Hello, Mrs. Newsom. I'm glad you could make it. I was a little worried when I didn't see you in the audience."

"I was busy with something else," Phyllis explained. She had put the blue ribbon in her purse and thought about taking it out, but that seemed too much like showing off. "But we hurried over here as soon as it was finished."

Bailey leaned her head sideways. "Come on. I'll show you backstage. I warn you, though, it's not all that impressive."

She stepped through the door, and Phyllis followed her. Phyllis halfway expected to see Joye Jameson standing there, since Bailey had been talking to someone, but there was no sign of the star. Instead, Reed Hayes, the show's producer, stood a few feet away behind the set's rear wall, talking to someone on a cell phone. Phyllis supposed Bailey had been talking to him.

"As you can see, not all that fancy," Bailey went on. Indeed, there was a lot of bare wood, equipment that Phyllis didn't recognize, and electrical cables. Off to one side was an area partitioned off with temporary walls that didn't reach all the way to the hall's tall ceiling. Phyllis wondered if that was Joye's dressing room. That seemed likely, as she didn't see any other place a star might go after the show.

"So tell me who your friends are," Bailey said. Phyllis introduced everyone, including Chet.

"It's a real honor to meet you, ma'am," the security guard said. "I've seen you on the show many times."

"And I've seen you around the hall here, Mr. Murdock," she said. "The fair seems to have good security. That's always reassuring."

"We do our best," Chet said. "A few minutes ago we had to answer a call about a disturbance on the other side of the hall." He nodded toward Phyllis. "Mrs. Newsom was involved in that."

"Oh, no," Bailey said. "Was there some sort of trouble? I thought I heard a commotion from over there, but I wasn't sure."

"It was nothing to worry about," Phyllis replied with a shake of her head. "One of the contestants in the funnel cake competition was a little upset that he didn't win; that's all."

"You were at the funnel cake competition?" Bailey asked, suddenly seeming even more interested.

Peggy said, "She wasn't just at it. She was in it."

"And she won," Carolyn added, obviously proud of her friend. "That's why that troublemaker was so upset. He tried to steal Phyllis's blue ribbon."

"You have the blue ribbon?" Bailey said.

Phyllis hadn't wanted to boast, but since Bailey had asked

her . . . She opened her purse and took out the ribbon. "Yes, it's right here."

A new voice said, "You won the prize for the best funnel cake?"

Phyllis turned and looked to see who had spoken, and a shock of recognition went through her as she saw Joye Jameson standing only a couple of feet away. For a second she couldn't find her voice, but then she held up the blue ribbon and said, "Yes, I did."

"Then, lady, have I got a deal for you!"

And with that, Joye threw her arms around Phyllis in a big hug.

Chapter 10

For a few seconds, Phyllis was too surprised to say anything. When she was able to speak again, all she was able to get out was "Oh, my goodness!"

Joye let go of her, stepped back, and laughed. "You must think I'm a crazy woman, grabbing you like that," she said. "I'm just glad I didn't have to go looking for you. You fell right into my lap, so to speak."

"Why would you, uh, be looking for me?" Phyllis asked.

"Well, not for *you* in particular, I suppose. I meant the winner of the funnel cake competition. But that's you! Your funnel cakes are the best in Texas!"

"Oh, I wouldn't go so far as to say—" Phyllis began.

"I would," Carolyn interrupted her. She put an arm around Phyllis's shoulders. "There's no need for false modesty. You won fair and square, and it's even more of an impressive accomplishment when you consider that you'd never even made funnel cakes until last week!"

Joye Jameson's eyes widened. "Is that true? Oooh, this story just gets better and better." She looked at the others. "Who are your friends?"

Phyllis was glad Joye had asked. It gave her a reason to get the focus of the conversation off of her for a moment. She introduced everyone, including Chet Murdock. The security guard pumped Joye's hand and said, "Gosh, it's an honor to meet you, Ms. Jameson. I haven't missed one of your shows in . . . well, since the show started, I guess!"

"That's very kind of you, Mr. Murdock. Or do guards have ranks, like captain or lieutenant?"

"No, just call me Chet. That'd be fine. More than fine. It would be great!"

"Okay, Chet," Joye said, smiling and looking a little like a person on the verge of being overwhelmed by a large, friendly puppy. She turned back to Phyllis and took her right hand in both of hers. "You know we're going to feature the winning funnel cake recipe from the competition on my show?"

"Oh, my," Phyllis said again. She was the one feeling overwhelmed now. "I remember you saying that on TV . . . but I never even thought . . ."

"Now, is that going to be all right with you?" Joye asked. "You don't mind, do you?"

"Mind?" Carolyn repeated. "Of course she doesn't mind. She'd be honored."

Phyllis felt a little flash of annoyance. Carolyn needed to let her speak for herself. And yet, strictly speaking, her old friend wasn't saying anything that wasn't true.

"Carolyn's right," Phyllis said. "I'd be very pleased—"

"Oh, but that's not all I'm going to do," Joye broke in,

sounding like someone on a late-night infomercial trying to sell greatest-hits CDs. For a second Phyllis wondered crazily if Joye had ever done anything like that before becoming a cooking show star. Joye continued, "I have something else even more exciting in mind. Do you want to know what it is?"

"I suppose so," Phyllis said, feeling a little breathless from this whole conversation.

"I'm not just going to talk about your funnel cakes. I'm going to make some myself . . . and you're going to help me!"

"You mean . . ." Phyllis had to force the words out. "I'm going to be on TV?"

Carolyn squealed. The excited sound was so unexpected, especially coming from her, that Phyllis had to turn and stare at her in disbelief for a second.

She didn't have much time to be surprised, though, because Joye went on, "That's exactly what I mean. You'll do it, won't you, Phyllis? It's all right if I call you Phyllis, isn't it?"

"Of course—"

"Then it's a deal! Tomorrow we make the prizewinning funnel cakes for the whole world to see!"

"Wait, I didn't mean—"

Phyllis stopped short as she was about to say that she'd been replying to the question about whether it was all right to call her by her first name, not the business about being on television. There was no reason why she shouldn't take Joye Jameson up on that invitation, she realized. She didn't have anywhere else she had to be, and the idea of appearing before millions of viewers wasn't as intimidating as she would have thought it might be. Actually, the bleachers being used as seating for the audience at the broadcasts held just a few hundred people. Those were the only ones Phyllis had to worry about, since she couldn't see all the others out there on the other end of the broadcast. Decades of standing in front of a classroom full of students had long since dulled any fears Phyllis had of speaking in public.

Joye was looking at her with an inquisitive frown. "Didn't mean what, Phyllis?" she said.

"Nothing," Phyllis said. She smiled. "I'd be happy to appear on the show with you."

A part of her still didn't believe she was hearing those words come out of her own mouth, but it was too late to bring them back now. She was committed.

Sam echoed that sentiment by saying, "All right, it's a done deal, like the lady said. You don't need any ex–basketball coaches on your show, do you, Miss Jameson?"

Joye laughed and said, "Sorry, but not right now, Mr. Fletcher. Although we might do something about sports-related cuisine in the future. That's actually not a bad idea. Maybe something about dressing up your nachos and hot dogs with new and exciting ingredients. Thank you for the suggestion."

"You're welcome," Sam said with a grin.

Joye turned to Bailey and assumed a more brisk and businesslike attitude as she said, "You and Reed will talk to Phyllis and work out all the details?"

"Of course," Bailey said. "Don't worry, we'll handle it."

"You always do," Joye said. Phyllis might have been mistaken, but she thought she heard the slightest undertone of something—she couldn't have said what—in the star's voice. Joye took Phyllis's hand again and was all smiles once more as she went on, "This is going to be great. I can't wait for tomorrow."

"Neither can I," Phyllis said, although the more skeptical part of her was still wondering what she had gotten herself into.

Joye went back to her dressing room. Bailey motioned for Reed Hayes to come over, and when the producer had joined them, she asked him, "Did you hear what Joye was talking to Mrs. Newsom about?"

"I couldn't help but hear," Hayes said. He nodded to Phyllis and went on, "Hello, Mrs. Newsom. I'm Reed Hayes, the producer of *The Joye of Cooking*."

"It's nice to meet you, Mr. Hayes," Phyllis said. "Producing a show like this must be a wonderful job."

"You'd think so, wouldn't you?" Hayes said. Before Phyllis could consider the implications of that question, he went on, "I'll have some papers for you to sign tomorrow before we go on the air, releases and other legal documents like that, you know. I'd have had them ready for you today, but, well, I didn't know Joye was going to ask you to appear on the show until just now."

"If it's any problem—" Phyllis began.

"No, no, it's not a problem at all. It might be nice if our star let me in on her plans from time to time, but hey, I'm only the producer, right?"

"Reed," Bailey said with a slight warning note in her voice.

Hayes smiled and shook his head. "Don't mind me. There's just a lot to keep up with, and my bark, as they say, is worse than my bite. I'm happy to have you appear on the show, Mrs.

Newsom, really. If you could be here tomorrow an hour before we go on the air, that would be great."

"To sign those papers, you mean?" Phyllis asked.

"Yeah, that and to get your makeup done, get you miked up and checked out, things like that. The show doesn't just happen. There's a lot of preparation."

"I'm sure there is. I'll be here on time," Phyllis promised.

Carolyn asked, "What about the rest of us?"

"I'm not sure the invitation extended to all of you . . . ," Hayes said. "The set would be kind of crowded with so many of you up there."

"I didn't mean that," Carolyn said. "I just wanted to know if we can come watch Phyllis be on TV."

"Of course," Bailey said. "You'll be more than welcome. We'll even set up some chairs, so you won't have sit in the bleachers with the rest of the audience. Won't that be all right, Reed?"

Hayes nodded and said, "Yeah, no problem."

Eve said, "We'll be like VIFPs."

Carolyn asked, "What does that stand for?"

"Very important friends of Phyllis, of course."

"All right, now you're just embarrassing me," Phyllis said. "I don't want to be treated like some sort of celebrity. All I'm going to do is be on TV for a few minutes." She looked at Bailey. "It will be for just a few minutes, won't it? Miss Jameson won't expect me to be on the show for the whole hour, will she?"

Bailey smiled and shook her head. "No, there'll be other segments besides cooking the funnel cakes. I don't know whether that will take two segments or just one. We'll work out those details with the director this evening at the daily production meeting. But you don't have to worry about that. We'll need you for ten to twenty minutes, tops."

"I'm not worried about it, just curious," Phyllis assured her. "I'll be available for however long you need me."

"Great. Oh, and one more thing . . . Be sure and bring that blue ribbon with you tomorrow. We'll want to show it off."

"I'll have it," Phyllis promised. "Actually, you really ought to have Carolyn on, too. She won a blue ribbon for her dark and nutty Nutella drop cookies in that competition."

"I'll take that up with Joye. You'll be here with Phyllis tomorrow, Mrs. . . . . Wilson, was it?"

"Wilbarger," Carolyn corrected her. "But I don't think that anybody needs to make a fuss over me. There are a lot of different winners in the cookie contest. There's only one best funnel cake in the state of Texas . . . and the woman who came up with it is the person who needs to be on TV!"

Chapter 11

$\mathcal{S}$uch modesty was unusual coming from Carolyn, who had always thoroughly enjoyed any recognition she received for her cooking and baking skills. But she was adamant about not stealing Phyllis's thunder, as she put it . . . so adamant that Phyllis began to wonder if it wasn't so much modesty as stage fright that prompted her friend's reaction. Just the very notion of appearing on TV seemed to make Carolyn nervous.

Phyllis couldn't really blame Carolyn for feeling that way. Over the next approximately twenty-two hours, she did her best not to even think about the millions of people who would be watching her. It really was sort of like an elephant in the room, though, hard to ignore and even harder to keep out of her thoughts.

At Peggy's house the next morning, Sam asked Phyllis, "Do you need to take all the ingredients for the funnel cakes with you?"

She shook her head. "No, Bailey promised that she would

get the recipe and that they would have everything on hand for Joye and me when the show starts."

"Must be nice to have somebody around to take care of all the little details like that."

"Yes, I'm not sure Bailey gets enough credit for what she does to keep things running smoothly," Phyllis said. "I don't think I've ever heard her last name mentioned on the show. Joye just refers to her as Bailey or her assistant, when she mentions her at all. But like that security guard said, it looks to me like Bailey does an awful lot."

"I expect she's well paid. It's television, after all."

Phyllis knew what he meant, but she wasn't sure he was right. From what she had heard, the stars and the executives got the big money, while everyone else in Hollywood made decent but hardly spectacular wages.

As the time to leave for the fair approached, Phyllis felt herself getting more nervous. She kept the feeling under control as much as possible, telling herself that everything was going to be all right. She was just going to do a little cooking in someone else's kitchen; that was all.

To get her mind off of it, she sought out Sam and found him in the kitchen getting a cup of coffee. She said, "I really owe you an apology. I've been so caught up in this funnel cake business, it totally slipped my mind that you have a contest tomorrow to worry about."

He grinned. "I'm not worried about it. Got my Spam sushi recipe all ready to go."

"It's a pretty complicated dish. Are you sure you'll be able to put it together there at the fair?"

"Sure. It takes a little longer than some things, I suppose, but a little pressure doesn't bother me."

"I can understand that," Phyllis said. "You've coached in a lot of basketball games that came right down to the last shot, haven't you?"

"Well, that's true." Sam grew uncharacteristically solemn. "But when you've spent months in a hospital watchin' somebody you love slip away, you learn that most things folks get all worked up about don't really mean a whole heck of a lot after all."

She put a hand on his arm and nodded. "Yes, I know what you mean," she told him. Like the others in their little circle, they had each lost a spouse, and the pain of that loss was something they would live with every day for the rest of their lives. To try to lighten the mood a little, she went on, "If there's anything I can do to help you with the contest, all you have to do is let me know."

"I appreciate that, but I reckon just havin' you there to root for me will be plenty."

"I'll certainly do that," Phyllis promised. She leaned forward to kiss him on the cheek.

From the kitchen doorway, Peggy said, "I knew it! I knew that tall drink of water had to be smooching with at least one of you. Better keep an eye on him, Phyllis. He looks like a lounge lizard to me."

Phyllis was a little embarrassed, but Sam burst out laughing. "I've been called a lot of things in my life, but as far as I remember, lounge lizard has never been one of 'em!"

"All I'm saying is that one man living in a house with three women . . . well, that's a recipe for hanky-panky," Peggy insisted.

Phyllis said, "It certainly is not. Not when the man is an absolute gentleman like Sam."

"Yeah, I'm chivalrous as all get-out," he said, nodding.

"It's none of my business," Peggy said with her eyes sparkling mischievously. "You just go on with what you were doing, Lothario. Don't mind me."

"I was, uh, gettin' some coffee."

"Uh-huh. Coffee."

"Oh, goodness gracious," Phyllis said. She knew Peggy was just joshing, so she wasn't really offended by the comments, but she was starting to get slightly annoyed. "Talk about making something out of nothing. I just gave Sam an affectionate peck on the cheek; that's all."

"And that's all you've ever done?" Peggy wanted to know.

"Well . . . I didn't say that." Phyllis felt her face growing warm as she blushed. Somebody her age shouldn't be doing that, she told herself sternly.

"I'll get out of your way," Peggy went on, backing out of the doorway.

"There's nothing to get out of the way of," Phyllis insisted.

Sam lifted his coffee cup and said, "Think I'll go upstairs and check my e-mail."

"Fine." Left alone in the kitchen, Phyllis sat down at the table. A few second later, she began to chuckle.

It was several minutes before she remembered to be worried again about her upcoming TV appearance, and she was grateful for the respite.

Since they had already seen all the exhibits at the fair during the past two days, there was no reason to go early today. They even ate lunch at Peggy's house, rather than at the fair, although they ate a little early to allow themselves plenty of time to get there.

Phyllis didn't eat much. She wasn't really hungry, and the last thing she wanted to do when she was nervous was to overeat.

On the way to Fair Park, Sam glanced over at her as he drove and asked, "Doin' all right?"

"Yes, I'll be fine. I just don't know why I agreed to do this. That's always the way it is. Someone asks me to go somewhere or do something, and I think it sounds like it would be fun or interesting, so I say yes. But then when the time actually comes, I just dread it and don't want to go."

"But when you go ahead, you wind up enjoyin' yourself, don't you?"

"Well . . . usually," Phyllis admitted.

"That's the way this'll be," Sam said confidently. "You'll get there and you'll have a fine time. Just keep tellin' yourself that."

"I'll try," Phyllis said.

Traffic cooperated, so it was only twelve thirty when they reached the fairgrounds. Phyllis was supposed to be at the broadcast set at one o'clock, so that gave them plenty of time to park and walk into the grounds. The fair was busy, even though it was the middle of the week.

Carolyn pointed at several school buses in the parking lot and said in an ominous tone, "Field trips."

"I know," Phyllis said. "That sight brings up a lot of memories."

"And not good ones, for the most part."

Eve said, "I'm just glad we didn't have to worry about that in high school. The seniors always took a trip somewhere, but it wasn't like what the elementary schools did. I suppose the administration thought that by the time the kids were in high school, they were getting enough of an outside education on their own."

"That's sure the truth," Sam said.

Peggy said, "You know, I sort of envy the four of you, having all those shared experiences with the schools. Me, I helped my husband run his furniture stores. I don't have any old furniture store buddies."

Carolyn patted her cousin on the shoulder. "We'll be your buddies, Peggy."

"Yeah, while you're here. But what happens when the fair is over and you go back to Weatherford?"

"Well . . . we could come and visit again. Or you could come and visit us."

"People say they'll do things like that, but we all know that when the time comes, they usually don't."

"This will be different," Carolyn said. "You'll see."

Peggy didn't seem convinced, but she didn't say any more about it.

As they approached the Creative Arts Building, Phyllis spotted a familiar figure standing to one side of the entrance. Gloria Kimball was as sleekly blond and beautiful as ever as she stood there with a microphone in her hand. Her bearded, shaggy-looking cameraman had his video camera balanced on his shoulder as he pointed it at her. The two of them were probably recording another segment for the local TV station, Phyllis thought.

As she and the others started into the building, a woman's voice suddenly called, "Mrs. Newsom! Wait just a minute!" Phyllis looked over in surprise and saw Gloria Kimball walking quickly toward her, followed by the cameraman. Gloria went on, "Mrs. Newsom, could I have just a minute of your time?"

Surprised that Gloria Kimball even knew who she was, Phyllis was a little flustered as she stopped. Her friends came to a halt as well. Phyllis always tried to be polite unless someone gave her a reason not to be, so she said, "Well, I suppose so. But only a minute. I have to be somewhere."

"Of course you do," Gloria said with the same sort of smile usually sported by Joye Jameson. TV personalities seemed to be able to summon the expression at a second's notice. Phyllis wondered if their cheeks and jaws sometimes ached from smiling so much, or if they got used to it. "I'm sure you're a very busy woman, since you're famous now."

"Oh, I'm not—"

"What else could you call it when you've created the best funnel cake at the State Fair of Texas? Don't be modest, Mrs. Newsom. That's quite an accomplishment. I'm Gloria Kimball, by the way."

Carolyn said, "Oh, we know who you are. We used to watch you every day on *Gloria's Kitchen*, and we still see you sometimes on Channel 44."

"You were always one of our favorites," Phyllis added.

Gloria practically preened at being told they recognized her. "I'd really love to ask you a few questions about that special funnel cake of yours, if you wouldn't mind."

"Well, I suppose that would be all right," Phyllis said. "But like I told you, I'm sort of in a hurry—"

"This won't take but a minute." Gloria lifted the handheld microphone, and before Phyllis fully grasped what was happening, the woman had moved beside her and slipped an arm around her shoulders. "We're here live with Phyllis Newsom, the winner of the annual funnel cake competition here at the State Fair of Texas."

Live? This was going out on the air? Phyllis tried not to gulp nervously at the thought.

Without missing a beat, Gloria turned from the camera and said to her like they were old friends, "Phyllis, tell me about this wonderful funnel cake of yours."

"Well, I, ah . . ." Phyllis took a deep breath and steadied herself. This was something of an ambush, she thought, but she could handle it. She began describing the maple pecan funnel cakes she had made the day before at the competition.

"Oh, they sound absolutely delicious!" Gloria said. "I don't suppose there's a chance you'd make some for me someday?"

"Well, I don't—"

"Tell me, how did it feel to win the contest? The way I understand it, in previous years the competition was an informal one among the concessionaires here at the state fair, but this year it became an official event and was opened to the public."

"That's the way I understand the situation, too."

"But the concessionaires, the professionals, if you will, still competed in the contest, so you were taking on the very best funnel cake makers in the world! You must have been thrilled to defeat them!"

"I wouldn't call it so much a defeat. I'm sure their funnel cakes were all wonderful."

"But not as good as yours," Gloria said, "because you won the blue ribbon! Can we see it?"

The ribbon was in Phyllis's purse, but she wasn't sure she

should take it out and display it on camera. It had just occurred to her that maybe it wasn't a good idea for her to be talking to Gloria Kimball like this. After all, she had agreed to be on *The Joye of Cooking* and talk about her funnel cakes there, as well as helping Joye Jameson make a batch of them, so that was sort of like promising an exclusive to a reporter, wasn't it? Did TV personalities ever try to scoop one another?

Those questions were going through her mind as she glanced over at the entrance to the Creative Arts Building. Bailey Broderick stood there with a stunned, angry expression on her face, and as soon as Phyllis saw the young woman, she knew that she had indeed made a mistake.

Chapter 12

"I'm sorry. I really have to go now," Phyllis said.

"If you could spare us just a few more minutes—" Gloria began.

Phyllis shook her head and muttered again, "I'm sorry."

Gloria moved her arm and stepped away from Phyllis, hardly missing a beat as she faced the camera and went on, "We've been talking to Phyllis Newsom, blue ribbon winner of the funnel cake competition of the State Fair of Texas, and my, didn't those funnel cakes sound delicious! And remember, you heard about them first right here on *The 44 News*."

Phyllis heard Gloria's voice clearly behind her as she walked toward the building, and she winced slightly at what had just gone out over the air. Beside her, Sam said quietly, "You probably shouldn't have done that, huh?"

"Probably not," Phyllis agreed.

But it was too late to do anything about it now. Still, she was a little worried about what had happened. She wouldn't blame Bailey at all if the young woman withdrew the invitation for her to appear on *The Joye of Cooking*. Even though Phyllis had been halfway dreading being on TV, she would be disappointed if the opportunity was taken away now.

As she came up to Bailey, she said, "I'm so sorry about what just happened—"

"I can't believe it," Bailey said.

Phyllis tried to defend herself. "I'm not used to all this, and I just didn't think—"

"The nerve of that woman, ambushing you like that." Bailey glared at Gloria Kimball, who was still facing the camera and talking into the microphone. "You know why she did it, don't you?"

Phyllis was relieved that Bailey seemed to be more put out with Gloria than with her. She said, "No, not really. I guess she just saw the opportunity to get a story."

"She did it because she hates Joye."

The flat statement surprised Phyllis. She said, "But Joye used to be Gloria's assistant. I thought they were friends."

A curt, humorless laugh came from Bailey. "Gloria hates Joye's guts. She thinks Joye forced her out and stole the show from her. I don't know all the details, but there was definitely a falling-out between them. When you see them making nice with each other on the air, like they did the other day, that's just for appearance's sake." Bailey shook her head. "But you didn't hear any of that from me, okay? It's really none of my business."

"We won't say anything," Phyllis promised. She looked around at the others, and they all nodded their agreement.

"Okay, fine," Bailey said. "We'd better get inside." As they started into the building, she added, "And maybe it would be better if none of us said anything to Joye about what Gloria just did. I understand how she ambushed you, and I'm sure Joye would, too, but let's not tempt fate by mentioning it."

"That's fine with me," Phyllis said. "I already feel bad about letting her take advantage of me like that. But isn't Miss Jameson bound to find out what happened sooner or later?"

"Yeah, but later is better. After the broadcast. Trust me, we don't want to upset her this close to going on the air."

Phyllis glanced over at Carolyn, who raised her eyebrows. It sounded like Joye Jameson had a temper, which agreed with what the security guard, Chet Murdock, had told them.

Bailey led the way across the big hall, where more cooking contests were going on again today, along with competitions for jams and jellies, pickles, canned vegetables, and nonfood items such as needlepoint, dolls, and quilts. The sight of beautiful handmade quilts on display made Phyllis think fondly of her late friend Mattie, who had been an expert quilter.

The bleachers were empty at the moment, but people were already lining up to attend the broadcast. Phyllis saw that Chet Murdock was one of the guards keeping an eye on the audience and gave him a friendly smile and nod as Bailey took her and her friends around to the back of the set.

Reed Hayes was waiting for them. He wasn't wearing a headset this time, but he had one of those little Bluetooth phones tucked into his ear and was talking to someone on it, although anyone who didn't notice the tiny gizmo might think he was just talking to himself. For a long time, Phyllis had seen people using those things and thought that they were perhaps not right in the head, before she finally figured out they were actually talking on the phone.

Hayes's job seemed to consist of talking to people all the time, Phyllis thought. She had never seen him when he wasn't connected in one way or another.

When he noticed that Bailey had arrived with Phyllis and her friends, the producer ended the conversation he was having and came over to them. "Hello, Mrs. Newsom," he said. "I've got those papers for you to sign." He held out a clipboard with several legal documents on it.

"What am I signing?" Phyllis asked as she took the clipboard from him.

"Standard boilerplate," Hayes said. "Liability waiver, waiver of personal appearance fee—"

Carolyn said, "You mean she doesn't get paid for being on the show?"

"Our guests generally aren't compensated," Bailey said. "Unless, of course, they're members of the Screen Actors Guild or something like that and union rules require it."

"In other words, you only pay stars. Nobodies don't get paid."

"Carolyn, it's all right," Phyllis said. "I never expected to be paid for being on the show. Goodness, just getting to cook with Joye Jameson is payment enough, don't you think?"

"Well, there is that, I suppose," Carolyn admitted. "And it's a pretty big deal."

"That's right, ladies," Hayes said. "Now, Mrs. Newsom, if you could just sign there where the X's are . . ."

A pen was attached to the clipboard. Phyllis used it to sign the three documents, although she took the time first to scan over them and make sure they were what Hayes said they were. She knew the producer was impatient, but she wasn't going to sign anything without being certain what it was.

When she handed the clipboard and papers back to Hayes, he said, "Great. Now Bailey can take you to makeup. Charlie will be along to see about getting you miked up, too."

As Hayes walked away and started talking on his phone again, Phyllis asked Bailey, "Who's Charlie?"

"Charlie Farrar, our director," Bailey said.

"The show's director handles things like that?" Phyllis was a little surprised.

"He's something of a perfectionist," Bailey explained. "Likes to check all the equipment himself." She smiled. "Besides, we have a pretty small crew, so people double up on jobs sometimes. Our budget isn't as big as what you might think it would be."

Peggy said, "I thought TV shows always cost millions of dollars to put on."

"Well, when you count what the talent makes . . ." Bailey stopped and shook her head. "But we don't cut any corners. We're just efficient; that's all."

Phyllis saw proof of that during the next forty-five minutes. Everyone involved in the broadcast seemed to know exactly what they needed to do and when they needed to do it. It was a beehive of activity, bordering on chaos to her inexperienced eye, but even she could tell that it was controlled chaos.

Charlie Farrar, the director, was a slender man with a lined, pale face and a shock of dark hair with threads of silver through it. His eyes were baggy, but whether that was from lack of sleep or just his natural appearance, Phyllis couldn't tell. He had a tiny microphone that was attached by an almost invisible wire to a battery pack that Phyllis would wear clipped to her belt. He told her how to put it on, then handed the equipment over to her and watched as she clipped everything in position.

Farrar wore a headset, too, and when Phyllis had the microphone on, he told her, "Count to five, Mrs. Newsom. Just use your normal voice."

"One, two, three, four, five," Phyllis said.

"How was that, Jerry?" Farrar asked, and Phyllis realized he was talking to someone over the headset. "Levels okay? Good." He nodded to Phyllis. "Just talk naturally to Joye and we should be fine."

"Is it all right to talk to my friends until then, or will that mess anything up?"

"Nah, that's fine. Your mike's dead right now. Jerry out in the truck killed it after we checked it. We'll turn it on again when we're ready for you."

"All right. Thank you, Mr. Farrar."

"Just part of the job," he said. He turned away and started talking to Jerry over the headset again.

Phyllis's makeup was done already, and the girl who had put it on hadn't really done anything except touch up what Phyllis already had in place.

"Well, now I suppose we wait," Phyllis said.

"Not for long," Sam said. "It's only five minutes until the show starts."

"But I don't know how far into it I'll be on," Phyllis pointed out. "No one's said anything about that yet."

Bailey had disappeared earlier, going off to take care of

yet another responsibility that had been given to her, but after delivering her warm-up speech to the audience in the bleachers, she came backstage and hurried up to Phyllis and the others, giving them a breathless smile.

"Almost ready," she said. "Mrs. Newsom, you can just wait right here, if you would. The rest of you need to come with me. I'll show you where you're going to be sitting."

Phyllis took advantage of the opportunity to ask, "Do you know when I'll be going on?"

"The second full segment," Bailey said. "That'll be about fifteen minutes in. I'll cue you."

Phyllis nodded her thanks. Everyone wished her good luck, Carolyn and Eve hugged her, and Phyllis gave Carolyn her purse to hold while the show was going on. Then Bailey ushered the others away around the end of the set.

Phyllis took a deep breath. With everything that had been going on around her, she had been somewhat distracted, but now that a lull had descended on the set, she felt that nervous anticipation inside her again. She told herself that the experience was going to be fun, but at the same time, she knew she would be very glad and relieved when it was over.

The prerecorded theme music took her a little by surprise. She saw Joye Jameson come out of the dressing room and stride purposefully toward the door leading onto the set. She seemed distracted, and Phyllis wondered if even someone as experienced as Joye got butterflies before a broadcast.

Joye noticed her standing off to the side and smiled at her. Phyllis returned the smile. Joye didn't pause or even slow down, of course. She opened the door and stepped out onto the set, waving a hand as she did so, and applause swelled up from the audience to compete with the theme music.

Phyllis could hear every word clearly as Joye greeted the audience and told a brief anecdote about having her picture taken in front of Big Tex. The show went to a commercial, and Bailey opened the door and stuck her head through.

"Doing all right back here?" she asked Phyllis.

"Just fine," Phyllis said. She thought she sounded a lot more calm and confident than she really felt.

Bailey gave her a smile and a thumbs-up. "I'll be setting up for the funnel cake segment off camera while Joye's interviewing her first guest. We'll have everything ready."

"You're amazing, keeping up with everything you do."

"Tell that to my boss."

Phyllis didn't know if Bailey meant Joye or Reed Hayes or both, and there was no time to ask because the young woman was gone again.

Joye's first guest was a local politician who talked about how much money the state fair pumped into the economy and then ate some cotton candy, getting the sticky stuff all over his face and prompting quite a bit of laughter from the audience. They sounded like they were in a good mood, Phyllis thought, and that was promising. She hoped they would be equally receptive of her.

The first full segment was over before Phyllis knew it, seeming to fly by. During the commercial, Bailey came backstage and closed the door. She motioned Phyllis closer.

"When we come back, Joye will talk a little about the funnel cake contest and then introduce you," Bailey said. "When I point at you, you just open the door and go on out. You can smile and wave at the audience, but after you've done that, try not to pay much attention to them. Just talk directly to Joye like you would if you were in a friend's kitchen. That's the feeling we want to get across. If you can, just forget all about the fact that you're on TV."

"I don't know if that's going to be possible."

"You'll be surprised how quickly you relax and get into it. Just have fun, Phyllis. That's what we're all here for."

Phyllis nodded, swallowed, and then took a deep breath. It helped a little, but not much.

Then Joye was talking again, saying something about the funnel cake competition and how it was different this year. The words sort of ran together in Phyllis's ears.

But she heard it quite plainly when Joye said, "And now here's the winner of this year's contest! Let's all give a big state fair welcome to Phyllis Newsom!"

Bailey pointed at her. Phyllis grasped the doorknob, turned it, and stepped out onto the set. The lights around it seemed so much brighter than they had earlier, and they made her pause for a split second before she was able to force her muscles to keep moving.

There was no getting out of it now. She was on.

Chapter 13

Phyllis was surprised by the applause. Of course, the audience was clapping only because Joye Jameson had told them to and because the applause signs were flashing at the sides of the stage, out of view of the cameras, but still, this was the first time in her life that such a crowd of people—and strangers, at that—had greeted her with such enthusiasm.

Her eyes adjusted to the lights as she crossed the stage toward Joye, who held out a hand to her. Phyllis clasped it, but instead of shaking hands with her, Joye hugged her and said with a dazzling smile, "Thank you for being here."

"It's my pleasure," Phyllis said, although pleasure wasn't exactly the way she would have described any of the emotions going through her at this moment. Being here did have a certain exhilaration to it, though. She remembered what Bailey had told her about smiling and waving to the audience, so she did that quickly before returning her attention to Joye.

"So you're here to tell us all about your blue ribbon–

winning funnel cakes," Joye said. "First of all, what made you decide to enter the contest? Did you know you'd be going up against some world-class competition in those professional funnel cake concessionaires?"

"Well, not really," Phyllis said. "I didn't think about the competition, and I certainly didn't expect that I would win. I just thought it sounded like it would be something fun to try."

"Well, that's a great attitude, I must say! This wasn't the first cooking contest you've been in, though, was it, Phyllis?"

"No, not at all. My good friend Carolyn Wilbarger and I have entered dozens of them over the years, since we've been retired from teaching, and we've won or placed high in quite a few of them, especially Carolyn."

Phyllis had spotted Carolyn, Sam, Eve, and Peggy sitting in front of the bleachers in folding chairs, and she saw the way Carolyn smiled at the mention of her name. Now people around the world had heard of Carolyn and her cooking skills.

"We're here to talk about you and your funnel cakes," Joye said, and even though her tone and smile were as bright as ever, Phyllis sensed that she was being scolded slightly for straying off script, so to speak. "Tell us what it is about them that makes them so special."

Before Phyllis could say anything, a man in the audience stood up and yelled, "They're not special! She's a thief! That blue ribbon should belong to me!"

People sitting around the man gasped and turned to look at him. Phyllis couldn't see him all that well because of the lights in her face, but she recognized Ramón Silva's voice.

Silva began forcing his way through the crowd as he descended toward the floor. He kept shouting about how his funnel cakes should have won the contest.

Other people were yelling now, too. Not everybody knew exactly what was going on, and in this violent day and age, any sort of unexpected public disturbance could provoke a panic. No one knew when some sort of lunatic might pull out a gun and start shooting or try to set off a bomb.

That wasn't Ramón Silva's intention, of course. He was just upset because he'd been defeated by what he considered an amateur, Phyllis knew. But he had the crowd worked up and there was no telling what was going to happen.

Reed Hayes ran out from behind the set, calling, "Security! Security!"

Chet Murdock and the other guard were already in motion. They reached the front of the bleachers at the same time Ramón Silva did. Silva shouted, "My blue ribbon! Mine!" and swung a punch at Chet, who ducked under it and tackled him. Chet probably outweighed the short, slender concessionaire by at least fifty pounds. Silva went down under the impact and crashed onto the first couple of rows of seats with the security guard on top of him.

"That's it for you, buddy!" Chet yelled. "This time you're goin' to jail!"

Silva wasn't fighting anymore. Instead he just lay there and groaned, possibly injured because of the way he had fallen with Chet on top of him. Chet stood up, and he and the other guard hauled Silva to his feet. The members of the audience had all drawn back to give them plenty of room.

Joye left Phyllis standing there beside the counter where the ingredients for the prizewinning funnel cakes were set out and hurried over to Reed Hayes. "Did we get to commercial in time to miss all that?" she asked the producer.

"Let me check with Charlie." Hayes spoke into his headset, then nodded to Joye. "Yeah, he cut the feed as soon as the guy stood up and started to yell. The viewers probably knew something was going on, but the whole ugly scene didn't go out over the air."

"Good," Joye said. "Who let that damned crazy bastard in here, anyway?"

To Phyllis, the ugly words sounded strange coming from Joye Jameson's mouth. She didn't think she had ever heard Joye say anything stronger than *heck* or *darn* on TV. She couldn't blame her for being upset, though. Silva's outburst had almost ruined the entire show.

"I swear, somebody's going to lose their job over this," Joye went on, sounding furious now. "I can't be expected to put on a show when I'm surrounded by maniacs and incompetents! I don't get paid enough for that!"

"You don't think you get paid enough, period," Hayes muttered.

"What was that?" Joye grabbed the lapel of his coat. "What did you say to me, Hayes?"

Phyllis tried not to stare. The unflappable facade of the beautiful TV host was definitely showing some cracks right now.

Bailey came up beside Joye and Hayes and said quietly, "The cameras may be off, but you still have an audience full of people out there, Joye."

That appeared to get through to Joye instantly. She let go of Reed Hayes's coat and took a deep breath. Her expression became serene again, even though she wasn't smiling just yet.

"You're right, of course," she told Bailey. She turned to face the audience. The people who had come to watch the broadcast were all still on their feet, buzzing with confusion and apprehension, even though Chet Murdock and the other guard had taken Ramón Silva away. Phyllis didn't see them anywhere.

Bailey stepped to the edge of the stage and lifted her voice to say, "Everyone please take your seats! Sit down, please, so we can start the show again!"

Phyllis was a little surprised they were going to continue after Silva's disruption, but she realized she shouldn't have been. After all, the old saying was that the show must go on.

Phyllis hadn't budged from her position during the incident. Joye came back over to her. Even though Joye was smiling again, Phyllis could tell that she was furious. Joye kept her outrage under firm control, however. She lifted her chin a little and said, "Close-up on me, Hank."

Normally it would be the director who issued orders like that, but Phyllis supposed Joye had the power to override Charlie Farrar if she really wanted to. In any case, the burly Hank pointed his camera right at Joye, who added, "Give me a countdown."

Hank held up an open hand, closing each finger and the thumb in turn until he had a clenched fist. Joye's smile brightened even more, and as she looked directly into the camera, she greeted the viewers at home by saying, "I hope you'll excuse us for those technical difficulties, folks. You can't put on a show like this without having a few little glitches now and then, I suppose."

Hank's camera pulled back slightly, probably in response to a command from Charlie Farrar out in the truck.

"Now, you were about to tell us all about those delicious funnel cakes of yours, Phyllis," Joye said.

Phyllis drew in a deep breath. The audience was settling back down on the bleachers. They had come to see a show, and everyone involved still intended to deliver. Phyllis had no choice but to go ahead, too.

She began talking about getting ready for the funnel cake competition. She explained about some of the different recipes she tried, the ones with pumpkin, chocolate, and fruit. Then she explained why she had decided on the recipe she'd used in the contest. She didn't want to stray too far from the taste of the traditional funnel cake, and the maple pecan recipe seemed to fit.

Joye said, "As you may have noticed, we just happen to have all those ingredients right here on the show, Phyllis."

Phyllis smiled and nodded, feeling more comfortable now. "I did notice that."

Joye turned to the cameras and the audience and said, "When we come back, Phyllis and I will be making a batch of those wonderful maple pecan funnel cakes, and a few lucky people from the audience are going to get to come down here and sample them with us on national television. Won't that be fun?"

Applause and cheers came from the audience. The red light on Hank's camera went off.

Joye turned sharply toward Bailey and Reed Hayes, who hurried toward her from the side of the set. "We'll be going into a third segment—" Hayes began.

"I don't care," Joye said, interrupting the producer. "The first one doesn't really count because of that trouble. I came here today to make funnel cakes, and by God, I'm going to make funnel cakes!"

"Well, it shouldn't be too big a problem, I suppose," Hayes said. "We have that segment of you riding some of the midway rides coming up, and we can cut it, can't we, Charlie?" He waited to hear the director's response, then said, "Charlie says we can cut it and show it tomorrow."

"Fine," Joye snapped. "Just do whatever it takes."

The commercial break sped by. Bailey told Phyllis, "Move on over behind the counter. You and Joye will be ready to start mixing the batter for the funnel cakes when we come out of commercial."

Phyllis nodded. She was starting to pick up the rhythm of the broadcast, she thought. Everything about it still seemed odd and unnatural to her, but at least she had a better idea now of what was going on and what was expected of her. She glanced at her friends, who smiled at her and gave her encouraging nods.

It would be all right with her, Phyllis told herself, if she was never on television again.

Hayes said, "We're back in three . . . two . . . one . . ."

The red light on Hank's camera came on.

"We're back," Joye said, "and my friend Phyllis Newsom and I are about to mix the batter for a batch of her prizewinning funnel cakes. Why don't you walk us through it, Phyllis?"

"All right, Joye," Phyllis said, figuring she might as well fall into the show's pattern of familiarity. "We're going to mix the batter and then pour it into two inches of hot oil using a funnel. We use a metal ring to keep the batter contained so we don't end up with a funnel cake the size of the pan."

Phyllis started cracking the eggs and emptying them into the mixing bowl, setting the empty shells in another empty bowl. She started the mixer and she and Joye added the ingredients, explaining to the audience what each ingredient was and how much was used.

While they were doing that, Bailey checked the temperature of the oil and adjusted the burner under the pan that was waiting to one side. Phyllis didn't rush what she was doing, but she also didn't waste time getting the batter mixed, knowing that the oil was already at the right temperature to fry the batter and the metal ring was in the middle of the skillet. She made sure that Joye handled some of the steps, too, having seen *The Joye of Cooking* enough to know that the host always participated in whatever was being prepared.

When the batter was ready, Phyllis said, "All right, we can go ahead and pour our first funnel cake now." She paused. "Would you like to do the honors, Joye?"

Joye laughed and said, "No, thanks. You're the blue ribbon winner here, Phyllis, so you go right ahead."

Phyllis had her finger over the opening in the bottom of the funnel, the way the professionals did it. She moved it away and let the batter begin to pour into the hot oil, moving it around and back and forth to form the classic shape inside the ring. Joye kept up a running commentary while she was doing that, but Phyllis focused all her attention on the task at hand and tuned out what Joye was saying. After everything that had happened, she didn't want to ruin the first funnel cake in front of millions of viewers.

When she was finished, she set the empty funnel aside, picking up the tongs instead. "You have to turn it like a pancake or a waffle, right?" Joye asked.

"That's right," Phyllis said. "The process is somewhat similar. More like a donut since it's fried, but we have to remove the metal ring first."

She removed the metal ring and set it aside, then grasped the funnel cake with the tongs and turned it over to finish cooking. When she judged it was ready, she removed it from the oil and set it aside to drain and cool.

"We can get another one cooking while we're putting the maple syrup and pecans on that one," she said.

"This is very interesting. I love watching you work," Joye said.

"Thank you. It's not really work, though," Phyllis said as she drizzled the maple syrup and sprinkled the chopped pecans over the first funnel cake. "Cooking has always been fun for me."

"Me, too! That's the way it is with the best cooks."

When Phyllis had the first funnel cake finished, an overhead camera moved in to get a close-up of it. Joye enthused over how beautiful it was, and then as the main camera, manned by Hank, took the shot again, Joye smiled into the lens and said, "I think I'm going to give it a try. Would that be all right, Phyllis?"

"Well, it might still be a little hot," Phyllis said. "Just be careful and don't burn your mouth."

"Oh, I won't." Joye tore a piece off the funnel cake, popped it into her mouth, and began to chew. While she was doing that, she said, "Oh, my. I know it's not polite to talk with your mouth full, but this is de—"

Phyllis had the tongs in her hand and had removed the ring and was about to turn the second funnel cake, but as she heard Joye stop short without finishing the word *delicious*, she glanced over at the host. Shock surged through Phyllis's mind as she saw Joye stagger, catching herself with one hand on the counter while her other hand went to her throat. Joye's mouth hung open, and her lips moved like those of a fish out of water as she gasped for air.

"Joye!" Bailey cried as she rushed in from the side.

With a harsh strangling sound, Joye collapsed, twisting off her feet as she fell to the floor behind the counter. For the second time in this episode, the audience members leaped to their feet in alarm and began to shout.

"Cut the cameras! Cut the cameras!" Reed Hayes yelled as he rushed forward from the edge of the stage.

Phyllis knew that Joye was having a violent allergic reaction of some sort. During the last few years she had taught, she and her fellow teachers had received training on such things. Too many students now had allergies and were prone to attacks if they were exposed to the wrong thing, and the teachers had to know how to deal with those potentially serious problems.

Bailey dropped to her knees beside Joye, who was writhing around on the floor as she struggled to draw air through her swollen throat. Bailey pulled something from her pocket that Phyllis recognized as an autoinjector—a small penlike syringe already prepared with a dose of epinephrine that could save the life of someone suffering from a serious allergic reaction. With swift, efficient motions that told Phyllis Bailey had practiced and prepared for this emergency, the young woman pulled the cover from the needle and stuck it into Joye's thigh. Bailey's thumb depressed the plunger. As she pulled the needle out, she sat back a little and a look of relief crossed her face as she waited for the medication to take effect.

That look turned to an expression of horror as Joye began to spasm even worse. Her arms and legs flailed, and her choking sounds rose to a frantic babble. Hayes knelt on her other side, and Hank came around the set to loom over the three of them. "What's wrong with her?" the burly cameraman cried. "That thing was supposed to stop the attack!"

Sam was out of his chair, standing beside Phyllis now with one hand gripping her arm to support her. Carolyn, Eve, and Peggy gathered anxiously around her as well. The audience crowded forward to see what was going on, and Chet Murdock and the other guard, who had returned from dealing with Ramón Silva, couldn't hold them back. The other guard was calling for more help on a walkie-talkie.

Joye's body jerked and her back arched up from the floor. She held that pose for a second, then slumped down loosely. People screamed and shouted. It was obvious to everyone what had just happened, but Hayes confirmed it by holding a hand to Joye's neck for a long moment, searching for a pulse, before he looked up and announced bleakly, "She's dead."

Chapter 14

An hour later, Phyllis, Sam, and the others sat alone in the bleachers and watched with grim expressions on their faces as several paramedics wheeled a gurney bearing a zipped-up black body bag away from the broadcast set.

Several uniformed Dallas police officers stood around the set, guarding it while the crime scene technicians continued scouring the area for every possible bit of evidence. Off to one side stood Bailey Broderick, Reed Hayes, Charlie Farrar, the cameraman Hank, and the rest of the crew. A couple of officers were keeping an eye on them to make sure none of them left before the detectives in charge of the case had a chance to talk to them.

At the moment, those detectives, a man and a woman, were interviewing Chet Murdock and the other security guard who had been on duty when the fatal allergic reaction had struck down Joye Jameson.

"I don't get what they're doing," Peggy said. "They're

acting like there was some sort of foul play here, instead of just a terrible accident."

"We don't know for sure that it was an accident," Carolyn said. "We've known people who appeared to die of natural causes before, but then it turned out to be something else . . . haven't we, Phyllis?"

"I don't want to even think about that," Phyllis said honestly. The knowledge that Joye had died right after eating a piece of her funnel cake was already nagging at her. She didn't see how it was possible that the two things could be connected, and yet the conclusion was inescapable. Somehow, that funnel cake had caused Joye's reaction . . . and her death.

Sam said, "I imagine the cops are goin' to these lengths because it was somebody famous who died. They know it'll get a lot of press coverage, and they don't want there to be any questions later on about them not doin' their job the way they should have, so they'll cover every possibility."

"I suppose so," Carolyn said. "But if you ask me, they're acting like they think Joye's death is suspicious."

"Any unexpected, unexplained death is suspicious by nature," Phyllis said. "That's all that's going on here."

She wished she could believe that. But deep down, she thought Carolyn was right. The entire building had been locked down as soon as the police arrived, although plenty of people had gone in and out first. There was no way the security guards on duty could have stopped that.

Now everyone was gone except for the five of them, the police, and the show's crew. The audience members and the other people who had been in the exhibit hall when the police arrived had been questioned briefly, a process that didn't amount to much more than getting contact information. Since Phyllis had been right there on the set with Joye, the police wanted her to wait and talk to the detectives, and her friends hadn't wanted to leave without her, so they were all still here, too.

The female detective who had been questioning the crew came over to the bleachers and said, "Mrs. Newsom?"

"Yes?" Phyllis replied as she stood up.

"Would you come with me, please?" As Carolyn started to get up, too, the detective put out a hand to stop her and added, "Just Mrs. Newsom, please."

"Phyllis, you don't have to talk to them without a lawyer," Carolyn said. She had an instinctive distrust of the police, probably because she and her daughter had both been suspects in a murder case several years earlier.

"I don't need a lawyer," Phyllis said. She hoped that was true. She hadn't forgotten how she herself had been locked up in jail less than a year ago.

As she stepped down from the bleachers to join the detective, the woman said, "Actually, if you'd like to have an attorney present, that's all right."

That surprised Phyllis. She said, "Am I being read my rights?"

"Oh, no. This is just informal questioning. We're just trying to find out what happened; that's all. But no one who wants a lawyer is going to be denied one."

Phyllis shook her head and said, "I'm fine."

The detective motioned toward the broadcast set. "Let's go over here."

The two of them stepped up into the working kitchen that had been built for the TV show's trip to the state fair. Phyllis couldn't help but glance at the spot where Joye had collapsed and died, but then she forced herself to look away.

The detective must have seen what she did. She said, "I'm sorry to have to put you through this, Mrs. Newsom. That must have been a terrible experience, watching Ms. Jameson die right in front of you like that."

"It was terrible, all right," Phyllis said.

"We'll get this over with as quickly as we can. I'm Detective Charlotte Morgan, by the way. My partner over there is Detective Al Hunt."

Detective Morgan was probably forty years old, Phyllis estimated, and rather attractive, although there was a certain hard-bitten cynicism visible in her face, no doubt put there by all the awful things she saw in her job. Blond hair fell just past her shoulders. She wore jeans and a brown leather jacket. Her partner, Detective Hunt, was a stocky, gray-haired man in a rumpled suit who came a lot closer to fitting the popular image of a cop.

"So," Detective Morgan went on, "just tell me about what happened here today."

"Well, I was on the show to make funnel cakes . . . You know about the funnel cake competition and how I won it yesterday?"

"Yes, ma'am, Mr. Hayes and Ms. Broderick told us about that. Unless you saw something unusual earlier, you can just take up the story from where you came out and started making funnel cakes with Ms. Jameson."

That was what Phyllis did, going back through the fifteen

minutes or so she had been on the set with Joye. She included every detail she could think of. Detective Morgan took notes, and from time to time she glanced up as if she were surprised about something.

Phyllis figured out what that something was when Morgan commented, "You must have an exceptional memory, Mrs. Newsom. Most witnesses are a little more vague about things."

There was a good reason Phyllis had gotten in the habit of being as observant as she was, but she was hesitant to explain it. On the other hand, it wouldn't take any time at all for the detectives to find out about her background if they wanted to.

"I've been around several criminal investigations in the past," she said.

"Oh, really?"

"My son works for the sheriff's department over in Parker County," Phyllis said. "I'm acquainted with a number of people in the department, and in the Weatherford Police Department, as well."

"This isn't really a criminal investigation," Morgan pointed out. "Not at this point, anyway."

"No, of course not. But because of, well, being around those sorts of investigations in the past, I've learned to keep my eyes open."

The detective studied her for a moment, then said, "Let me get this straight. You're a retired schoolteacher, right?"

"That's right."

Detective Morgan was starting to look even more cynical now. "And an amateur detective?"

"I never said that."

"Look, Mrs. Newsom, I realize that when some people get to be a certain age, they have to find something to occupy their time—"

Phyllis felt a flash of anger. "That's not it at all, Detective," she said.

"I don't mean any offense. I'm just doing my job." Morgan closed her notebook. "I think I've got all I need from you right now, Mrs. Newsom. You gave your contact info to the uniformed officer who canvased everyone, didn't you?"

"Yes, I did. I gave him the address where we're staying here in Dallas, my address in Weatherford, and my cell phone number."

"Then that's all we need. Thank you." Morgan started to turn away, then paused. She waved a hand at the counter, where all the ingredients for the maple pecan funnel cakes were still sitting, along with the one from which Joye Jameson had taken a bite and the pan of oil, now cold, with the scorched second funnel cake still in it. "Does any of this stuff belong to you? Because we're going to have to take it all in as evidence, and we can give you a receipt for it . . ."

Phyllis shook her head. "No, the TV show provided everything for the funnel cakes we were making today. There's nothing out of the ordinary about any of it, though; I can tell you that much."

"What kind of oil is that?"

"Corn," Phyllis said. "That's the first thing I thought of, that it might be peanut oil, because I know there are people who are violently allergic to peanuts. But my recipe calls for corn oil, so I'm sure that's what they used."

"We'll have it tested and make certain of that, but thanks, anyway."

"Detective . . . I'm curious about one thing."

Morgan looked like she was growing impatient, but she asked, "What's that?"

"You have the footage that was being broadcast, don't you? So all you have to do to know what happened is to look at it."

"The camera doesn't always catch everything. We have to ask questions to know what we're looking at."

That answer made sense, Phyllis thought. She nodded and said, "Thank you."

"If we need anything, we'll be in touch."

"What about my friends? Are you going to interview them, too?"

Morgan glanced over at the bleachers where Sam and the others were sitting. She asked, "Where were they during the show?"

"In some folding chairs in front of the bleachers where they're sitting now."

"Then they didn't really see anything more than what the rest of the audience would have seen," the detective said. "No, we shouldn't need them. You're all free to go."

"Thank you," Phyllis said again, and this time Detective Morgan went back over to rejoin her partner. Sam, Carolyn, Eve, and Peggy came down the steps to meet Phyllis as she walked off the set.

"Are they going to interrogate us, too?" Carolyn asked.

Phyllis shook her head. "No, the detective said we were all free to go."

"Do they know what caused Joye's allergic reaction?"

"If they do, Detective Morgan didn't say anything to me about it," Phyllis replied.

"It looked like a peanut allergy to me," Carolyn went on. "Back when we were still teaching, they really drilled the dangers of peanuts into us. We had in-service training with the school nurse about it every year. And you know, I've always wondered where all those peanut allergies came from. I don't recall ever knowing anyone who was allergic to peanuts while I was growing up, do you?"

Carolyn looked around at the others, who all shook their heads. "Everybody I knew ate goobers," Sam said.

"I don't understand it, either," Phyllis said, "but I don't doubt that it's real."

"Oh, neither do I," Carolyn said. "I just can't figure out why it's so prevalent now."

One of the officers at the building's exit had to check with Detective Hunt on the radio before he would allow them to leave. As they stepped out into the beautiful autumn afternoon, which was a mixture of clouds and sunshine, it was hard for Phyllis to believe that death had struck so suddenly and unexpectedly in the building behind them. Joye Jameson had been so beautiful and vivacious, and a couple of minutes later she was gone. It was tragic, Phyllis thought, and not just because Joye was a television star. She would have felt the same way about anyone who had died like that.

The fair was still going on, of course, even though the Creative Arts Building had been evacuated and put off-limits to the crowds thronging through Fair Park. Phyllis and her friends started making their way toward the parking lot but hadn't gone very far when she heard someone behind her call, "Mrs. Newsom!"

Phyllis turned to see Bailey Broderick hurrying toward them. The young woman looked upset, and understandably so. Her boss and mentor had just died right in front of her eyes not much more than an hour earlier.

"Bailey, dear, I'm sorry—" Phyllis began.

"What did you do?" Bailey interrupted her. "What did you do to kill Joye?"

Chapter 15

That accusation left Phyllis speechless for a moment, but Carolyn immediately stepped into the breach.

"How dare you say something like that?" she demanded of Bailey. "Phyllis didn't do anything to hurt that poor woman!"

"Seems to me you're a little out of line there, Miss Broderick," Sam added.

Bailey didn't back down. Still addressing Phyllis, she said, "Joye was eating your funnel cake, and then she died. What am I supposed to think? What's anyone supposed to think?"

Phyllis had regained her composure now. She said, "You had that injector ready, Bailey. Clearly you know that Joye was allergic to something. All of the ingredients were provided by the show, so you know everything that went into that funnel cake."

Bailey stared at her for a second before saying, "Wait a minute! Are you accusing *me* of doing something wrong?"

"Not a very good feeling, is it?" Carolyn asked, clearly speaking from experience.

"Hold on, everyone," Phyllis said. "Bailey, I'm not accusing you. Since you obviously knew about Joye's condition, I'm asking you what she was allergic to. Was it peanuts?"

Bailey nodded. "As a matter of fact, it was."

"I thought so. When people have such a violent reaction it's usually either peanuts or shellfish that causes it, and there was nothing even remotely connected to shellfish in that recipe."

"There weren't any peanuts, either," Bailey pointed out. "If there had been, Joye wouldn't have gotten anywhere near those funnel cakes."

"So she knew she was allergic, too."

"Of course."

"Had you ever had to use an allergy pen like that on her before?"

"Once," Bailey said. "A couple of years ago when we were in New Orleans for Mardi Gras. Just before we went on the air, while we were still backstage, she accidentally ate some candy that had peanuts in it. She reacted badly enough that I had to use the pen, although not as violently as she did today." A frown creased the young woman's forehead. "But that time the pen stopped the reaction in its tracks. I can't figure out why it didn't work this time. In fact it just seemed to make things worse."

"No, I can't figure that out, either," Phyllis said. "But I'm sure the police will get to the bottom of it."

"They're treating this like they're suspicious of all of us," Bailey went on with worry creeping into her voice. "Like they think somebody hurt Joye on purpose. I guess . . . I guess that's got me all on edge. Otherwise I wouldn't have gone off on you like that. I'm sorry, Mrs. Newsom."

"Don't worry about it, dear. We're all upset."

Carolyn's snort made it clear that Phyllis was more forgiving than she would have been in the same circumstances.

Phyllis nodded toward the Creative Arts Building and said, "I take it the police are through in there and have told everyone they're free to go?"

"Actually, the detectives are still talking to a few of the crew members, but they were finished questioning me." Bailey laughed humorlessly. "They told me not to leave town, though. I guess that means I'm a suspect."

"I'm sure that's not the case. They don't know yet if there was even any wrongdoing."

Peggy said, "Somebody did something wrong—that's for sure; otherwise, that little gal wouldn't be dead."

Bailey winced at the plainspoken words. Before she could say anything else, a man called her name, and they all turned to see Reed Hayes coming toward them.

"There you are," Hayes went on as he came up to them. "I wondered where you'd gotten off to. Are you all right?"

"What do you think?" Bailey asked. Her voice held a little quaver of emotion now.

Hayes put his arms around her, reminding Phyllis that Bailey and the producer were supposed to be involved in a romantic relationship. She hadn't seen much evidence of that so far whenever she was around them, but Hayes summoned up a little tenderness now as he hugged Bailey and patted her on the back.

"I know you're upset," he told her, "but you've got to pull it together. We're all counting on you, Bailey."

She nodded, sniffled a little, and said, "I know."

"Counting on her for what?" Carolyn asked bluntly. Phyllis was wondering the same thing, but her friend had saved her the trouble of asking.

"We still have another broadcast to do tomorrow," Hayes said. "Bailey will have to fill in for Joye."

"Couldn't you just show a rerun instead?" Phyllis asked.

"Our contract with the syndicate calls for us to produce a minimum of four new shows per week unless it's a scheduled hiatus," Hayes explained. "In an emergency situation like this, they'd probably grant us an exception . . . but they'd hold it against us when we sit down to hammer out the new contract in a couple of months, and I don't want to give them any extra advantage."

"I didn't know you were about to negotiate a new contract," Phyllis said.

Hayes still had one arm around Bailey's shoulders. He shrugged with his other shoulder. "No reason you'd know about it. You're not in the TV business."

"That's true," Phyllis said. "I'm certainly not."

"Wait a minute," Carolyn said. "You're going to continue with the show?"

"For now. We don't have any choice. We have a contract. As for whether or not it goes on in the long run . . ." Hayes squeezed Bailey's shoulders. "I suppose that all depends on how Bailey does in the meantime."

"Reed, I've told you I . . . I just don't know about this . . . I mean . . . taking over the show—"

"Who else is going to do it?" he asked her. "There's no one else who can."

"Maybe Gloria Kimball could come back," Carolyn suggested. "I don't think she would mind."

Hayes sent a sharp glance her way. "That's not going to happen," he said. "No matter how much Gloria might like the idea." With a hand on Bailey's arm, he started to steer her back toward the building. "Come on. We've got to talk to Charlie about tomorrow's show."

Bailey let him turn her around, but she lifted a hand in farewell to Phyllis. "Again, I'm sorry for what I said, Mrs. Newsom."

"It's all right," Phyllis told her. "You have a lot of other things to worry about now."

Once more she and her friends started toward the parking lot. As they walked, Carolyn said, "You know, some people might consider it a lucky break for Miss Broderick that something happened to Joye. Now she gets to step in and take over the show for a while. It's like a ready-made audition for her to be a star."

"I don't think I like what you're hinting at," Phyllis said.

"Maybe not . . . but you can't deny that the same thought crossed your mind, didn't it?"

Phyllis had to admit that was true enough, although she just shrugged and didn't say so out loud.

Maybe it was just because she had stumbled into those murder cases in the past, but once she had gotten over the initial shock of seeing Joye Jameson die right before her eyes, she had begun to ask herself who might benefit from Joye's death. Bailey Broderick was the obvious answer to that question.

Bailey had labored for several years in near anonymity, and from what Phyllis had seen, she worked hard to make sure the show was a success while receiving no credit for her efforts. Anyone in that situation might be expected to feel a little reasonable jealousy. Throw in the fact that Bailey would now be taking over the show for the next couple of months, and it certainly appeared that she had a good reason for wanting Joye Jameson dead.

On the other hand, Phyllis had seen no indications of any hostility between Joye and Bailey. Maybe a little apprehension on Bailey's part over the fact that Joye could be a temperamental boss, but if that was a reason for murder, then a lot of the world's bosses would be in danger. Other than that, the two women had seemed to get along very well.

There had been a hint of friction between Joye and Reed Hayes over Joye's salary, Phyllis recalled, but again, nothing that wasn't extremely common in the business world. Instinctively, she had an easier time regarding the producer as a potential killer, rather than Bailey, but there was absolutely nothing to base that feeling on, Phyllis told herself.

Anyway, the whole thing was absurd. As far as anyone knew now, Joye's death was just a tragic accident of some sort, and Phyllis was sure that would turn out to be true, once all the evidence was in. She was just wasting her time by letting her mind play with these fantasies of murder.

"Will you folks be heading back to Weatherford now?" Peggy asked as they reached the parking lot and headed toward Phyllis's Lincoln.

"I've still got that Spam cook-off tomorrow," Sam reminded her.

"Oh, yeah. Well, I wouldn't want you to miss that, Stretch. And I've got to admit, I've enjoyed having the company this week. That house of mine will seem emptier than ever once the four of you are gone."

Carolyn said, "Maybe we'll stay until the weekend, if that's all right with you. I'm not sure we'd want to brave Friday afternoon rush hour in Dallas."

Sam laughed. "Since I've been doin' the drivin', I'm darn sure I don't want to brave Friday afternoon rush hour in Dallas. I think Saturday mornin' will be just fine for us to go home."

"Sounds good to me," Peggy agreed. "Like I said, I've enjoyed having you here."

They got in the car, left the fairgrounds, and headed back to Highland Park. Phyllis didn't really pay attention to the urban landscape on both sides of the highway. Instead, she was still distracted by thoughts of everything that had happened this week. Her mind kept returning to the way she had seen Bailey and Hank the cameraman possibly sneaking off for a clandestine meeting. Could that have had any bearing on what had happened later?

Sam glanced over at her and said quietly, "You're thinkin' about it, aren't you?"

"I can't seem to help myself," Phyllis said. "I guess I really am the terrible old busybody some people take me for."

"Not hardly," Sam said. "You're just puzzled by what happened, like the rest of us."

"There shouldn't have been any peanuts in that funnel cake. There *weren't* any peanuts or peanut butter or anything like that added to it. I know that. I was right there. It had to be the oil. That's the only possibility. But I watched Bailey put the oil in the pan. It was supposed to be corn oil."

Carolyn leaned forward and said over the seat, "The label on the bottle *said* it was corn oil. But that doesn't mean that it actually was."

Phyllis nodded and said, "I know. There might have been a mistake at the factory, I suppose. The wrong label could have been put on the bottle. That would make it just a terrible accident."

"Or someone could have switched the corn oil for peanut oil," Carolyn persisted. "And that would make it . . ."

"Yes," Phyllis said. "That would make what happened to Joye Jameson murder."

Chapter 16

Like the proverbial genie in the bottle, once the word was out there, it was impossible to put it back. Phyllis couldn't honestly say that she had thought about murder as soon as Joye began to choke. She had been too startled and then too horrified for that. But Joye had been dead for only moments when the possibility that her death wasn't accidental occurred to Phyllis.

When they got back to the house in Highland Park, Peggy turned on the television and started flipping through the channels as they all sat in the den, still somewhat stunned by what had happened. All she found was normal afternoon programming—judge shows, talk shows hosted by washed-up celebrities, reruns of fifty-year-old sitcoms, and infomercials—until she abruptly stopped pressing the button on the remote as a familiar face appeared.

Gloria Kimball looked into the camera with an earnestly sorrowful expression on her face as she said, "—happened to be near the Creative Arts Building, Mike, just as word began to spread that something terrible had happened to Joye Jameson."

The shot went to a split screen, with a perfectly coiffed, spray-tanned, and equally earnest male news anchor in the studio on the left and Gloria outdoors with the fairgrounds in the background on the right. The anchorman said, "Yes, and we've confirmed now, Gloria, that Joye Jameson, host to the popular *Joye of Cooking* syndicated TV series, passed away this afternoon during the live broadcast of an episode from the State Fair of Texas. Can you add any more to that, Gloria?"

Carolyn said, "Anybody who was watching Joye's show knows that."

"Not necessarily," Phyllis said. "They know something happened to cause the show to cut away to a commercial, but it never came back after that, so they might have thought the problem was just technical difficulties."

On the TV screen, Gloria Kimball said in answer to the anchorman's question, "Yes, Mike, I can. It appears that Joye Jameson had a fatal allergic reaction to something in the funnel cake she had just tasted, a funnel cake made by the winner of this year's funnel cake competition, one Phyllis Newsom. As a matter of fact, I spoke with Mrs. Newsom earlier today in an interview about her victory that our viewers probably saw."

Phyllis winced. She had never been interested in celebrity or fame, and certainly not notoriety like this.

Sam pointed out, "Hey, she said, 'one Phyllis Newsom.' There's bound to be more of them in the world than just you."

"Not helping," Phyllis muttered.

The anchorman went on, "So you're saying, Gloria, that

Joye Jameson was killed by this . . . this fatal funnel cake made by Phyllis Newsom?"

"Good Lord!" Carolyn burst out. "I think you should sue them, Phyllis."

Phyllis just shook her head wearily and waved off Carolyn's suggestion.

"Oh, it's much too early in the investigation to speculate about that, Mike," Gloria said.

Peggy asked, "Could they possibly call each other by their first names more often? Nobody talks like that in real life."

"It's TV news," Sam said. "It just sort of has a noddin' acquaintance with real life."

Gloria continued, "I'm sure it'll be a while before the medical examiner's office announces an official cause of death. But in the meantime"—her face got even more solemn—"my very good friend, my protégée, if you will, is gone, struck down in the prime of her life by a cruel fate."

Carolyn said, "If what Bailey told us is true, Gloria's probably dancing a jig on the inside right now."

Phyllis thought about that. From what Bailey had said, Gloria Kimball did indeed hold a bitter grudge against Joye over what had happened several years earlier. No one could tell that from the way she was acting now, though.

"Thank you for that live report from the state fair, Gloria," the anchorman said. "You'll let us know if there are any other breaking developments?"

"Of course, Mike."

"Thanks again, Gloria." The split screen went away, leaving the anchorman on camera by himself. He went on, "I'm Mike Wallichevsky for *The 44 News*, and we'll be right back with a story you won't want to miss about a gorilla that can predict what the stock market is going to do." He smiled. "You may want to get some bananas together to invest."

"That's about enough of that," Peggy said as she turned the TV off. "I think I'm gonna go start supper."

"I'll come and help you," Carolyn said as she got to her feet. "How about you, Phyllis?"

After a couple of seconds, Phyllis said, "What?"

"I asked if you wanted to help us fix supper."

"Oh. I'm sorry, I was a little distracted. No, I don't really feel up to it, Carolyn, if that's all right."

"That's fine," Carolyn assured her. "After everything that's happened this week, I'm sure you could use a little rest and relaxation."

"Yes," Phyllis said, "I think I'll go up and check my e-mail and try to get my mind off of everything."

About half an hour later, Sam knocked quietly on the partially open door of Phyllis's room. She was sitting in an armchair by the window, her computer open in her lap. She looked up, saw Sam standing there, and smiled.

"Come on in," she said.

Sam sat on the foot of the bed and said, "I had a feelin' you were doing more than just checkin' e-mail up here. You've been researchin', haven't you?"

"That's right. My Google-fu is powerful, as you always like to say."

"Yeah, but somehow it doesn't sound quite so goofy when I say it."

"So you'd like to think, anyway," Phyllis said, still smiling.

"I believe I'll change the subject by askin' you what you found out."

Phyllis nodded. "I was looking into the background of Joye Jameson's show—"

"That goes without sayin'."

"And I was amazed," Phyllis said, "at how much, well, gossip you can find out about celebrities online."

"Celebrity gossip on the Internet." Sam shook his head. "Who'd'a thunk it?"

"That's about enough joking around from you, Mr. Fletcher. Do you want to hear this or not?"

Sam held up his hands in mock surrender. "All right, I'll behave," he promised.

"Good. Anyway, I went all the way back to the days of *Gloria's Kitchen*. It's true that Joye was Gloria Kimball's assistant. I remembered that, but I didn't know that Joye worked on the show for five years in that position before Gloria had a problem on the air one day."

"What sort of problem?" Sam asked.

"Well, the consensus of opinion seems to be that she was drunk, although some people believe she was using drugs. In fact, after the incident Gloria herself claimed she had a poor reaction to some prescription medication. But regardless of the cause, she made something of a spectacle of herself. There are clips from that episode on YouTube."

Phyllis tapped the computer's touch pad a couple of times and turned it so that Sam could see the screen. The video played, and as it opened, Gloria Kimball, looking only slightly younger than she did now, was walking unsteadily across a set much like the one at the state fair.

"This was on the show's regular soundstage in Hollywood," Phyllis said.

Gloria tripped, apparently over nothing, and had to catch herself on a kitchen counter. "My nex' guess is . . . is movie star Frank . . . Frank Stanton. Gorgeous boy, jus' gorgeous. Here he is now. C'mon out, Frankie."

A good-looking young man about twenty years old came onto the set, smiling but looking a little worried and wary at the same time. He had good reason to feel that way, because Gloria greeted him by throwing her arms around him and kissing him on the mouth. The actor tried to disengage himself from her embrace gracefully, but Gloria hung on. Joye Jameson was visible in the background of the shot, looking shocked.

"That kid's half her age," Sam said.

"Yes, evidently Gloria was a cougar before the term even became popular," Phyllis said. She turned the computer around to face her again and stopped the video. "It goes on like that for another minute or two before the director finally cuts away."

"Who was the director?" Sam asked.

Phyllis frowned and said, "You know, I don't know. There are no credits on this clip. You think it was Charlie Farrar?"

"I don't have any idea," Sam said with a shrug. "It just occurred to me; that's all."

"It might be interesting to find out. Hang on a minute while I look."

Sam sat on the bed while Phyllis navigated to another site. After a few moments, she said, "According to this, Charlie Farrar worked as an assistant director and director on *Gloria's Kitchen*, but it doesn't list individual episodes that he directed. Still, it's certainly possible he was there that day."

"Didn't mean to distract you," Sam said. "Go on with what you were tellin' me about how Gloria fell from grace and Joye took over."

"Well, after that incident, Gloria was off the show for a while, although it was still called *Gloria's Kitchen* at that point. She supposedly had medical issues, which everyone took to mean she was in rehab."

"Yep. You can see why."

"Joye filled in for her, and after several weeks of that, the name of the show changed without explanation to *The Joye of Cooking*, and Joye was the star from then on. There was some minor speculation that Joye had sabotaged Gloria somehow, maybe by slipping her some sort of drug without her knowing, and of course there was a little talk about how Joye must have been sleeping with the producer, too, in order to take over the show so quickly and completely."

"That producer bein' Reed Hayes?"

"Yes. He wasn't the original producer on *Gloria's Kitchen*, but he'd been with the show for several years at the time, and he's still running it."

Sam rubbed his chin and said, "So back then Hayes was sleepin' with Gloria Kimball's assistant, and now he's Bailey Broderick's boyfriend."

"It was *rumored* he was sleeping with Joye. There's no proof of that, as far as I've been able to discover so far. Of course, I just started looking into it." Phyllis paused. "And I appreciate you not asking me why I'm doing this."

"Shoot, I understand," Sam said. "You're curious. I am, too. I've got to say, though, in the time that I was around 'em, I didn't get any sort of ex-lovers vibe from Hayes and Joye. For what it's worth."

"For what it's worth, neither did I," Phyllis said. "Maybe a little animosity, but I figure that was strictly business. Which leads right into my next point . . . Joye was rumored to be demanding a large increase in her salary in this new contract that's coming up. Large enough that it's possible the syndicate would have canceled the show rather than giving in. Evidently the battle over that behind the scenes has been pretty bitter. Joye was even threatening to leave and start her own network if she didn't get what she wanted."

Sam frowned and asked, "Was she a big enough star to do something like that? No offense, but I'd barely heard of the lady until recently."

"She was a big enough star with her target audience that she probably could have found the backing she needed. Whether or not she would have been successful . . . well, who knows? You can't predict TV."

"Or much of anything else about life," Sam said.

Phyllis smiled. "That's true. But that keeps it interesting, don't you think?"

"Well . . . there's a good reason for that old Chinese curse. You know, the one that goes, 'May you live in interesting times.'"

"And we certainly do," Phyllis said.

From downstairs, Carolyn called, "Supper's ready!"

"There's more," Phyllis said, "but we'll talk about it later."

Chapter 17

$\mathcal{D}$uring supper, neither Phyllis nor Sam mentioned anything about what they had been discussing upstairs, but it was never far from Phyllis's mind, and judging by the thoughtful expression on Sam's face, he was mulling it over, too.

The mood at the dining room table was subdued. Phyllis tried to liven it up slightly by saying, "Sam, tell us again about the recipe you're going to use in the contest tomorrow."

He grinned. "Well, as you might expect, growin' up in Texas when I did, I never knew much about sushi, even though it was invented right here in the Lone Star State."

"What?" Carolyn asked. "I never heard of such a thing! Sushi wasn't invented in Texas."

"Sure it was," Sam insisted. "We've had it around here for as far back as I can remember."

Phyllis tried not to roll her eyes. She had a pretty good idea what he was about to say.

"We call it bait," Sam said with a smile.

Carolyn stared at him for a couple of seconds, then sighed exasperatedly in an eloquent expression of her opinion regarding his sense of humor. Phyllis could tell that Eve and Peggy were trying not to laugh, though.

"Anyway," Sam went on, "what I'm gonna fix for the contest isn't really sushi, but that's what I'm callin' it. It's Texas-style Spam sushi, a little like a California roll but even more like Hawaii's Spam *musubi* recipe. It has sushi rice that's easy to make in a rice steamer, and it's put together in a form. You can buy *musubi* forms, but I made mine by cuttin' out the bottom of a Spam can. You put down a strip of seaweed on a plate or cuttin' board, place the form in the middle of the seaweed, add some sticky rice, then a slice of Spam that was fried in bacon grease, and has a mixture of cream cheese and green onions spread on it. To that you add slices of avocado and jalapeño peppers. More rice is added to the top of that, but you have to flatten it all as you go along. The last step is to push it out of the form and wrap the seaweed around the whole thing. If the seaweed overlaps, dab a little water on it to make it stick together, and that's pretty much it."

When Sam was finished, Peggy said, "You know, I'm not much of a sushi eater myself, but that actually sounds pretty good. I'd give it a try."

"We've all had it," Phyllis said. "Sam prepared it for us at home last week."

"It is pretty good," Carolyn added with a tone of grudging admiration in her voice.

"I'll fix some more for all of us," Sam promised. "After I've won the blue ribbon for it tomorrow."

Eve asked, "Aren't you worried about being greedy? I

mean, three blue ribbons in one household is a bit much, isn't it?"

Sam grinned and said, "Nah, we can't help it if we're all culinary geniuses."

Carolyn said, "I just hope you don't run into any competitors as crazed as that funnel cake fellow . . . what was his name?"

"Ramón Silva," Phyllis said.

"That's right. I hope there isn't anyone like him in the Spam contest."

Sam shrugged. "I won't let it bother me. Haters gonna hate; that's how I look at it. Doesn't make any difference in how I roll."

"I suppose," Carolyn said.

The conversation put another thought into Phyllis's head. She turned it over in her brain as the meal continued and tried not to let the others see how distracted she was.

She was glad when supper was over. After everything was cleaned up, Carolyn, Eve, and Peggy went into the living room to watch a movie on DVD. Phyllis begged off, saying that she was tired, and Sam mentioned that he was going upstairs to read.

"No offense, ladies, but that movie y'all are about to watch looks a little weepy, and if I want to sit around and cry, I can watch clips from the Cowboys' last few games."

Phyllis was glad that Peggy didn't make any suggestive comments about Sam going upstairs at the same time. With all the thoughts of murder crowding into her brain, romance was just about the last thing on her mind.

Sam went on down the hall to the room he was using,

waited a few minutes, and then walked back quietly. Phyllis had left her door open. As he slipped in, he said, "Sneakin' into a gal's room makes me feel like a teenager again."

"I'm afraid I don't remember that far back," Phyllis said.

Sam sat on the end of the bed as he had before. "All right, what was the rest of it you were gonna tell me?"

"It's about Hank Squires."

Sam frowned in thought for a moment, then shook his head and said, "Uh . . . who's Hank Squires?"

"You know. Hank the cameraman, from *The Joye of Cooking*."

"That big fella who works the main camera? The one who's startin' to go bald on top?"

"That's him," Phyllis said. "He used to be married to Joye Jameson."

Sam stared. A few more seconds ticked by before he said, "That doesn't hardly seem right. He's built sort of like the Incredible Hulk, and she was just a little bitty thing."

"You see couples like that sometimes," Phyllis said with a shrug. "I was surprised when I found out about it, too, to be honest. But they were definitely married. I read about it on several websites. They got a divorce several years ago, and it's the timing of that divorce that's the interesting part."

"I know you're gonna tell me."

"The divorce became final three weeks before the incident on *Gloria's Kitchen* that led to Joye taking over the show."

Sam thought about it, then shook his head again. "I don't get the connection."

"If the marriage had lasted a little longer, Hank would have wound up married to a rich, famous TV star."

"Son of a gun," Sam said. "You're right. She was just a nobody when they split up, but that was about to change."

"Yes. And remember, Joye was rumored to be having an affair with Reed Hayes at the time."

"What was listed as the grounds for the divorce? Got any idea?"

"I was able to look that up on a state of California public records database. The grounds were irreconcilable differences, which, of course, can mean almost anything. The divorce appears to have been quite amicable despite that, though. They split the marital property down the middle, and no spousal support was awarded for either party."

Sam grunted. "No alimony, huh? That would've been a heck of a note, if Joye got rich and famous but Hank had to keep on payin' her part of what he earned as a cameraman on her show. That'd sure chap a fella's behind."

"Yes, but that's not what happened," Phyllis reminded him. "So we can't consider it a motive for murder. And the two of them must have stayed friends; otherwise, Hank wouldn't have continued to work on the show."

"Yeah, that makes sense," Sam agreed. "Although if there really was an affair and he knew about it, he might've kept his feelin's bottled up inside all these years, lettin' 'em stew and fester. Throw in the fact that Joye was rich as sin and he was still a workin' stiff . . . well, it might have been enough to push him over the edge sooner or later."

"I suppose you're right about that. And there's one more thing that has me curious. Yesterday I saw Hank and Bailey acting rather suspiciously, as if they might have been sneaking off to meet each other."

Sam's bushy eyebrows rose in surprise. "You mean you think the two of 'em might be carryin' on together? Bailey's supposed to be datin' Reed Hayes."

"Hence the sneaking around if she actually is involved with Hank Squires."

Sam shook his head and said, "That's pretty hard to figure, too. Those two don't strike me as the sort to get mixed up with each other."

"Remember how unlikely you thought it was that Hank and Joye Jameson were married."

"Yeah, there's that, all right," Sam agreed. "I guess you never can predict who somebody's gonna wind up fallin' for, can you?"

"Not with any degree of accuracy." Phyllis gave him the details of what she had observed in the Creative Arts Building the day before, then said, "Of course, there could be a perfectly legitimate explanation for what they were doing. Like I mentioned, the restrooms are down that hall. Maybe I just imagined that Hank and Bailey were acting furtively."

"I've never known you to imagine anything like that. You're usually pretty doggone sharp about what you see."

"It's one more thing to consider, anyway," Phyllis said. "And so is that business with Ramón Silva."

"Now you've lost me again," Sam said. "You're talkin' about the fella who was mad because you won the blue ribbon for your funnel cakes?"

"That's right. We know he was there at the broadcast."

"Yeah, he made a big enough scene everybody in the place knew he was there. But how could that tie in with what happened to Joye Jameson? He was mad at you, not her."

"Yes, but if something was wrong with my funnel cakes, it would bolster his claim that he should have won the contest instead of me," Phyllis said. "Tampering with them would be a way of making that happen."

Sam's eyes narrowed in anger. "He better not have. That'd be a mighty sorry thing to do. I wouldn't think that substitutin' peanut oil instead of corn oil would make enough of a difference to ruin your funnel cakes, though."

"No, it wouldn't have. But we don't know that's what he did . . . if, in fact, he did anything."

"But it was peanut oil that caused Joye's allergic reaction," Sam said.

"We've been assuming that because it seems to make sense given Joye's medical history, but we don't know if it's true. Maybe Silva tampered with the ingredients some other way to make the funnel cakes taste bad, and whatever he did triggered the allergic reaction in Joye just like peanuts would have. We don't know the actual cause of death. It'll take an autopsy to determine that."

"And I doubt if those detectives are gonna be anxious to share the results with you."

Phyllis sighed. "I know. It's easier to figure these things out when Mike is involved."

"Maybe he knows somebody in the Dallas PD who wouldn't mind givin' us a heads-up."

"I can't ask him to do that," Phyllis said with a shake of her head. "He's already gotten in trouble with Sheriff Haney and the district attorney for passing along too much information to me in those other cases."

"Shoot," Sam said, "that DA just holds a grudge against

you because he's arrested folks and then had to let 'em go when you proved they were innocent by catchin' the real killers. He's mad because he thinks you made him look bad."

"That was never my intention."

"Of course not. You just wanted to get to the truth."

Phyllis nodded. "That's right. But this case is really none of my business. I can't stop myself from speculating, but I have to stay out of it. I'm sure Detective Morgan and Detective Hunt will find out what happened." She paused. "At this point, we don't even know for sure if it was murder or just an accident."

"As long as nobody tries to blame you for it, that's all I care about," Sam said. "Although I don't like that some folks are gonna just assume your funnel cake killed her, no matter what really happened."

"Well, you can't control what the public thinks, so there's no point in trying."

"What do *you* think?" Sam asked. "I don't mean as an intellectual exercise. I mean, what does your gut say about what happened?"

For a long moment, Phyllis didn't answer. Then she looked at him and said, "It's not a very elegant way to put it . . . but my gut tells me that Joye Jameson was murdered."

Chapter 18

*J*oye Jameson's death was front-page news in the paper the next morning, plus there were features about it on all the morning news shows, including apparently heartfelt tributes from a number of friends, coworkers, and business associates in Hollywood. The hosts of other popular cooking shows were interviewed, and all of them sang Joye's praises.

"Of course, what would you expect them to say?" Peggy commented as the five of them watched TV before it was time to head for the fair. "In Hollywood they're always nice when somebody dies, even if they were trying to stab the person in the back the week before."

"They're all performers," Carolyn said. "They're always putting on an act."

Phyllis didn't feel quite that cynical about the entertainment industry, but she suspected that a lot of the glowing words they heard on TV were insincere.

Several of the networks interviewed Gloria Kimball,

which was understandable since she was the original host of the show that had brought Joye Jameson so much fame and fortune. In one of the interviews, a solemn Gloria said, "I knew the first time I met Joye that she would be a huge success. She was so smart and had so much drive, so much passion for what she was doing. She was an absolute pleasure to work with, and we became fast friends."

The interviewer asked, "So there was never any resentment on your part over the fact that Joye took over the show you'd been hosting?"

Gloria looked offended. "Of course not! And that's not exactly the way it happened. Joye only stepped in because of my medical issues at the time. I asked her to help out, and no one was more pleased by her success when she did than I was."

Peggy said, "Oh, now, that's hogwash. I'm surprised those two didn't wind up in a catfight sometime."

"For all we know they did," Carolyn said. "In Hollywood, they cover up things like that."

"They used to," Sam said, "but I reckon that's a lot harder nowadays when everybody's got a phone in his pocket that's a high-def video recorder, too. Even a few years ago when Joye took over the show, most folks already had phones that would shoot video."

"And there are all those show business gossip websites," Phyllis added. "I'm sure that if Joye and Gloria had ever come to blows, rumors of it would have been reported."

Carolyn looked at her and said, "Since when do you know about show business gossip websites?"

Phyllis didn't want to tell the others that she had been unable to stop herself from doing some theorizing about Joye's death, which had led her to investigate the backgrounds of the people involved in the show. She shrugged and answered vaguely, "How can you not hear about them if you ever watch TV?"

"That's true," Sam said. Phyllis suspected he was stepping in to help her out, and she was grateful to him for it.

On the big screen, the interviewer was saying to Gloria Kimball, "You were the first one to break the news of Joye Jameson's death, weren't you?"

"That's right," Gloria said. "But it's a story I wish I'd never had to report."

Peggy said, "That's quite a coup for a local news outfit like Channel 44, breaking the story of a national celebrity's death. Especially when it's got a reputation for lightweight tabloid stuff like *The 44 News*."

"Yes, it was lucky for Gloria Kimball that she happened to be on hand, wasn't it?" Carolyn said. She looked at Phyllis. "Unless it wasn't just luck. What do you think, Phyllis? Maybe Gloria wanted to have a major news story break while she was close by."

"I'm sure I wouldn't know," Phyllis said, although she couldn't help but think that the speculation added another layer to a possible motive for Gloria to tamper with those funnel cake ingredients. Since she and Joye had worked together for several years, it wasn't far-fetched at all to think that Gloria had probably known about the younger woman's peanut allergy.

Sam put his hands on his knees and pushed himself up from the armchair where he was sitting. "Guess I'd better start gettin' ready for the contest," he said. "I've got the rice steamer and all the nonperishable ingredients gathered up. I'll put the rest of the stuff in a small ice chest to keep it cool."

"I'll give you a hand," Phyllis said as she stood up. She didn't want to talk about Joye Jameson's death anymore. She had decided she was just going to stay out of this case, and that would be a lot easier to do if she wasn't thinking about it all the time.

When they were ready to go, they got in Phyllis's car and Sam took the wheel for the drive to Fair Park. Phyllis looked over at him and said, "You're still not the least bit nervous, are you?"

"Nope. Why should I be? I'd like to win, sure, but whether I win or lose, my life will go on pretty much the same."

From the backseat, Carolyn said, "I wouldn't be too sure about that. Anyone who wins a cooking contest achieves a certain level of fame."

"Well, maybe. But I don't think anybody's gonna be beatin' down my door just because I happen to cook some Spam better than a few other fellas."

"You might be surprised," Phyllis said. "I think there's a good chance you'll wind up being interviewed on TV if you win."

"On *The 44 News*," Peggy added.

"You think so?" Sam said with a little frown. "I didn't really think about that."

Eve said, "Leave the poor dear alone. You'll just make him nervous when he wasn't to start with. He has the right attitude, you know. In the long run, it doesn't really make any difference who wins or loses."

"Eve's right," Phyllis said as she reached over to pat Sam on the shoulder. "You just keep on feeling the way you do, Sam. We should all be as easygoing as you."

"Uh-huh," Sam said, but he seemed a little distracted now, as if he couldn't stop thinking about the fact that winning the contest would make him at least a little celebrated, if only for a short time. The proverbial fifteen minutes of fame . . .

They arrived at the Creative Arts Building well ahead of the time when the contest would begin, but that would give Sam the opportunity to take care of any necessary preparations. Everything appeared to be back to business as usual at the fair. Thousands of people strolled around on the roads and pathways, the various exhibits were thronged with crowds, and a number of different contests were going on.

As they entered the building, Phyllis glanced toward the area where the broadcast set was located. As Reed Hayes had said, the show's contract called for a new episode today, so Phyllis wasn't surprised to see quite a few people moving around the set. She was able to pick out Hank Squires from the crowd since he was taller than anyone else on the crew. She looked to see if Bailey was anywhere near the big cameraman, but she didn't spot the young woman.

She wasn't supposed to even be thinking about the case, Phyllis reminded herself. Sam needed her support right now, so she focused her attention on him instead.

"Is there anything I can to do help?" she asked as he carried his ice chest and a bag containing the other ingredients toward the contest site.

"Nah, this is my chore to take care of," he replied, "but I appreciate you askin'. You and the other ladies can go on and do whatever you want to. I got this."

Eve asked, "Can we wish you good luck?"

"You bet," Sam said. "I'll take all of it I can get."

Eve came up on her toes and kissed him on the cheek. "Good luck, then," she said.

Carolyn gave him an awkward, grudging hug, and Peggy punched him lightly on the arm. "Good luck, High Pockets," she said. "Knock 'em dead." She frowned. "Well, not literally. That wasn't a very good choice of words, was it?"

"Don't worry about it," Sam told her. "I reckon I know what you mean."

Phyllis kissed him on the cheek, too, and said, "We'll be here in the building somewhere if you need us. And we'll certainly be back for the results of the judging."

"I'd appreciate that, too," he said. "I'll probably need the moral support."

Carrying the makings for his Texas-style Spam sushi, he went to join the other contestants. Phyllis and her companions began walking around the rest of the hall, looking at some of the other foods that had already won competitions.

Their path eventually took them near the broadcast set. Phyllis saw a familiar face. The friendly security guard, Chet Murdock, stood beside the set, arms crossed as he looked around the big room. He smiled as Phyllis came up to him.

"Hey, Mrs. Newsom," he said. "How are you today?"

"I suppose I'm all right, Chet," she said. "Still upset about what happened yesterday, of course."

Chet's smile went away and was replaced by a solemn expression. "Yeah," he said, "I think we all are. That was just such a terrible thing. I couldn't believe what I was seeing. I felt like there was something I ought to do to help Ms. Jameson, but there wasn't anything. We get a little first aid training and they give us lessons in CPR, but we're not equipped to handle a real medical emergency like that."

"The fair has actual medical personnel standing by, though, right?"

"Yeah, sure. But it all happened so fast they wouldn't have had a chance to get here, even if they'd been close by. Ms. Jameson's only chance was that pen thingy Ms. Broderick had, and when that didn't work . . ." He shrugged. "After that, it was too late."

"Yes, it was," Phyllis agreed.

"I've gotta say, I'm a little surprised to see you back here today. After what happened, I thought you might be done with the fair, at least for this year."

"My friend Mr. Fletcher is in the Spam cook-off today," Phyllis explained. "I wanted to be here for that."

"Oh, yeah, sure, that makes sense."

Phyllis gave in to temptation and asked, "You haven't heard anything about the official cause of death, have you?"

Chet made a face and shook his head. "Eh, the cops don't share stuff like that with us lowly security guards, I'm afraid."

"I meant no offense—"

"Oh, no, none taken. Anyway, it's not like being a guard is my career or anything, so you can say whatever you want. I'm going to be a chef, or maybe even have my own cooking show one of these days. Being around the set is inspiring." His expression fell. "Or at least it was, you know, until . . ."

"Yes, I know," Phyllis said, nodding. She let a few seconds of shared solemnity go by, then asked, "What are you doing here right now, Chet? It looks like you're protecting the set."

"That's exactly what I am doing," he said. "It's my job to make sure nobody wanders up and starts messing with anything. Only people who work for the show are allowed on the set or in the backstage area. There's a guard back there, too."

"Were you doing that yesterday before the show?"

"Yep. We keep the place secure. That's the job."

"So the only ones who had access to the set were people who work for the show? No one else was around it yesterday?"

He frowned slightly. "That's what I just said, isn't it?"

"I was just curious," Phyllis said.

Chet smiled again. "For a second there, you sounded like those cops. They asked me the same thing." He chuckled. "You don't moonlight as a homicide detective when you're not making funnel cakes, do you?"

"Oh, no," Phyllis answered. If Chet didn't know about her history, she certainly wasn't going to get into it.

What he had told her was interesting, though. If he was right, that eliminated Ramón Silva and Gloria Kimball as suspects, since they couldn't have gotten near the funnel cake ingredients to tamper with them. Unless, of course, one of them had managed somehow to slip past Chet. Phyllis couldn't rule out that possibility. She didn't know how good Chet Murdock was at his job, although from what she had seen of him so far, he seemed at least competent.

It also meant that if the ingredients had been tampered with, the person who had done it was most likely a member of the show's crew. That brought her thoughts back to Hank Squires. Although as a cameraman he wouldn't have any legitimate reason to be fooling around with any of the food on the set, everyone was probably so accustomed to seeing him around that they wouldn't even notice him, despite his size. People often didn't really pay attention to the things they were used to seeing.

But the same would be true for everyone else involved in the show. No one would have thought twice about Bailey Broderick doing something with the funnel cake ingredients.

She handled food on the show all the time. Even Reed Hayes probably wouldn't have aroused any suspicion. Because he was the show's producer, it was his job to make sure all aspects of it were running smoothly, including the cooking demonstrations.

"There you are," Carolyn said from behind Phyllis. "We wondered where you had gotten off to."

"I was just talking to Mr. Murdock here," Phyllis explained.

The guard smiled and nodded to the others. "Ladies. Good to see you again."

"Sam's contest is about to get under way," Eve said. "I know he told us we only had to be there for the results, but I'd like to watch the whole thing."

"So would I," Carolyn added.

"I couldn't agree more," Phyllis said. "Let's go watch Sam cook some Spam."

"We're right with you, Dr. Seuss," Peggy said.

Chapter 19

The Spam cook-off was popular. A large crowd had gathered to watch as the contestants began preparing their dishes. As Sam had mentioned, there were quite a few male competitors in this contest, but a number of women had entered it as well.

The spectators had to stay back a short distance, but the judges were allowed to circulate among the contestants and talk to them, asking them questions about their recipes. Phyllis watched and listened with great interest. She wanted to know some of the other possible uses for Spam that these competitors had come up with.

She saw Spam enchiladas like Sam originally thought about making, Spam pizza, Spam kebabs, Spam sliders, Spam stuffed in jalapeños and wrapped with bacon, Spam with noodles, and Spam stir-fry. Competitors were wearing Spam shirts, and some even wore Spam hats.

"Sam's really concentrating, isn't he?" Carolyn commented. "I'm not sure I've ever seen him looking so serious."

"Yes, he's usually pretty happy-go-lucky," Eve agreed. "Right now he almost looks like he's performing brain surgery."

Phyllis wasn't sure she would have gone quite that far, but Sam was taking the contest seriously, no doubt about that. He wore an intense frown on his face as he prepared each of the ingredients for his recipe, then began putting them all together to form his Texas-style Spam sushi. He used his homemade form, layering the sticky rice, Spam, and other ingredients, and ending with some more sticky rice. When he pulled off the form and wrapped the assembled entry with the seaweed to finish, he looked like a pro. Watching him made Phyllis's heart beat a little faster. She had never realized how alluring it was to watch a man cook.

A couple of the judges stopped to watch him and talk to him. Sam responded in a low voice, so that Phyllis couldn't make out the words, but both judges smiled and chuckled. She sighed in relief. The judges seemed receptive both to what Sam was making and whatever he had said to them.

She wondered if it had been the joke about sushi being invented in Texas.

The contest didn't actually take very long, but to Phyllis it seemed longer than it really was. After a while, she figured out why she felt so tense, a lot more so than she had felt in any of the contests she had entered over the years. It was because of how much she cared about Sam and wanted him to win. Even though he had tried to pass the contest off as unimportant, she knew him well enough to be aware that he wanted to do a good job at anything he put his mind to. That was why he had been a successful coach and educator, why he was such an excellent woodworker, and why he knew more about computers than she ever would. He had the drive to excel at whatever he was doing.

On the other hand, he had enough self-confidence that if he didn't win or at least place highly, he wouldn't be devastated. But it would certainly be nice if he received some recognition for his efforts.

Phyllis glanced over at her friends. She could tell that they were rooting for Sam, too. She sent positive thoughts his way. It couldn't hurt.

Eventually the time allotted for preparation was over. The contestants had to present their dishes to the judges. As the evaluations started, Phyllis caught Sam's eye, smiled, and gave him a thumbs-up. He returned the smile somewhat wearily, as if his efforts had taken a lot out of him.

When the judges came to Sam's entry, each of the three men ate a bite of the Spam sushi. Then they each took another, which Phyllis thought was a good sign. They wouldn't have eaten a second sample if they weren't considering Sam's entry for one of the top spots, she told herself.

The judges moved on, and Sam looked relieved. Phyllis understood the feeling. He had given the competition his best shot, and whatever happened now, it was out of his hands. All he could do was wait for the results.

That didn't take long. When they had sampled all the dishes, the judges consulted among themselves for a few moments, then nodded in agreement. One of them took the blue ribbon from a folder and moved toward the far end of the group, where he presented the ribbon to a contestant who had prepared a Spam and black bean pizza with a cornmeal crust. Everyone applauded, including Phyllis and her friends. Even though Sam hadn't won, they weren't going to be bad sports about it. Phyllis knew Sam, with his background in athletics, wouldn't want that.

The judge took the second place red ribbon from the folder and turned around to walk the other way along the line of contestants. He was going toward Sam this time, and Phyllis felt her pulse quicken. Finishing second in the only cooking competition he'd ever entered would be a tremendous achievement, especially at this level, she thought.

Her heart leaped as the judge stopped in front of Sam, extended the ribbon to him, and then shook hands. A grin broke out across Sam's rugged face as he pumped the judge's hand. Phyllis heard the man say, "Excellent job, Mr. Fletcher."

"Thank you, sir," Sam said. Still grinning, he held up the ribbon so everyone could see it.

The presentation of the third-place ribbon was anticlimactic as far as Phyllis was concerned, although she was sure the woman who won it was pleased. As the contest concluded, she led the others over to Sam and put her arms around him as she said, "Congratulations!"

Sam surprised her by kissing her on the lips. "You were my inspiration," he said as he broke the kiss. "I never would have even entered if it wasn't for you and Carolyn. I can't thank the two of you enough."

"I don't mind accepting your thanks," Carolyn said, "but you don't have to kiss me."

"Dang, how do I get the job of being an inspiration?" Peggy wanted to know.

"Trust me, dear," Eve told her. "That position is permanently filled, I think."

Since that banter made her feel a little uncomfortable, Phyllis said, "So can we try this batch of your award-winning Texas-style Spam sushi now?"

"Help yourselves," Sam told her. "I didn't fix enough for us to make lunch off of it, but it's a pretty good appetizer."

After snacking on the Spam sushi, which was delicious, Phyllis thought, they helped Sam pack up his supplies, and he took everything back to the car.

They met back at the food pavilion for some actual lunch. As they were eating, Carolyn asked, "Are we heading back to Peggy's house now?"

Phyllis said, "Actually, I thought we might go back to the Creative Arts Building and take in the TV broadcast."

"You want to go back there?" Carolyn asked, her eyes widening in surprise. "After what happened yesterday?"

"I'd like to see how Bailey does. I'm sure she'll be nervous, so the more friendly faces there, the better."

"Everyone will be friendly," Carolyn said. "The general public won't care that it's her first show. Some of them won't even know it."

"I'll bet almost everyone in the audience will know what happened," Phyllis said.

Peggy added, "It'd be hard not to if they've watched TV in the past twenty-four hours."

Carolyn shrugged. "I don't mind going. It's a little morbid, though. I feel a little like we'll be watching a train wreck."

"I certainly hope it's not that bad," Phyllis said.

When they finished eating, they walked back to the Creative Arts Building. It was possible they might not be able to get into the show, Phyllis thought. Joye Jameson's death might have brought out an even bigger crowd than usual. Carolyn was right: In a way it was like a train wreck, or an accident on the side of the road that turned all the other drivers into gawkers. She felt an instinctive liking for Bailey Broderick, and she hoped for the young woman's sake that the broadcast went well.

A lot of people were already lined up to climb into the bleachers and watch the broadcast. Phyllis and the others joined the throng. She waved at Chet Murdock, who was standing next to the steps leading to the bleachers, guarding the rope that kept the audience from filing in yet. Chet grinned and returned the wave.

"Maybe your chunky friend there would let us go to the front of the line," Peggy suggested.

"Goodness, I wouldn't ask such a thing of him," Phyllis said. "I doubt if he'd do it, anyway. He seems quite devoted to his job, even if he doesn't want to make it his career."

By this time she had been around the show enough so that she could estimate the crowd, and she knew that they would get in to see the broadcast. As she was standing there, Phyllis noticed a woman ahead of them in line turning around to cast glances toward her. After that had happened several times, she began to wonder what was going on.

It didn't take long to find out, because the woman said, "Hey, aren't you the woman who made funnel cakes on this show yesterday?"

"That's right," Phyllis said, feeling a tingle of apprehension go through her.

"The one whose funnel cakes killed Joye Jameson?"

Carolyn's voice was loud with anger as she said, "Now,

hold on just a minute there! Phyllis's funnel cakes had nothing to do with what happened to Joye."

Actually, that wasn't true, thought Phyllis, or at least it probably wasn't. But she wasn't surprised that Carolyn was defending her.

"That's not the way I saw it," the stranger said. "Poor Joye took one bite of that funnel cake, and boom! Down she went. What else are we supposed to think killed her?"

"There was nothing harmful in that funnel cake," Carolyn insisted.

Phyllis put a hand on her arm and said, "It's all right, Carolyn. I don't want you getting into an argument on my behalf."

Carolyn snorted. "It's not an argument. Just the ignorant ranting of a person who doesn't know what she's talking about."

"Hey, lady," the woman said as she took a step toward Carolyn, "I got your ignorant ranting right here—"

Sam moved between them and held up his red ribbon. "Came in second place in the Spam cook-off," he said. "They gave me this red ribbon and fifty dollars. How about that?"

"Good for you," the stranger said. "But if you're with that bunch, I wouldn't eat anything you fixed. It might be poisonous."

Carolyn's face flushed an even darker red, and trouble might have been unavoidable if Chet Murdock hadn't come along the line and said, "All right, let's all settle down here. We're letting the audience in now, so move along, folks, move along."

The audience members climbed into the bleachers. Several more people were staring openly at Phyllis now, and she knew they had either heard what the woman had said or recognized her from the previous day's broadcast. The unease she felt confirmed that she had no real interest in being a celebrity, certainly not a notorious one like she appeared to be for the moment.

They sat down on one of the benches about halfway up the bleachers. Phyllis did her best to ignore the looks being sent her way and talked to Sam instead, asking him, "So are you going to enter some more cooking contests now?"

"I don't know about that," he replied dubiously. "I'm not sure I know how to cook anything except Spam and chocolate peanut butter oatmeal cookies."

"Well, if you do decide to, I'll be glad to give you some pointers."

"I'll keep that in mind," he promised. "I can make a mean pot of chili, come to think of it, and Texas is known for its chili cook-offs. It might be fun to go to one."

Bailey was the one who had warmed up the crowd before the other broadcasts began, and Phyllis wondered if she would continue with that job even though she was now the star of the show, at least temporarily. As the time for the broadcast to begin approached, Bailey came out onto the set and picked up a microphone. The audience quieted down and applauded for her, even without being told to. She was dressed in jeans and a pullover sweater, a more informal outfit than Joye Jameson had usually worn, but it looked good on Bailey and fit her personality.

"Thank you. Thank you, everyone," she began. "Welcome to *The Joye of Cooking*." Her voice caught a little as she said the name of the show, but she pushed on immediately. "We'll be getting started in a few minutes, and before we do I'd like to mention a few things, like the applause signs . . ."

She used her free hand to point toward the signs, but as she did, her voice trailed off. Phyllis looked where Bailey was pointing, and as she did, she saw the same thing that must have caused the young woman to fall silent. Detectives Morgan and Hunt of the Dallas Police Department stood at the side of the broadcast set, and judging by the grim expressions on their faces, they weren't here to carry out any sort of pleasant task.

Of course, the rest of the audience probably didn't recognize the detectives, so they must have wondered why Bailey had stopped in the middle of her speech.

Charlotte Morgan looked over at Al Hunt, who shrugged and nodded as if telling her to go ahead. Morgan stepped up onto the set and started toward Bailey, who suddenly appeared confused and frightened. Phyllis thought Bailey looked like she wanted to turn and run, but she didn't move. She seemed to be rooted to the spot. Plenty of noise came from the rest of the hall, but utter silence had fallen over this side of the big room. Reed Hayes came through the door at the back of the set and said in a stricken voice, "Bailey . . . ?"

She didn't turn to look at him. Phyllis could tell that Bailey couldn't take her eyes off Charlotte Morgan. The detective stopped in front of her and said, "Bailey Broderick, you're under arrest for the murder of Joye Jameson."

Chapter 20

That eerie silence hung over the set for several long seconds after Detective Morgan's pronouncement, but then it exploded into a hubbub of sound from the audience and also from some of the crew members. From his position behind the main camera, Hank Squires yelled, "No! That's crazy!"

Hank stepped out from behind the camera and started toward the set. Detective Hunt got in his way. Even though Hank towered over the policeman, he stopped his advance. He kept glowering over Hunt's head at Detective Morgan, though.

Reed Hayes said, "Bailey, don't say a word to these people. Not one word, do you understand? I'll call the show's lawyers right now."

Phyllis wasn't sure what good it would do to call a firm of show business lawyers in Hollywood when Bailey was being arrested for murder in Dallas, but other than that, she thought Hayes's advice was good. She knew the detectives would try to rattle Bailey and get her to say something incriminating, so not saying anything at all probably was the best course of action for her right now.

Phyllis realized she wouldn't even be thinking such a thing if she weren't convinced that Bailey was innocent. That was a mighty big conclusion to jump to, but her instincts told her that Bailey hadn't killed Joye Jameson. Phyllis had been right there, only a few feet away, and she had seen the genuine shock and sorrow in Bailey's eyes when Joye collapsed and died.

Carolyn leaned over to Phyllis and said, "This is insane! I don't believe that girl had anything to do with it."

"Neither do I," Phyllis agreed. "Of course, we don't know her that well—"

"I'll say you don't," Peggy put in. "You've only talked to her two or three times."

Eve said, "Phyllis has excellent judgment about these things."

"Maybe so, but she's out of her bailiwick here."

That was certainly true, Phyllis thought. This wasn't the familiar, comforting small-town confines of Weatherford. This was cold, impersonal, crowded Dallas. The detectives weren't going to listen to her. Nobody really cared what she thought.

Charlotte Morgan was still talking to Bailey, no doubt reading her her rights. Morgan took out a pair of handcuffs. Looking pale and shaken, Bailey turned around. Morgan cuffed her wrists behind her back and then took hold of her right arm. The detective led Bailey off the set.

"Looks like they're gonna have to show a rerun today after all," Peggy said.

Phyllis glanced at the clock. It was only a few minutes until the show was supposed to begin. Reed Hayes was probably on the phone to his bosses, letting them know what had happened so they could step in and order that rerun. Phyllis didn't really know how these things worked, but she figured there was a good chance the syndicate always had an old episode ready for any sort of emergency that kept a new episode from going on the air. That seemed like a reasonable precaution to take with a show that was broadcast live.

In the meantime, the audience didn't know what to do. Some of them probably realized there wasn't going to be a show today after all, since the host had been led off in handcuffs, but the others might still expect to be entertained. Everyone stayed in the bleachers, sitting there uncertainly, as more time passed and the hands on the clock moved beyond the top of the hour.

Reed Hayes had disappeared during the commotion. Phyllis wondered if he had gone to the jail to do whatever he could for Bailey. Hank was still there, pacing back and forth angrily and running a hand over his balding head. The director, Charlie Farrar, came in from the truck and joined the rest of the crew around the set, but he looked just as lost as they did.

After a while Hayes emerged from the backstage area, so he hadn't left after all. He conferred with Farrar and then motioned for Chet Murdock to join them. Hayes looked like he was giving orders to the security guard. Chet nodded.

When Hayes was finished talking to him, Chet came over to the bleachers and held up his hands. "Can I have your attention?" he said, raising his voice to be heard. "Everyone? Can I have your attention, please?"

Gradually the members of the audience quieted down. When they had, Chet went on, "The producers of *The Joye of Cooking* regret to inform you that there will be no show today. They hope you will continue to watch the show when new episodes resume in the near future. Thank you."

Groans and mutters of disappointment came from some in the audience, but most of the people just stood up and started to leave the bleachers in an orderly fashion, including Phyllis and her friends. When they reached the floor, she said to Sam, "I want to talk to Mr. Murdock for a minute before we go."

"Sure," he said. "I don't suppose we're in any hurry."

Phyllis made her way over to the guard. When he saw her, he said, "Hey, Mrs. Newsom. Do you believe that? I never saw anybody arrested in the middle of a TV show before." Chet shook his head regretfully. "I never saw anybody arrested for murder before, period."

"I know," Phyllis said. "It's terrible. I don't think Miss Broderick is guilty, either."

"You don't?" Chet asked with a surprised frown on his face. "I don't think the cops would have arrested her without some pretty strong evidence against her, do you?"

Carolyn and the others had followed Phyllis. When Carolyn heard what Chet said, she let out a disgusted snort. "That just shows how much you know about the police, young man," she said. "We've seen them arrest innocent people again and again and charge them with murder."

"You have?" Chet still looked confused. "Are you ladies like . . . crime buffs or something?"

"Phyllis solves murders," Carolyn said, pointing at her.

Phyllis would have just as soon she hadn't done that, but there was no stopping her.

Chet's eyes widened. "You do?" he asked Phyllis. "You're a detective? Really?"

"I've helped the authorities figure out a few things," Phyllis admitted. "But I don't think the police here in Dallas would be interested in anything I had to say."

"You don't know that," Chet said, getting excited. "You should offer to help them if you think Ms. Broderick isn't guilty."

"What do you think?" Phyllis asked. "You're around the set here a lot. You might have noticed something that could have a bearing on the case."

Chet made a face and shook his head. "Well, yeah, I'm here, but . . . to be honest sometimes my mind sort of wanders a little. As long as there's no trouble I don't really pay that much attention. I probably shouldn't admit that, but like I told you, I don't plan on making this my life's work."

"Of course," Phyllis said. "But if you think of anything—"

She stopped short. She had been about to give Chet her cell phone number and ask him to call her if he thought of anything that might be connected to Joye Jameson's murder. But then she remembered that she wasn't investigating this case. There wasn't really even a case to investigate anymore, since the police had already made an arrest.

Phyllis finished by saying, "If you think of anything, you should call the police and talk to Detective Morgan or Detective Hunt. I'm sure they'd appreciate any help you could give them."

"I'm not so sure they would, but I'll keep it in mind," Chet promised.

Phyllis nodded and said, "It was nice meeting you this week, Mr. Murdock. I hope you get to do what you want in life."

"Thanks," the young man said with a smile. "You, too."

Phyllis returned the smile, thought about her family, her friends, and her teaching career, and said, "I already have."

Traffic was heavy on the freeways, even though it wasn't officially rush hour yet. Phyllis thought that rush hour in Dallas could almost be considered to exist twenty-four hours a day. However, Sam was a steady, patient driver and got them back to Peggy's house without any problems.

"This week certainly hasn't turned out like I expected it to," Carolyn commented as they sat in Peggy's living room.

"You mean you didn't think you'd win any of the contests?" Peggy asked.

Carolyn said, "Hmph. Of course I did. I always expect to win when I enter a contest, and I'm never surprised when Phyllis does." She looked pointedly at Sam and added, "Some results I couldn't have predicted, though."

Phyllis was about to tell her that that wasn't a very nice thing to say, when Sam chuckled and responded, "You got that right. You didn't really have any evidence to go on, since I never cooked much of anything around you ladies before."

Well, if he wasn't upset about Carolyn's comment, she wasn't going to leap to his defense, Phyllis decided. Besides, he had a point. Before this whole business about going to the state fair had come up, for all they had known, any food he prepared might have been terrible. Once he started trying out various Spam recipes, it was obvious that Sam really was a decent cook, but the rest of them still didn't know how his skills would stack up against those of the other entrants in the contest.

Peggy turned on the TV, and it wasn't long before an early newscast began. Not surprisingly, the arrest of Bailey Broderick was the lead story.

"Police have made an arrest in the death of television cooking show host Joye Jameson," a perfectly groomed anchorwoman said. "Bailey Broderick, twenty-seven, has been charged with murder in the death of Jameson. Broderick has been an assistant producer on the program *The Joye of Cooking* for several years. So far, police have released no information about a possible motive in the killing. Ms. Jameson, who passed away yesterday afternoon during the broadcast of her show, was originally thought to have succumbed to a fatal allergic reaction to something in a funnel cake she had just eaten."

Phyllis hoped the anchorwoman wouldn't mention that *she* had cooked that particular funnel cake.

"We'll have more on that story as it develops," the woman on the TV screen went on. "In our other top story tonight, a cold front is headed our way, and this weekend it's going to bring us our first really fall-like temperatures of the season. For more on that, let's go over to meteorologist Chip Cavaletti in the weather center."

The ringing of the doorbell made Peggy pick up the remote control and mute the sound on the TV. "Who in the world can that be?" she muttered as she lifted herself to her feet, obviously reluctant to leave the comfort of her recliner. "I'm not expecting anybody."

She went up the hall to the front door and opened it.

Phyllis looked past Peggy and saw a middle-aged man standing there. As far as she recalled, she had never seen him before.

The stranger was about as average looking as a man could possibly be. Medium height, a little stocky but not really fat, with an open, pleasant face topped by a mostly bald scalp. A fringe of slightly wavy brown hair ran around his ears and the back of his head. The one thing that stood out about him was his gray suit, which Phyllis, while not an expert on such things, thought must have been pretty expensive. It just looked like it cost a lot of money.

"Mrs. Newsom?" the man asked. His voice was friendly and went well with the rest of him.

"Nope," Peggy said. "But she's here." She assumed the role of gatekeeper. "What do you want with her?"

Phyllis had gotten to her feet when she heard the man ask for her. She came up behind Peggy with Sam, Carolyn, and Eve following her and said, "That's all right. I'll talk to the gentleman." She smiled at him. "I'm Phyllis Newsom."

"David Miller," he said, introducing himself. His name was as nondescript as the rest of him. "I'm an attorney—"

Peggy said, "You guys are going from door to door now to drum up business? I remember when you weren't even allowed to advertise!"

"So do I, ma'am," David Miller said, "but that's not why I'm here." He slid a business card case from his coat pocket, took out a card, and extended it to Phyllis. "My client asked me to come and talk to you, Mrs. Newsom."

Phyllis took the card, saw that the address on it was a piece of prime real estate in downtown Dallas, and asked,

"Who's your client, Mr. Miller, if you're allowed to tell me that?"

"Certainly. I'm representing Ms. Bailey Broderick. It's my job to keep her from being convicted of killing Joye Jameson, and she seems to think that you might be able to help me."

Chapter 21

It was beginning to seem as if the surprises this week held would never come to an end, Phyllis thought as she looked at the bland-faced attorney. After a couple of seconds went by, she said, "I think you should come in, Mr. Miller. Obviously we need to talk." Remembering that this wasn't her house, she glanced over at Peggy and added, "If that's all right . . . ?"

"Oh, sure," Peggy said. "You can't send him away after a bombshell like that. Come on in."

Phyllis and Peggy ushered Miller into the living room. Phyllis asked, "Do we need to speak in private?"

"These are your friends?" Miller said as he looked around at the others.

"That's right."

"I wouldn't insult you or them by implying that they can't be trusted. However, there are issues of confidentiality . . ."

Peggy said, "The rest of us will go back in the den, and the two of you can stay in here. Don't worry, it's not bugged."

"The possibility that it might be didn't even cross my mind, I assure you," Miller said.

"You want something to drink?" Peggy asked. "I've got iced tea and Coke, or I can put on a pot of coffee. I'm not a boozer, though, so I can't offer you a beer."

"Nor am I," Miller assured her. "Thank you, but I'm fine."

Sam said, "You let us know if you need us, Phyllis."

When the others were gone and Phyllis and Miller were seated in comfortable chairs, she said, "I really don't see how I can be of any assistance to you, Mr. Miller. You made it sound like Bailey sent you here to talk to me. How can that be?"

Instead of answering Phyllis's question, Miller asked one of his own. "You just called my client by her first name. Does that mean the two of you are friends?"

"Well . . . no, not really. We've only spoken a few times, and then not for long. I suppose I just think of her as Bailey because I've seen her on TV so many times. You know, like Regis. That's just the way people think of him, whether they've ever met him or not. I'll bet most people who come up to him on the street say 'Hello, Regis,' not 'Hello, Mr. Philbin.'"

Even to herself, Phyllis sounded like she was babbling. She must have come across that way to David Miller, too, because he said in a tolerant tone, as if humoring her, "I'm sure you're right, Mrs. Newsom."

That annoyed Phyllis. She said bluntly, "What is it you want from me, Mr. Miller?"

"According to my client, you were closer to Joye Jameson than anyone else when she was stricken with her fatal attack."

"That's right, I suppose. I hope your client isn't trying to say that I deliberately caused that allergic reaction."

Miller waved away that suggestion. "No, not at all. She thought that you would be able to testify as to how genuinely surprised she was when Ms. Jameson collapsed, and how she made an immediate attempt to save Ms. Jameson's life."

"She did," Phyllis replied without hesitation. "Bailey wasn't just surprised. She was completely shocked, and I'd be glad to testify to that opinion."

"Ah, but there's the problem," Miller said. "It's only your opinion. It isn't evidence. Perhaps Ms. Broderick was doing a fantastic job of acting."

Phyllis shook her head. "No, I'm convinced it's the truth. And aren't you supposed to be on her side?"

"Of course. But if you were on the witness stand, don't you think the prosecutor would raise the possibility that Ms. Broderick was acting?"

"Oh," Phyllis said. "You're right. That's exactly what would happen." She frowned. "That brings us back around to me not understanding how I can help you."

"I told you why my client suggested that I talk to you. To be honest, even though you were an eyewitness, I'm not sure your testimony would help our case that much. I probably would have gotten around to talking to you eventually, but I wouldn't have come right over here from the jail if I hadn't thought of something else."

"I'm sure I don't know what that could be," Phyllis said.

"Your name struck me as familiar somehow," Miller said with a faint smile tugging at his lips. "So I did a little quick research. It didn't take long to figure out where I'd heard of you before."

He took out his phone, touched the display screen a couple

of times, and turned it so she could see what he had called up. It was a search engine screen, and her name was in the search box, with a number of results below it.

"You're the crime-solving grandma from Weatherford," he said.

Phyllis bristled. "I really don't appreciate being referred to that way," she said.

"I'm sorry, I meant no offense. I was just quoting one of the websites about you."

"You mean some newspaper story about the cases I've been mixed up in?"

"No, although there are certainly quite a few of those available online, if anybody wants to take the trouble to look. I was talking about one of the fan sites."

"The what?"

"The Phyllis Newsom fan sites. There are several devoted to your crime-solving activities."

"Wait a minute," Phyllis said. "There really are such things?"

Miller looked at her for a second, then said, "Don't tell me you've never set up a Google Alert for your name."

"I don't know what you're talking about."

"It's a thing where Google sends you an e-mail with a link every time somebody mentions your name on a website or a blog or anything like that."

Phyllis shook her head. "I had no idea such things existed."

For a moment Miller looked like he didn't believe her. Then he chuckled and said, "I didn't think you were serious. But you are, aren't you?"

"Completely," Phyllis assured him.

"Well, if nothing else, it's a refreshing attitude in this

day and age. You're something of a celebrity among true-crime buffs, Mrs. Newsom. More importantly for my purposes, though, you're someone who's obviously quite observant, or you wouldn't have been able to solve those other murders. I want you to take me through everything you remember leading up to the moment when Joye Jameson took a bite of that funnel cake you'd just prepared."

"Everything? Right here and now?"

"It's never too soon to start putting together a strong defense," Miller said. "I promise you, at this very moment there are assistant district attorneys already working on the case they'll present to the grand jury when they ask for an indictment against Ms. Broderick. I don't want them to get too much of a jump on me."

"I can certainly understand that. Do you want to ask questions or . . . ?"

"Just tell me what happened, start to finish, in your own words." Miller took a pad and pen from his briefcase so he could make notes while Phyllis was talking.

Phyllis led the attorney through the events of the previous afternoon, starting with when she and her friends had arrived at the broadcast set. Miller took copious notes, evidently preferring that method to recording what she told him. He didn't interrupt her to ask any questions, but when she was finished, he said, "The cooking oil you used for the funnel cakes was already there on the set when you arrived?"

"It was," Phyllis confirmed. "The people on the show had my recipe. Anyone could get it from the state fair, I suppose. Someone—and I assumed it was Bailey—assembled all of the ingredients and had them ready when I got there."

Miller nodded. "Yes, that agrees with what Ms. Broderick told me. Making preparations like that is part of her job."

"The bottle of cooking oil was sitting on the counter when we got there," Phyllis said. "It wasn't a new, unopened bottle, either. I'd say a cup or so of oil had been used from it."

"You see, right there is a good reason for me to be here," Miller said. "I might not have even thought of something like that to ask about it, but to you, noticing it is just second nature."

"Well, to be fair, when you cook a lot you pay attention to such things. You don't want to start something and then realize halfway through that you don't have enough of one of the ingredients. If my friend Carolyn had been making the funnel cakes, she would have been able to tell you the same thing."

"That may well be," Miller said, "but I'll bet she wouldn't make the instinctive leap to the next question that information brings to mind."

"You mean, where was the oil kept before the show?" Phyllis asked.

"Exactly. That's something I'll need to find out from my client. I didn't have a chance to do a lengthy interview with her. I'll do that in the morning, after the bail hearing." Miller leaned back in his chair. "Right now, I'm trying to get everything straight in my mind, so I have an accurate picture of the events. I really appreciate your help with that, Mrs. Newsom."

"I'll do whatever I can," Phyllis said. Something else occurred to her. "There's bound to be security camera footage from the Creative Arts Building. Maybe that would show you if someone was messing around with the ingredients. I'm convinced someone substituted peanut oil for corn oil."

"From what I've heard about the case, I agree, although I don't have my hands on the autopsy report yet. That's something else I hope to accomplish over the weekend. There's a chance that may have to wait until Monday."

"There's something else bothering me . . ."

As Phyllis's voice trailed off, Miller urged her, "By all means, go ahead. Given your history, Mrs. Newsom, I'd say your instincts are to be trusted."

"Why didn't the injector work?"

"The one that Ms. Broderick used in an attempt to counterattack Ms. Jameson's allergic reaction?"

"Yes. The epinephrine should have stopped the reaction, shouldn't it? That's what those pens are made for, and according to Bailey, she used one once before when Joye had a bad reaction."

Miller nodded slowly and said, "That's true. That's something else the autopsy report might answer."

"Don't the authorities have to turn copies of all their findings over to you?"

"Yes, they do, but we're a long way from a trial yet," Miller pointed out with a slight smile. "And the police have been known to drag their feet during the discovery phase. But I'll find out everything that they have; you can count on that. Do you think the autoinjector is important?"

"Someone could have tampered with it, too."

Miller thought about it and nodded. "That would explain why it didn't work, wouldn't it? Maybe they substituted something else for the epinephrine so it wouldn't counteract the allergic reaction."

"I saw Bailey take the pen out of her pocket. We need to find out where it was before that and who could have gotten to it." Phyllis paused. "I'm being presumptuous, aren't I? Telling a high-powered defense attorney how to handle an investigation. Good grief."

Miller smiled again. "What makes you think I'm high-powered, as you put it?"

"Well, the production company that makes *The Joye of Cooking* hired you—"

Miller stopped her by shaking his head. "No, I'm not working for the production company."

"You're not? Reed Hayes said he was going to call his bosses in Hollywood. I assumed they found you here in Dallas."

"No, Mr. Hayes retained my services on behalf of Ms. Broderick. I'm acquainted with some people in California. Executives at the production company may have recommended me to Mr. Hayes, but they're not paying me. I suspect they thought that would be a conflict of interest. Their primary responsibility lies with the late Ms. Jameson, after all. She was their star."

"Of course," Phyllis said. "I should have realized that."

"I'll take that 'high-powered' business as a compliment, though. Most people find me incredibly dull."

Phyllis had a hunch that was exactly the way David Miller wanted people to regard him. That might cause them to let down their guard around him. She would have bet that his opponents in court tended to underestimate him, too, at least the first time they faced him. She had seen the keen intelligence in his eyes, though, and trusted him to do a good job of defending Bailey.

Miller closed his notebook and said, "I think I've got everything I need for now. I'm sure I'll be talking to you again later. I can find you here or reach you at your cell phone number?"

"That's right. I—" Phyllis stopped. "How did you know I was staying here with Carolyn's cousin?"

"You gave your cell phone number and this address to Ms. Broderick the other day, when Ms. Jameson asked you to appear on the show. They wanted it for their paperwork, and also in case they needed to contact you. Then Ms. Broderick gave the information to me when she told me she wanted me to talk to you."

"Yes, I remember now."

"Don't worry, I didn't track you down through any nefarious means. Although I have some acquaintances who probably could have hacked the GPS in your phone and pinpointed your location within a few feet. That's one thing about being in my line of work—"

"You know some shady characters?"

Miller laughed as he got to his feet. "I've never heard it described any better." He put out his hand. "Thank you, Mrs. Newsom. It's been a pleasure talking to you. I sense that we're kindred spirits, if you will. We both like to get to the bottom of things and discover the truth."

"That's right," Phyllis said as she shook his hand. "I hope that'll be enough to find Joye Jameson's killer."

Chapter 22

When the lawyer was gone, Carolyn asked, "What in the world was that all about?"

Sam said, "Maybe Phyllis can't tell us. The fella did say there were confidentiality issues."

"He didn't trust you because he doesn't know you," Phyllis said. "I do."

Peggy said, "Hey, you've only known me for a little less than a week."

"Yes, but you're Carolyn's cousin. If she trusts you, then so do I."

"Peggy is absolutely trustworthy," Carolyn declared. "We've known each other since we were children."

"Good enough for me," Phyllis said. "Mr. Miller wanted to get my version of what happened at the fair yesterday afternoon. So I told him all of it the way I saw it." She paused, unsure whether to mention the rest of the conversation. But these were her friends, so she was sure they would understand. "He'd also heard of me because of my involvement in those other cases—"

"So he wants to hire you as a detective," Peggy broke in. "You should get a private investigator's license."

"Phyllis Newsom, private eye," Sam drawled. The brief glare Phyllis shot in his direction just made him chuckle.

"No, Mr. Miller didn't want to hire me," she said. "He just sort of picked my brain a little. And I'm not going to be getting any sort of license other than my driver's license when it's time to renew it. I don't need a new line of work, thank you very much."

Carolyn asked, "Did the two of you come to any conclusion about who might have murdered Joye Jameson if Bailey Broderick didn't?"

"Unfortunately, no. The police haven't turned over their evidence yet, so at this point Mr. Miller doesn't even know why they thought they had sufficient grounds to arrest her. He's hoping to find out more over the weekend, including getting a copy of the autopsy report."

"If they've even done an autopsy yet. From what I hear, those things get backed up all the time."

"With Joye Jameson bein' a celebrity, I'll bet they got to it right away," Sam said. "It'd mean some bad publicity if they didn't."

Carolyn said, "Hmph. If Dallas was really worried about bad publicity, you'd think they'd do something about the traffic!"

Since it had been such a busy day, Phyllis and Carolyn just prepared Lousiana-style muffulettas for supper. When they were finished, Peggy said, "I'm not sure I want you people to go home tomorrow. I haven't eaten this good in years."

"I'm going to leave a batch of cookies for you," Carolyn said.

"And we'll make a big breakfast before we leave in the morning," Phyllis added.

"That sounds good," Peggy said. As she spoke, the doorbell sounded. "Again?" she asked, rolling her eyes. "I don't remember the last time I had this many people ringing my doorbell."

While Peggy got up to see who was at the door, Phyllis and Carolyn began clearing the table. Eve said, "Let me help. Since I don't cook, I never feel like I'm pulling my weight when you two are around. Good looks and a sparkling wit are only worth so much, you know."

They were about to start out to the kitchen when Peggy appeared in the dining room door with an odd expression on her face that Phyllis noticed right away. Peggy said, "Somebody else here to see you, Phyllis. You're popular today."

"Who is it?" Phyllis asked.

Peggy glanced around the room nervously, then whispered, "The cops."

"What!" Carolyn said.

Peggy nodded. "Well, just one cop, actually. That woman detective."

Phyllis figured she meant Detective Charlotte Morgan. "I'll talk to her," she said. She didn't know what this was about, other than being connected to Joye Jameson's murder, obviously, but there was only one way to find out.

"She's waiting in the living room," Peggy said.

"Did she have a warrant?" Carolyn asked.

Peggy frowned. "You know, I, uh, didn't think to ask."

"Whatever they want, always make them show you a warrant. That's my rule now."

"I think we can dispense with the warrant this time," Phyllis said. "I don't have anything to hide."

"We should come with you," Carolyn insisted. "Just in case that woman tries any strong-arm tactics."

"I'm pretty sure I'll be fine," Phyllis told her. "But if I need help . . . well, you're all within earshot, aren't you?"

"We certainly are, and we'll be right here close by until the police are gone."

Phyllis nodded her gratitude and went past Peggy. She walked along the hall from the dining room and turned to go through the entrance into the living room.

Charlotte Morgan was sitting on the divan with a smartphone in her hand, swiping a fingertip over the screen. She looked up as Phyllis came into the room.

"Mrs. Newsom," she said as she slipped the phone back into her purse. "Thank you for seeing me."

"I always try to cooperate with the police. My son is a law enforcement officer."

"Sheriff's deputy over in Parker County, right?"

"That's right."

"You're used to having his help when you investigate crimes, aren't you?"

The blunt question annoyed Phyllis, but she kept her voice level and polite as she said, "I've never asked Mike to do anything that wasn't proper."

"But you took his help when he volunteered it, didn't you, including sharing evidence with you?"

Phyllis ignored that question and asked, "What can I do for you, Detective?"

"You don't seem surprised that I know about your history with criminal investigations," Morgan commented rather than answering Phyllis's question. They were trading being stubborn, Phyllis thought.

She didn't care for this fencing. Without mentioning David Miller's visit, she said, "I've recently discovered that there's quite a bit of information about me on the Internet."

"You didn't know that before?"

"Honestly, it never even occurred to me to look."

"Well, you must not have a vain bone in your body," Morgan said.

"Why did *you* look up those websites, Detective?"

"Until today you were a person of interest in Joye Jameson's death, Mrs. Newsom. I'm sorry if that offends you—"

"I'm not offended," Phyllis said. "I suppose you had to look into the background of everyone who was there on the set, as well as the crew members who were nearby."

"That's right." Morgan smiled, but the expression wasn't particularly friendly. "You know, the things you've been mixed up with in the past might just make this easier. You know something about how an investigation works."

Phyllis shrugged. "I know enough to figure that you came here for a reason, which you still haven't told me."

"All right." Morgan's tone hardened as she went on, "This is a high-profile case. A TV star and bestselling author dies under mysterious circumstances, and it's big news all across the country. My partner and I wanted to make sure we had all the possibilities covered, so until we knew for sure whether or not Joye Jameson was murdered, we proceeded on the assumption that her death was a homicide."

"Which clearly it was, or you wouldn't have arrested Bailey Broderick."

Morgan didn't respond to that. She continued, "We'd been keeping an eye on the people involved until we got the results back from the autopsy. Once the arrest warrant was issued, all the other surveillance was supposed to be pulled off. But the officers who were watching you were still on the job when Ms. Broderick's attorney came to see you."

"You were watching me?" Phyllis said. A note of outrage crept into her voice, even though she knew it wasn't really justified. There was nothing wrong with keeping possible suspects under surveillance; that was just smart police work.

But even though she knew that logically, she still didn't like being spied on.

"It wouldn't be proper for me to ask you what David Miller talked to you about—"

"And that's good," Phyllis said, "because I don't intend to tell you."

"But I will say that if you're thinking about conducting your own investigation into this case—playing detective, to put it bluntly—you'd be smart to forget it. You'll just wind up in trouble. This isn't a little town like Weatherford where you can get away with something like that." A hint of a smirk stole onto Morgan's face as she added, "And even over there, you got arrested for interfering with an investigation, didn't you?"

"You already know that or you wouldn't be asking the

question," Phyllis said. "That's the only reason you came to see me, to warn me to stay out of the case?"

"Why else would I be here? I'm not going to share all our evidence with you, if that's what you're waiting for, so you can solve everything for us poor dumb cops. Besides, we've already arrested the person who killed Joye Jameson."

"You're wrong," Phyllis said. "Bailey Broderick didn't do anything of the sort. I was right there, as close to her as I am to you right now, and I can swear she had no idea Joye was going to have that allergic reaction."

"She's got you fooled; that's all."

Phyllis shook her head. "I don't believe that."

Morgan stood up. "Well, luckily for me, it doesn't matter what you believe or don't believe," she said. "All that matters is the evidence. And trust me on this . . . Bailey Broderick killed Joye Jameson. There's absolutely no doubt about that."

"You can't stop me from talking to her attorney, you know," Phyllis said as Morgan turned toward the door.

"We wouldn't dream of interfering with the legal process like that," Morgan said. "Miller can come up with whatever defense he wants to. It's not going to do any good. I'll let myself out."

"Fine," Phyllis said. "Good evening, Detective."

The words sounded more civil than she wanted to be at that moment.

When Detective Morgan was gone, the others emerged from the hallway. Phyllis wondered if they had been listening to the entire conversation. She wouldn't be surprised, nor could she bring herself to be mad at them if they had.

"Boy, talk about a nasty little ice queen," Peggy said.

"I think there are even stronger words that could be used if we weren't all ladies," Eve said. She inclined her head toward Sam. "And one very chivalrous gentleman."

"I'm not feelin' too chivalrous at the moment," Sam said. "They've got a lot of nerve, stakin' out Phyllis like that."

"I didn't care for that, either, but I can understand why they did it," Phyllis said. "Until they knew for sure what had happened, they had to assume the worst about everybody."

Sam said, "She sounded mighty sure about Bailey Broderick bein' the killer, too."

"I was just thinking about that . . . and I believe in one way she might be right."

Carolyn frowned. "What? I don't believe it! Bailey Broderick is no murderer."

Phyllis smiled and shook her head. She said, "That's not what I meant. Bailey may have killed Joye, but I still don't believe she's a murderer."

They all frowned at her in confusion, but Phyllis didn't say anything else. She had to think about it some more first.

Chapter 23

$\mathcal{L}$ater that evening, Phyllis caught Peggy alone in the kitchen and said, "I have a favor to ask of you."

"Shoot," Peggy said.

"Would you mind if we stayed a few more days? Those of us who want to, I mean."

"Mind?" Peggy repeated. "Honey, haven't I been saying that I hate to see you go? Having company this week has been the best thing to happen to me in a long time."

Phyllis smiled. "I know, but I don't want us to wear out our welcome. You know the old saying about guests and fish?"

"How they both start to stink in three days? I'm sure that's true for some people, but to be honest, you folks don't really seem like guests. Carolyn's family, of course, and that's sort of the way I've started to feel about the rest of you. And like I said, I haven't eaten this good in ages! You think I want to go back to eating my own cooking so soon?"

Phyllis laughed and said, "Well, I suppose it's settled, then. I'll have to talk to the others and make sure none of them have to get back to Weatherford by a certain time."

"Old geezers like us don't have a lot of pressing engagements, except maybe with the funeral home." Peggy paused. "Let me ask you a question, though. Does staying here in Dallas have something to do with that murder case?"

"Well . . ."

"I knew it! You're going to solve it, aren't you? Carolyn told me how you're like a pit bull. Once you get your jaws locked on a mystery, nobody can pry you loose until you're ready to let go."

"I'm not sure I like being compared to a pit bull, but it's true that I don't think Bailey is guilty. And now that she's been arrested, the police aren't going to be looking for anyone else. They think they have the killer."

"You never did explain about that."

"No, I didn't," Phyllis said.

Peggy smiled. "That's right, be mysterious. You'll come clean sooner or later. And when you do, I'll be interested to hear what you have to say. So yeah, stay here as long as you like. I'll be glad to have you."

With that settled, Phyllis went to talk to the others. They were all in the living room. She said, "I don't want to cause trouble for anyone, but I've decided to stay here in Dallas for a while. The rest of you are free to go back to Weatherford, of course."

"I wondered how long it was going to take you to get around to that," Carolyn said. "You don't want to leave Joye Jameson's murder unsolved, do you?"

Eve added, "We all expected this, dear."

"And we don't mind stayin' as long as Peggy's willin' to put up with us," Sam said.

"Phyllis already checked with me," Peggy said as she came in the room. "I told her you could all stay as long as you want to. Heck, even being on the edges of a murder case is probably more excitement than I'll have the rest of my life."

Phyllis said, "It's pretty likely that the police or Mr. Miller will want to talk to me again, and it would be easier to do that if I was here in town, instead of coming all the way over from Weatherford every time they have questions for me. So there's a practical reason for staying, too."

"I don't care about that," Peggy said. "I just want to be around when you figure out who the real killer is."

"I hope your confidence in me isn't misplaced."

"It never has been so far," Sam said.

With that settled, Phyllis was able to turn in and get a surprisingly good night's sleep. It was a little after nine o'clock the next morning when her cell phone rang. She didn't recognize the number, but when she answered, she heard a familiar voice on the other end.

"How are you this morning, Mrs. Newsom?" David Miller asked.

"I'm all right, I suppose," Phyllis said. "Did you know that the police had Mrs. Stockton's house under surveillance yesterday evening when you came here?"

"What? That's an outrage!" Miller paused. "Sorry. Being upset about what the police do is just a matter of habit, I suppose. Actually, I'm not at all surprised to hear that, although I would have thought they'd have been pulled off that detail by then, since they'd already made an arrest."

"I think there was a mix-up in communications somewhere," Phyllis told him. "That's the impression I got from Detective Morgan, anyway."

"Charlotte Morgan talked to you?" This time, the attorney sounded genuinely surprised.

"That's right; she came by here yesterday evening."

"What did she want?"

"She looked me up on the Internet just like you did. She came to warn me not to interfere with the investigation into Joye Jameson's murder."

Miller grunted and said, "What investigation? They seem to think they have a solid case against Ms. Broderick already. The ADA at the bail hearing a few minutes ago claimed that she was a flight risk. He played the Hollywood celebrity card and tried to convince the judge that Bailey has enough money and influence to escape this jurisdiction. I was able to cut his legs out from under him, though, by playing the same card right back at him. If Ms. Broderick is really that big a celebrity, I said, then where could she go to hide?"

"No offense to anyone," Phyllis said, "but I don't think Bailey is really that big a celebrity. Nobody but a fan of *The Joye of Cooking* would even know who she is, and most people who watch the show probably wouldn't remember her name or even what she looks like."

"That's true. Anyway, the judge turned down the no-bail request and set it in the amount of five hundred thousand dollars. The bondsman I work with was able to handle that without any problem. We're on our way to my office right now."

"We?" Phyllis repeated.

"Ms. Broderick and myself."

"Oh, my goodness. You don't have me on speakerphone, do you? I wouldn't want Bailey to hear me saying that she's not really a celebrity yet."

"Don't worry about that," Miller told her. "I was wondering if you could join us."

"You want me to come to your office?"

"If that's possible. Do you know where it is?"

"You gave me your card yesterday. I'm sure my friend Sam could find the place . . ." Phyllis looked at Sam, who had been following her end of the conversation along with Carolyn, Eve, and Peggy. He nodded to indicate that he didn't mind taking her to Miller's office. "Yes, I suppose I can meet you there."

"Excellent. As soon as you can get here, then, if that's all right."

"We'll leave in just a few minutes," Phyllis promised.

Miller thanked her, then said good-bye and broke the connection.

"That happened a little sooner than I expected it to," Carolyn commented. "You're going to be right in the middle of this case, as usual, Phyllis."

"I'd just as soon there was nothing 'usual' about a murder case," Phyllis said. "I wish I knew why he wants me to be involved. You'd think a defense attorney wouldn't invite a civilian, so to speak, to help him with a case."

"I can tell you why he wants your help," Sam said. "He wants to be able to bring you into court and show you off to the jury. You're the famous crime-bustin' granny, and if you think his client is innocent, why, she must be."

"Publicity," Phyllis said. "He wants to try the case in the news media before it ever gets to court."

"It might work," Sam said. "Can't hurt to try." He chuckled. "The fella doesn't know what he's really lettin' himself in for, though. He'll find out when you drop that killer right in his lap."

Chapter 24

David Miller's office was in a glass, chrome, and steel high-rise in downtown Dallas. A modern art sculpture that reminded Phyllis of something that had been left out in the sun until it partially melted adorned the plaza in front of the building.

"I don't care for big buildings like this," Phyllis told Sam as they crossed the plaza. "And according to Mr. Miller's card, his office is on the twenty-second floor. I always worry about riding that high in an elevator. It's the only time I really feel claustrophobic."

"Statistics say it's safer than crossin' the street out here."

"And you know the old saying about that. There are lies, damned lies, and statistics."

Sam grinned. "Thirty-seven per cent of all statistics on the Internet are made up, you know."

"They are? Where did you—" Phyllis stopped in midsentence and narrowed her eyes at him. After a moment she sighed and shook her head.

Even though it was Saturday morning, there were several people in the lobby of the office building. Phyllis and Sam had to go past a security desk, and the guard on duty there stopped them and asked, "Can I help you folks?"

"We're here to see David Miller," Phyllis told him. "He's expecting us."

"I'll need to double-check that. Your names?"

"Phyllis Newsom and Sam Fletcher."

The guard nodded, picked up a telephone, and punched a couple of buttons on its base. After a moment he said, "Yes, I have a Mrs. Newsom and a Mr. Fletcher to see Mr. Miller . . . Thanks." He hung up the phone and told them, "You can go on up. The elevators are right over there. Mr. Miller's office is on twenty-two, in case you didn't know that already."

"Thank you," Phyllis told him. "Do you screen everyone who comes in all the time, or just on the weekends?"

"Pretty much all the time," the guard said. He smiled. "A lot of criminal defense attorneys have their offices here, and so do some divorce lawyers. You get people with grudges coming in every now and then."

"I'll just bet you do," Sam said.

He and Phyllis walked over to the bank of elevators. Phyllis looked up and said, "At least these aren't the kind with glass walls so that you can see how high you're going. I don't care for those, either."

"Don't the glass walls help with the claustrophobia?" Sam asked as he pushed the UP button.

"Maybe a little, but the fear of heights more than counteracts it."

One of the elevator doors opened, and a computerized female voice announced in dulcet tones, "Going. Up."

"I don't know if I'll ever get used to machines talkin' to me," Sam said as they stepped into the car. "Guess I've seen too many movies about how they're gonna take over someday. I'll bet they're already plottin' against us."

The door closed and the elevator rose so smoothly it almost didn't seem like they were moving. Phyllis knew they were, though, and her nervousness increased a little with every floor number that changed on the display beside the elevator controls. After a few moments, Sam said, "This'll give you a nosebleed."

The elevator came to a stop, and the disembodied voice said, "Twenty. Second. Floor." The doors opened.

"Thank goodness," Phyllis said. "It was starting to seem like there wasn't enough oxygen in here."

They stepped out into a reception area with marble floors and a horseshoe-shaped counter. There were places for several receptionists to work behind that counter, but at the moment only one was on duty, a very attractive young woman with short, sleek blond hair. She said, "Mrs. Newsom? Mr. Fletcher?"

"That's right," Phyllis said.

The woman stood up. She wore a white blouse and a fairly short black leather skirt, and she was tall, probably an inch over six feet. Not much of that height came from high heels, either, Phyllis saw as the receptionist walked out from behind the counter. Her shoes were low heeled and looked comfortable.

"Mr. Miller is expecting you," she said unnecessarily. "If you'll follow me . . ."

They went through a door into a carpeted hall with several doors on either side, all of them closed at the moment. At the end of the hall was a set of double doors. One of them was partially open.

The receptionist stopped at that door and said, "Mrs. Newsom and Mr. Fletcher are here." She opened the door wide and stepped back so they could go in.

Miller's office wasn't ostentatiously fancy, but it was comfortably and expensively furnished, Phyllis saw, and the wall behind the lawyer's big desk was mostly glass, which provided a spectacular view of downtown Dallas. The window faced north, and Phyllis felt like she could see halfway to Oklahoma when she gazed in that direction. She tried not to think about how high they really were.

Miller stood up from the big leather chair behind the desk. Bailey sat in a slightly smaller chair in front of the desk. Miller extended a hand and said, "Please come in and have a seat, and thank you for coming down here this morning." He glanced at the door and added, "Thanks, Karen," to the receptionist.

Phyllis shook hands with the lawyer and said, "I don't think you were formally introduced to my friend Sam Fletcher yesterday."

Miller shook with Sam as well. "No, but I know who you are, of course, Mr. Fletcher. Watson to Mrs. Newsom's Holmes, eh?"

Sam grinned and said, "I've tried to tell her that, but she claims not to see it."

"I just think comparing me to Sherlock Holmes is ridiculous," Phyllis said. "I'm not that fond of it when people bring up Miss Marple, either." She turned to the young woman seated in front of the desk and went on, "How are you this morning, Miss Broderick?"

Bailey sighed. The slightly haggard look on her face told Phyllis that she probably hadn't slept much the night before. That was no surprise. Phyllis remembered how difficult it was to sleep behind bars . . . and she hadn't been charged with something nearly as serious as murder.

"I'll be all right, I suppose," Bailey said, "at least when this is all over and my name has been cleared." She glanced at Miller, then looked at Phyllis again. "It's not that I don't appreciate the concern, Mrs. Newsom, but I'm still not completely clear why you're here . . ."

"Wasn't that obvious from the context of what we just said?" Miller asked. "Mrs. Newsom has something of a reputation as a detective. She's solved several murders."

Bailey's tired-looking eyes widened. "Really?"

Phyllis didn't think it would be wise to bring up her theory that Miller wanted her involved with the case more for the sake of publicity than for anything else. Bailey needed all the optimism she could muster right now.

Besides, Sam might be right: Maybe there really was something she could do to help them discover the truth about Joye Jameson's death.

Miller waved Phyllis and Sam into two of the comfortable leather chairs arranged in front of the desk, and as he sat down himself, he said, "I want to go over everything I've been able to pry loose from the police and the district attorney's office so far. I'm sure they're holding things back—they always do—and we'll have a fight on our hands getting everything from them. But for now we know that Joye Jameson died of anaphylactic shock brought on by an allergic reaction to peanuts. The allergen appears to have been introduced into her system by the oil in which Mrs. Newsom's funnel cake was fried."

Bailey looked at Phyllis and said, "You're lucky they didn't jump to a different conclusion and arrest you."

"Believe me, I know," Phyllis said, nodding.

Miller waved a hand. "Such a charge never would have stood up. I could have gotten that thrown out at the arraignment. Mrs. Newsom had no chance to tamper with the oil. It was already there when she arrived, and she was in front of hundreds of witnesses the whole time she was around it."

"Was all the oil in the bottle peanut oil instead of corn oil?" Phyllis asked.

Miller nodded. "That's my impression, yes, except for some residual traces of corn oil."

"So whoever did it poured out the corn oil and poured in the peanut oil, filling it to the same level it had been before."

"That's a reasonable assumption," Miller agreed.

"Is it all right for me to ask questions?"

"By all means, Mrs. Newsom. You're here so that I can take advantage of that keen brain of yours."

Phyllis ignored the flattery and turned to Bailey. "Do you remember when that bottle of oil was last used before Thursday's show?"

Bailey had lost some of her dull, dispirited look. She seemed to be taking an interest in what was going on, which was reasonable considering that her freedom was at stake.

"It was only used once," she said. "That was on Tuesday, when Joye fried some chicken. I opened it then."

"It hadn't been opened before? The seal was intact?"

"That's right."

"So no one could have tampered with it before that."

"No. If they had, Joye would have had a bad reaction to the chicken. She ate several bites from a piece of it during the broadcast."

Phyllis nodded and asked, "What did you do with the bottle after that episode?"

"I put it back in the cabinet that's built into the set. That's where we keep all the nonperishable ingredients and supplies, just like in a pantry. There's a big refrigerator/freezer backstage for the perishable stuff."

"Does that cabinet have a lock on it?"

Bailey nodded. "Yes, and we try to keep it locked up whenever no one's around."

Miller asked, "Who has the key to it?"

"Well, there are several keys. Joye has—I mean, had one. Reed. Our prop man, Dan Connolly. And I have one, too, of course. I probably have to get in there more than anybody else."

"Any others?"

"I don't know. It's possible. Somebody could have had a copy made."

Miller frowned and said, "It's probably not the best lock in the world, anyway. Somebody might have been able to get it open."

"Do you use the same set every time you broadcast from a remote location?" Phyllis asked.

"We've been using this one for about a year," Bailey said. "It breaks down into its components so it can be loaded on trucks and transported easily. Joye liked for the show to have the same look to it no matter where we were broadcasting from."

"So everyone on the crew and in the production staff is familiar with it?"

"Sure. The set is just part of the job."

"So everyone would have known where the oil was kept?"

Bailey shrugged and said, "I guess so. They would if they ever paid any attention to things like that. I couldn't tell you who did and who didn't."

"We'll try to find out," Miller said. "I or one of my associates will be interviewing everyone connected with the show." He paused for a second. "Getting back to the bottle of oil . . . Naturally your fingerprints would be on it."

Bailey nodded. "Of course."

"When Ms. Jameson fried that chicken on Tuesday, did she pour the oil into the pan, or did you?"

"Joye did," Bailey said. "I'm sure of it. But you can check the tapes of the show if you want to."

Miller smiled and said, "That's something else I'll be doing. I plan to watch every episode you broadcast from the state fair. There's no telling what might show up. Your friend Mr. Hayes is supposed to send a DVD over anytime now."

Bailey's eyes dropped for a second at the lawyer's mention of Reed Hayes. Phyllis noticed that and wondered if it meant anything. She didn't want to take that tack right at the moment, though, so she said, "What about other fingerprints? Would anyone have had a reason to be handling that bottle of oil besides you, me, and Joye?"

Bailey shook her head. "Not that I know of."

"Do you have any idea why the autoinjector didn't work?"

The question seemed to take Bailey by surprise. She shook

her head again and said, "I don't know. I guess I just supposed the reaction was too strong . . ."

"You told me you'd used one of them on Joye before," Phyllis reminded her.

Miller leaned forward and looked intrigued. "We hadn't gotten into this yet," he said. "I'm glad you brought it up, Mrs. Newsom."

Bailey said, "Yes, like I told you, a couple of years ago in New Orleans I used one of the pens when Joye got hold of some candy with peanuts in it. There weren't supposed to be any peanuts in the candy, but there was one hidden inside the chocolate—"

"Hidden?" Miller repeated. "You mean someone tried to murder Ms. Jameson two years ago?"

"No, no, nothing like that," Bailey said. "It was purely an accident. The lady who made it was a guest on the show. She made some with peanuts and some without, because we'd told her that Joye was allergic. It was just a mix-up. The poor woman was horrified that she'd gotten it wrong."

"I don't recall seeing that episode," Phyllis said.

"It never aired," Bailey explained. "Sometimes because of logistics and travel considerations, we do two episodes in a day, broadcast one of them live and tape the other. That was one we were taping to show the next day. Joye said she couldn't go on, and everyone went along with her, of course." Bailey smiled but didn't look particularly amused. "Everyone always went along with what Joye wanted, if they knew what was good for them."

Miller made a face and said, "Now, see, that's the sort of thing you don't want to be saying, especially in public or in court. It goes to motive. Makes it sound like you had a grudge against Ms. Jameson because she was overbearing and hard to get along with."

"She could be like that when she didn't get her way," Bailey said. "That's just the truth, and anybody who worked with her will tell you that, at least if they're telling the truth. She studied the tapes of every episode after it was broadcast, and she'd rip poor Charlie a new one if she didn't like some of the camera angles. The same with Reed if the running time was off at all. And of course any time I did something that she didn't like—"

"That's enough," Miller cut in. "We'll talk about all that, just not right now."

Despite what the attorney said, Phyllis was glad Bailey had been honest. Bailey's words had confirmed the hunch Phyllis had about the way Joye Jameson treated the people who worked for her. It was somewhat disillusioning—Joye had always seemed so *nice* on TV—but not that surprising.

"Let's get back to the autoinjector," Miller said to Bailey. "You used one during that earlier incident, the one in New Orleans?"

"That's right. And it stopped the reaction pretty quickly. Joye was choking, but she was able to breathe again in seconds after I injected her. The swelling in her throat went down right away."

"She had that reaction to one peanut?"

"She's pretty sensitive. I guess enough of the oil soaked into that funnel cake to set off the reaction."

Phyllis said, "I used paper towels to soak up the extra oil after I took the funnel cake out, but some of it certainly would have remained in the cake."

"You brought this angle up, Mrs. Newsom," Miller said. "Do you think it's important that the pen didn't work?"

"I thought maybe the killer tampered with it, too," Phyllis explained. "He or she could have substituted something for the epinephrine that wouldn't stop the allergic reaction."

"Coppering his bets, eh?" Miller said. "It's certainly possible. The forensics team probably analyzed whatever was left in the pen, but if they didn't, they need to. That might bring us around to the question of not only who had access to the bottle of oil but also the pen."

"That's not going to help us," Bailey said. "We already know one person who had access to both of them." She looked around at the others and heaved a sigh. "And that would be me."

Chapter 25

A long moment of silence followed that disheartening statement from Bailey. Finally, David Miller broke it by saying, "I think we could all use a break and some coffee. There's a small kitchen here in the suite. I'll have Karen make some for us."

"Why don't you let me do it?" Phyllis suggested as Miller reached for the intercom on his desk.

He stopped and shrugged. "Well . . . all right, I suppose." He pointed at a door to the left of the office. "There's a hall through there. The kitchen is on the right. Bathroom and a small bedroom to the left. Sometimes I spend the night here when I'm working on a case and don't have time to sleep much. It's easier than going home to an empty apartment."

Too much information, and slightly pathetic, too, Phyllis thought, but she didn't say that. Instead, she stood up, motioned for Sam to keep his seat, and said, "Bailey, why don't you come with me and give me a hand?"

For a second Bailey looked like she was going to refuse, but then she said, "Why not?" She stood up and followed Phyllis out of the office.

The kitchen was small, as Miller had said, but it was equipped with a state-of-the-art microwave, a compact refrigerator and freezer, a fancy European coffeemaker, a gleaming stainless steel sink, and a well-stocked cabinet. Phyllis found the coffee in the cabinet and started it brewing while Bailey folded her arms and leaned against the counter.

"So you're a detective," she said.

"I'm a retired schoolteacher who's been lucky enough to figure out a few things," Phyllis said.

"If it was just a matter of luck, I don't think Mr. Miller would have called you in as a consultant. He's supposed to be one of the best defense attorneys around. I know he doesn't really look like it, but that's what Reed says, anyway."

"I heard that the production company wouldn't provide a lawyer for you."

"How could they? Joye was their star. They have to be on her side . . . now. Even though she's dead." Bailey made a little noise in her throat. "Maybe especially because she's dead."

Phyllis pretended to keep most of her attention focused on the coffeemaker as she said in an apparently offhand manner, "What do you mean by that?"

"I mean they were ready to dump her over those contract negotiations. They probably never really would have, mind you. Star power is still important in Hollywood. But there were a lot of people pretty mad at her, from Reed on up to the suits at the very top. She really put Reed in a bad position by throwing several tantrums and walking out of meetings with the executives. He was caught right in the middle."

"That's not a good place to be," Phyllis agreed, still keeping her tone casual. "Speaking of star power, it appears they were grooming you for something like that until . . . well, until this unfortunate incident."

"No, you've got that wrong," Bailey said. "I was going to be strictly an emergency replacement; that's all. With Joye gone, they would have killed the show—" She stopped, closed her eyes for a moment, and pressed the fingertips of one hand to her forehead. "Good grief, that's a terrible way to phrase that, isn't it?" She looked up again. "They would have canceled the show, or brought in somebody else and rebranded it. It would have been essentially a new show. Who knows? They might have even brought Gloria back. They might do it yet."

"You think so?"

"I wouldn't say it was likely, but you can't rule it out. Enough time has passed since her little meltdown that it's possible. The viewing public has a pretty short attention span. And she's done pretty well for herself here with her local gig." Bailey thought about it and nodded. "Yeah. It could happen."

The delicious aroma of the coffee brewing filled the room now. Phyllis took a deep breath and enjoyed it, but she didn't let her mind stray from the real reason she had cajoled Bailey into coming to the kitchen with her. She said, "If Gloria did come back to the show, I'm sure Reed would be disappointed. He must have had high hopes for you taking over."

"Maybe." Bailey looked away again, like she had in Miller's office. "Reed always seemed to have more faith in me than I did in myself. But he would have been disappointed. I would have been a big disappointment to him." She ran her fingers through her hair and started to look agitated. "He shouldn't be wasting his money paying for somebody to defend me. It's not fair to him."

"Why not?"

"Because he's got it all wrong! I'm not . . . I'm not who he thinks I am. Things aren't what he . . . they just aren't . . ."

"Are you talking about your involvement with Hank Squires?" Phyllis asked quietly.

Bailey's head snapped up. "What are you talking about?" she demanded. "What do you know about Hank and . . . and . . ."

That shot in the dark had paid off, Phyllis thought. And she felt bad about taking it, too. If Bailey hadn't been in such a frightened, depressed state of mind, she might have been able to keep up the deception.

As it was, she crumbled. Tears began to run down her cheeks as she stared at Phyllis.

"I'm sorry," Phyllis said. "I saw something the other day that made me think there might be something going on between the two of you, but I wasn't sure."

"You tricked me."

"Only because I don't believe you killed Joye. I don't want to see you convicted for a murder you didn't commit. I want to help you, Bailey."

"Well, you can't do it by blaming anything on Hank! He's the sweetest, gentlest man—"

"Big men like that often are."

"He wouldn't hurt anybody, let alone Joye."

"He used to be married to her, you know."

"Of course I knew that," Bailey said. "Everybody on the show knew that."

"When a couple splits up, a lot of hard feelings can linger," Phyllis pointed out. "And in this case, right after their divorce Joye became a big success, while Hank was still running a camera."

"He loves running a camera. He didn't hold any sort of grudge against Joye. He was happy for her success. He told me so, more than once."

"Just because he told you that doesn't necessarily make it true."

"You must not have ever loved anybody," Bailey said. "I would have known if Hank was lying to me."

Bailey was incredibly young, thought Phyllis. She hadn't discovered that some people could look right in the eyes of a person they loved and tell a bald-faced lie. Phyllis sort of envied her that youth and innocence.

David Miller stuck his head in at the kitchen door. "How are we coming on that coffee?" he asked.

"It's just about ready," Phyllis told him.

Miller must have seen that Bailey had been crying. He looked back and forth between the two women and said, "Everything all right in here?"

"Fine," Bailey said as she turned to look at him, but she didn't sound fine. "Mr. Miller, I need to ask you something."

Miller smiled and said, "Of course. You're the client. Ask anything you want to."

"Is your defense of me going to be to blame somebody else for killing Joye?"

Miller seemed to be taken aback by the question. He said,

"One possible line of argument is always to create a reasonable doubt in the minds of the jurors—"

"By making them think someone else did it."

"Or to make them believe that you didn't."

"But you're going to have a hard time doing that, aren't you? Because I have a motive—the prosecutors will say I was Joye's long-suffering assistant who wanted to take over the show—and I certainly had the means and opportunity. I mean, I was right there! It would have been easier for me to switch that cooking oil than it would have been for anybody else."

"We'll try not to point that out—" Miller began.

"I'm sure the district attorney will make certain the jury knows about it," Bailey said. "So your only real chance of an acquittal is to point the finger of blame at somebody else, a specific somebody if you can."

"It's much too early to be worried about things like that. We've barely started putting together your defense."

"You won't get me off by accusing Hank or Reed," Bailey insisted. "I know neither of them is guilty, and I won't have them ruined by dumping a lot of suspicion on them."

Miller was starting to look angry now. "I'm not in the habit of letting the client dictate my tactics to me," he said. "I do whatever I believe to be in your best interests. That's my job."

"But you work for me."

"Actually, in this case I don't," Miller said. "I work for Mr. Hayes."

"You won't once he knows the truth," she snapped.

"What do you mean by that?" Miller frowned. "What haven't you told me?"

"Ask your consultant."

With that, Bailey pushed past Miller and stalked out of the kitchen. He turned to look after her and said, "Wait! Ms. Broderick!" Before starting after Bailey, he threw a glance at Phyllis and said through clenched teeth, "What did you *do*?"

Phyllis didn't know how to answer that. She had just been gathering as much information about the case as she could, the same way she always did when she was trying to figure out what had really happened. Sometimes that backfired, as it appeared to have done here.

Miller didn't wait for Phyllis to respond. He hurried along the hall after Bailey.

The coffee was ready, so Phyllis poured a cup for herself and one for Sam. There was no point in letting it all go to waste.

Chapter 26

By the time she got back to Miller's office, the lawyer was nowhere to be seen, and neither was Bailey. As Phyllis handed one of the cups to Sam, she asked, "Where did they go?"

"He took her into that little bedroom to talk to her and try to calm her down," Sam said. "She was mighty upset."

"I know," Phyllis said, "and it's my fault. I told her I knew she was cheating on Reed Hayes with Hank Squires."

"You mean you were right about that? Her and that big fella are really carryin' on?"

"Evidently. Bailey didn't take it well when she thought I was trying to blame Hank for Joye's murder. She told Mr. Miller she wouldn't allow him to throw suspicion on either Hank or Reed."

"I don't imagine that went over too well."

"I just hope I haven't ruined everything."

Sam put a hand on Phyllis's shoulder and said, "You're just tryin' to help the girl the best way you know how. Nobody can fault you for that."

She leaned against him and said, "Thank you, Sam. Sometimes I worry that I'm just as much of a meddler as some people seem to think I am."

"You don't have to worry about that. I've never seen anybody who tried harder to help people. That's not the same thing as meddlin'."

Footsteps in the hallway made them move apart. Miller and Bailey came into the office. Bailey still wore a slightly sullen expression, but she didn't seem quite as angry as she had been a few minutes earlier.

"Ms. Broderick and I have had a good talk," Miller said, "and we've agreed that she'll leave the particulars of the case to me. However, I've promised her in turn that we'll be careful about not trying to throw suspicion on anyone who's innocent."

Bailey said to Phyllis, "I asked him to fire you, but he told me you're not working for him. You're really here because you want to help me, not because you're getting paid?"

"Of course," Phyllis said. "Right from the start, I didn't think that you had anything to do with Joye Jameson's death, any more than I did. Neither of us knew about the peanut oil."

"I certainly didn't," Bailey said. "And if you're really on my side, then I'm sorry about getting mad earlier. I just don't want Hank or Reed getting hurt. Hank's such a good guy, and Reed . . . well, he's going to wind up getting hurt enough already."

"When he finds out about you and Hank, you mean?"

Bailey nodded. "Yeah. And he has a right to know the truth. I'm going to tell him."

Miller said, "I've warned Ms. Broderick that if she does

that, Mr. Hayes might withdraw his financial support from her defense."

"You wouldn't keep on with the case pro bono?" Sam asked.

Miller smiled uncomfortably and held out his hands to indicate their surroundings. "Please, Mr. Fletcher," he said, "does this look like a pro bono office to you?"

"Looks like the office of somebody who can afford to kick in the occasional fee," Sam said.

Miller inclined his head. "An honest, forthright answer, if a bit blunt. But we're getting ahead of ourselves. Ms. Broderick, it's the weekend. I'm probably not going to be able to get much more out of the district attorney's office until Monday. Why don't we just put everything on hold right now, including your plans for any dramatic revelations to Mr. Hayes? Can you do that for me, and for yourself?"

Bailey sighed and nodded. "I suppose so. A few more days won't make any difference."

"Well, they can, but let's assume that any difference they make will be a positive one. Perhaps some new evidence will come to light."

Phyllis took that opportunity to say, "Like the matter of whether or not the pen was tampered with, too. Where are they normally kept?"

"There's a supply of them in the production office, in the trailer outside," Bailey said. "And there were some in Joye's dressing room, too. She always liked to have one close by, which is understandable."

"Did she ever have to inject herself with one?"

Bailey frowned in thought. "I know she didn't anytime

that I was around her, and I don't recall her ever mentioning that she had. She knew how to, of course. Most of us on the staff did."

"The one that you used—where did you get it? From the office or the dressing room?"

"I got it from the dressing room that morning."

Miller asked, "Did Ms. Jameson keep the dressing room locked when she wasn't using it?"

Phyllis had been about to ask the same thing.

"Sometimes she did; sometimes she didn't," Bailey said. "If she was going to be gone for a while, she'd usually lock it up. If she just stepped out for a few minutes, she didn't."

"So anyone who was around the set conceivably could have slipped in there and tampered with the pen," Phyllis said.

Bailey shrugged. "I suppose so. But how would the murderer have known exactly which pen I would pick up and put in my pocket? They all look the same."

Sam said, "Maybe he tampered with all of 'em."

Phyllis wasn't surprised that he had come up with a potentially important point. Sam never said much during these investigations, but he listened and he was smart, and Phyllis had learned that when he spoke up, it was wise to pay attention to him.

She nodded now and said, "That would be the only foolproof way of making sure Bailey got one of the pens that wouldn't stop the allergic reaction. In fact . . ." She thought back to how absolutely certain Charlotte Morgan had been that Bailey was responsible for Joye's death. "What if it wasn't just a matter of keeping the pen from saving Joye's life?"

"What do you mean?" Bailey asked.

"You saw how Joye's reaction suddenly got even worse when you injected her," Phyllis said. "I've been considering another possibility. What if the killer replaced the epinephrine in the pens with a solution tainted with peanut oil? What if it was pure peanut oil?"

"Good Lord," Miller breathed. "That would be like a junkie mainlining with uncut heroin."

Bailey's eyes were wide with horror now. "So you're saying maybe I really did kill her," she said in an unsteady voice. "The murder weapon wasn't really the funnel cake. It was that injector I used on her."

"You were trying to save her life," Phyllis said. "We all know that. What you did may have killed her, but the real murderer is whoever switched the cooking oil and tampered with the pen."

Miller held up his hands. "Hold on a minute. All we know for sure is that the cooking oil was switched. We don't know that the pen Bailey used, or any of the pens, was tampered with."

"That would explain why the police arrested her, as well as the way Joye reacted to the injection," Phyllis said. "It would be hard to pin down whoever switched the oil, but there's absolutely no doubt who administered the injection. Everyone who was there saw Bailey do that."

"But why would I be stupid enough to kill her right in front of everybody like that?" the young woman asked.

Miller thought about it and said, "Maybe not stupid. With all the commotion going on, you could have slipped the empty pen in your pocket and disposed of it later. Or you could have had an empty pen already prepared and swapped it out with the one you used."

"I thought you were supposed to be defending me!"

"Devil's advocate, my dear, devil's advocate."

"You know, there's another way to look at this," Phyllis said. "The killer may have had two targets, not just one. He may have hoped that the police would discover the pen had been tampered with and then arrest Bailey, just as they actually did. He gets rid of Joye by arranging her death, and at the same time he gets rid of Bailey by framing her for that death."

"He?" Miller said. "Do you have someone in mind?"

"No," Phyllis admitted. "And actually, the person who might stand to gain the most from getting both Joye and Bailey out of the way is a woman."

"You're talkin' about that blond lady," Sam said.

"Exactly," Phyllis said. "Gloria Kimball."

Chapter 27

Miller seemed intrigued by the idea, even though he said, "I don't really know who that woman is. Does she have a strong enough motive to have done such a thing?"

"Well, she used to be a major star of daytime television," Bailey said, "and she blamed Joye for taking that from her."

"Did she? I mean, did Ms. Jameson take the job away from this Kimball woman?"

"I don't know," Bailey said. "I wasn't working for the show then. From everything I've heard, though, and from what I've seen of how Joye operates . . ."

When she paused, Miller said, "Go on. This could be important for your defense, Ms. Broderick."

"I honestly don't know. Joye might have done something to sabotage Gloria. Joye was very ambitious. When she started talking about the new contract, she made it clear that she wanted to be the highest-paid star of a cooking show on television. I'm sure she was every bit as ambitious several years ago when she was Gloria's assistant. So I really can't rule anything out when it comes to what she might have done."

Phyllis said, "And it doesn't really matter whether Joye actually did anything to ruin Gloria's career or not, as long as Gloria *believes* that she did. That's sufficient motive right there."

"And by framing Bailey at the same time," the lawyer mused, "she creates a possible opening for her triumphant comeback. As a theory, I like it. I like it a lot." Miller shook his head. "But that's all it is—just a theory. We don't have a shred of evidence to indicate that's what took place."

"We know Gloria was there at the fair," Phyllis said. "She was always close by anytime anything happened. She might've had a chance to tamper with the cooking oil and the injectors. The problem is that there were always security guards around the broadcast set and the backstage area, too. Gloria would have had to slip in and out without being noticed. I'm not sure how difficult that would have been for her."

"The security camera footage ought to help us with that," Miller said. "If we can find any shots of her skulking around where she wasn't supposed to be, not long before Ms. Jameson's death, then given her potential grudge against the victim . . ." Miller shrugged. "That might be enough right there to create reasonable doubt in the minds of the jurors."

Bailey said, "I'm not sure I want just reasonable doubt. Even if I'm acquitted, there'll always be people who believe that I was responsible for Joye's death. I'd rather that my name was cleared once and for all by finding out who really killed her."

"And I'd like to have a full head of hair, be six inches taller, and weigh forty pounds less," Miller said. "We do what we can with what we have, and in this case, my job is to keep you out of prison, no matter how I go about it. That said . . ." He looked meaningfully at Phyllis. "Solving the murder *would* be the most effective way of going about that."

"No pressure there," Sam said.

"I'll do my best," Phyllis said. "I'm sure we all will. Bailey, if you remember anything that might be helpful . . . anybody hanging around the set who shouldn't have been there . . . anything unusual that you overheard . . . you'll let us know right away?"

"Of course."

Miller looked at Phyllis again and asked, "Is there anything else we need to cover today?"

Phyllis thought about it, then shook her head. "Nothing that I can think of."

"We'll be in touch on Monday, then, after I've had a chance to rattle the district attorney's cage a little more." The lawyer turned his attention back to Bailey. "Ms. Broderick, how would you feel about staying here for the time being? The apartment is small, but it's quite comfortable."

"I don't know," Bailey said with a frown. "Why would I do that?"

Miller held up his hands in a reassuring gesture. "Please, don't think for a moment that I'm suggesting anything improper. I'd just like for you to be somewhere safe, somewhere the media can't get at you and provoke you into saying anything or doing anything that would sensationalize the case any more than it already is."

"I have a room in the hotel where everyone from the show has been staying—"

"Which the press already knows about, I promise you. I could put you up somewhere else, at some other hotel, but when you do that you always run the risk of leaks. There are too many people who are eager to trade information for money or celebrity."

"I suppose that makes sense," Bailey agreed. "But if I stay here I'll need a few of my things."

"My assistant Karen can pick up anything you need for the next few days. Trust me, she has excellent taste."

"You're making it too difficult to say no," Bailey responded with a smile.

"That was the general idea."

"All right, I'll stay. But I'll have to let a couple of people know where I am."

"Mr. Hayes and Mr. Squires?"

"That's right."

Miller thought it over for a moment and then nodded. "If you think they can be trusted, I suppose it's all right," he said.

"I trust them," Bailey said.

That didn't mean the two men were completely trust-worthy, Phyllis thought. Hank Squires seemed harmless enough despite his size, and as far as Phyllis could see, he had no reason to kill Joye Jameson and frame Bailey for the murder.

Reed Hayes was a different story. Joye had caused considerable trouble and embarrassment for him in recent weeks, during the contract negotiations. He might have decided that it would be easier to get rid of her, in a fashion that might well be deemed accidental, than to continue trying to deal with her. As for framing Bailey for the killing . . .

If Hayes had discovered her affair with the cameraman, he might have been hurt and angry enough to do such a thing. Bailey seemed to think that Hayes didn't know about her involvement with Hank, but she could be wrong about that. Hayes might have discovered it but kept his knowledge to himself while he plotted his revenge.

That sounded pretty melodramatic, Phyllis told herself as the thought crossed her mind. But melodrama was just an exaggerated version of real life. Human emotions—love, anger, resentment—existed, and sometimes they drove people to do things that were almost beyond belief. She had seen proof of that with her own eyes, more times than she liked to think about.

"I'll be in touch," Miller said as Phyllis and Sam got up to leave. "And thank you for coming down here today, Mrs. Newsom. I think the picture is considerably clearer than it would have been if we hadn't had your input."

"I'm glad to help," Phyllis said.

Bailey said, "Yes, I appreciate it, too. You don't owe me a thing. In fact there have been a few times when I wasn't very nice to you. And you're willing to go out of your way to help me."

"We all need people to pitch in from time to time. I like to do what I can."

As they left the lawyer's private office, Miller called on the intercom for his blond assistant to come in. Phyllis and Sam passed her on their way out. Karen paused long enough to ask, "Do you need my help with anything, Mrs. Newsom?"

"Just take care of Miss Broderick," Phyllis said. "This case is liable to get worse before it gets better."

·   ·   ·

The ride down in the elevator was about as nerve-racking as the trip up to the twenty-second floor. Phyllis was glad to leave the car and get solid ground under her feet again.

As they left the building, a chilly wind swept across the plaza with its modernistic sculpture. "Feels like that cool front got here," Sam said. Gray clouds thickened overhead.

"Yes, it certainly seems more like autumn now," Phyllis agreed, somewhat distractedly. She was thinking about everything they had learned during the meeting with Bailey and Miller. There was no shortage of suspects in this case, but they needed more information. At this point, Phyllis couldn't see anything that would allow her to prove Bailey Broderick was innocent. It was a frustrating feeling.

That frustration stayed with her the rest of the day, and by Sunday it had reached an annoying level. The overcast skies had hung around all day Saturday, but now the clouds had blown on out, leaving an almost cold but clear and sunny day.

"Do you have any plans for today?" Phyllis asked Sam later that morning as they ate breakfast in the kitchen.

"Figured I'd watch the Cowboys lose to a team they ought to beat or win a game they ought to lose. I forget who they're playin', so I don't know which it'll be today. Why? If you've got somethin' better in mind, I'm open to suggestions."

"I want to go back out to the fair."

Carolyn was standing at the counter, waiting for some toast to pop up from the toaster. She looked over her shoulder and said, "I don't. I've had enough of the traffic and the crowds. I knew there had to be a good reason I don't go to the state fair very often."

"I don't figure Phyllis wants to go for the fair itself," Sam said. "She's got something else in mind. Like solving that murder." He leaned forward. "That's it, isn't it? You've figured it out, and now you just have to confirm your deductions."

Phyllis smiled and shook her head. "I wish that were true. I don't have any more idea who killed Joye Jameson than I did the moment she collapsed."

"Well, that won't last long, I'll bet."

Phyllis wasn't so sure, but she was still a long way from giving up. Her determination to uncover the truth had come in handy many times before, and she told herself that this case wouldn't be any different.

Eve and Peggy didn't want to go back to the fair, either. Phyllis didn't blame them. They had already seen everything they wanted to see, and a person could only eat so many deep-fried foods. Phyllis felt bad about dragging Sam back down to Fair Park, and she said as much as they were driving along North Central Expressway.

"Aw, I don't mind," he told her. "I know you don't like drivin' over here in Dallas, and I sure don't like you goin' out and investigatin' by yourself."

"Yes, that's nearly gotten me in trouble a few times, hasn't it? Or it would have if you hadn't shown up when you did."

"Told you all along, you're the brains and I'm the brawn of this outfit."

"Don't underestimate your brains, Sam. I think it takes both of us to figure these things out."

He glanced over at her and nodded. "We make a good team, all right."

Something about his voice caught Phyllis's attention. From time to time in the past, they had talked about getting married, but the discussion had never reached serious levels. The thing of it was, she was very comfortable with what they had, and after being happily married to Kenny for so long, she wasn't sure she ever wanted to tie the knot again. And although he had never come right out and said it, she had gotten the feeling that Sam felt the same way. Then Eve had gotten married and that hadn't worked out well, so out of consideration for her friend's feelings, Phyllis certainly hadn't wanted to take that plunge herself, and over time the whole idea had sort of . . . faded away. She hoped it wasn't resurfacing now, because she didn't want to face it.

Sometimes it was easier to solve murders, she thought, than it was to untangle the mysteries of the human heart.

Chapter 28

"We're gettin' our money's worth out of those season passes we bought online before comin' over here," Sam commented as they walked through the fair's main gate. "If we'd had to buy new tickets every day, the price would've really added up by now."

"Well, I didn't know we'd be coming here *quite* so often," Phyllis said, "but it seemed like a good idea since you and I were entering contests on different days."

Even on a Sunday during football season, the fairgrounds were busy. Phyllis and Sam walked past the giant figure of Big Tex, where people were taking the usual pictures of their families in front of the towering statue, and headed for the Creative Arts Building.

Phyllis couldn't have said exactly what she hoped to find there, but she might see something that would jog her thought processes into action.

On the way, they passed a massive RV parked outside the

building. A door in the side of the vehicle opened as they went by, and a familiar figure stepped out. Phyllis recognized him as Charlie Farrar, the director of *The Joye of Cooking*.

Everybody on the show referred to "the truck," where most of the technical equipment was located, along with the production office. Phyllis realized now that it wasn't a truck at all, but rather this big recreational vehicle. The term was probably a holdover from the days when actual trucks had been used to fill those roles.

She stopped and said, "Hello, Mr. Farrar."

The director paused and looked baffled for a second, but then recognition dawned on his face. "Mrs. Newsom," he said. "What are you doing here?"

Phyllis decided not to say anything about how she was working with David Miller to try to clear Bailey's name. "Just taking another look around. I'm still upset about what happened the other day."

"I'm not surprised," Farrar said. "We all feel that way. It was a tragic loss."

Phyllis remembered what Bailey had said about how Joye would lose her temper with Farrar over any camera angles she didn't like when she watched the tapes of the episodes. That didn't really seem like enough of a motive for killing someone, but you could never tell how people might react to things. Sometimes even the smallest incident was enough to set a person on a road that eventually led to murder.

Because of that, she asked a question to which she had already figured out the answer. "Is this what they call the production truck?" She waved a hand toward the RV.

"That's right. This is where all the technical magic happens."

"I'm surprised you're out here today. Aren't the broadcasts from the state fair over?"

"Yeah, we were only gonna be here a week, even before . . . well, you know what happened," Farrar said. "I was just doing some housekeeping. Backing up files, updating logs, things like that. Securing everything for the trip back to L.A." He paused. "After what happened, I was afraid for a while that the cops wouldn't let us leave, but then . . . well . . ."

"Once Ms. Broderick was arrested, the rest of you were free to leave town."

Nodding, Farrar said, "Yeah, that's pretty much the size of it. I feel really bad for Bailey and all, but I didn't want to be stuck here in Dallas, either. I'm sure we'll have to come back for the trial, but who knows when that'll be."

Sam asked, "What's gonna happen with the show now?"

"I wish I knew. Reed's been talking nonstop to the execs, trying to figure it out. We've got reruns slated for this week, but after that . . ." Farrar shrugged. "Your guess is as good as mine, friend. I wouldn't be surprised if they shut down production permanently."

"You mean cancel the show?" Phyllis asked.

"Yeah. That'll put some people out of jobs, including me. It's not like it'll be the first time, though. That's one thing about this business. No job lasts forever. Sooner or later everybody has to scrounge up more work. Luckily I have a couple of Emmys on my shelf at home. I'll be able to line up something else if it comes to that."

"I hope you're right," Phyllis said. "This may be out of

line, but . . . would you mind letting us take a peek in there? I've never seen the inside of a television production truck before."

Farrar laughed. "It's not like it's that interesting."

"Not to you, maybe, but it's all new to me."

"Well, sure, I can understand that. And I've got a few minutes." He took some keys out of his pocket. "But it'll have to be quick."

"You keep it locked up all the time?" Phyllis asked as Farrar inserted one of the keys in the door he had used.

"Have to. There's a lot of expensive equipment inside." Farrar opened the door. "Watch your step when you come in."

Phyllis climbed the portable steps that had been set down beside the RV. Sam followed her. They entered something that looked like the control center at NASA, at least to Phyllis's eye. There were a lot of monitor screens, computer keyboards, consoles full of dials and switches and levers and gauges.

The same thought must have gone through Sam's mind, because he said, "Looks like you could launch a rocket from in here."

"Well, we can communicate with satellites, but no rocket launches," Farrar said. "Do you want me to try to explain all the equipment to you?"

"That's not necessary," Phyllis told him. "In fact, just thinking about what all of it must do sort of makes my head hurt. I'm not that technologically inclined. But it certainly looks impressive."

Farrar pointed to the screens in front of one of the consoles. "The main thing is that each of those screens is fed by one of the cameras. That's where I sit and switch between them. That determines how they move and which shot goes out on the broadcast."

"You talk to the cameramen over headphones?" Sam asked.

"Yep."

Phyllis said, "That must be a stressful job, keeping track of all that. Like an air traffic controller."

"It can get pretty hectic. But I'm used to it, and hey, not to be overly modest, I'm good at what I do."

"And you have the Emmys to prove it."

Farrar grinned. "Yeah."

"What about the production office? It's in here, too, isn't it?"

"Yeah, in the back. But I can't let you look in there."

"Oh? Is it top secret?"

"Not really, but I don't have the key," Farrar said. "Reed and Bailey are the only ones who do. Oh, and Joye had one, too, of course. Joye went wherever she wanted to, whenever she wanted to."

And from the tone of the director's voice, it was clear to Phyllis that there was no love lost between Farrar and Joye, either.

"I'll bet you had to turn over tapes of all this past week's shows to the police," she said.

"That's right. Although we don't actually use tapes anymore. It's all digital now, stored on hard drives. We burned DVDs for the cops. It's funny, though, how people still use the word *tape* when they're talking about recording TV. Habit, I guess, because we used videotape for so long."

"Habits are hard to break," Phyllis agreed.

"If there's anything else you'd like to see . . ."

"Oh, no, we've taken up enough of your time, Mr. Farrar. Thank you for showing us around."

"Glad to," Farrar said. He ushered them back outside the RV. "If I don't see you again, Mrs. Newsom, it was nice to meet you. Although, come to think of it, we probably will see each other again, won't we? At Bailey's trial, I mean."

"Yes, I suppose so," Phyllis said, although she hoped it never came to that. She wanted the real killer to be exposed long before the case against Bailey ever came to trial.

As they walked away from the RV and headed toward the entrance of the Creative Arts Building again, Sam said quietly, "You weren't really interested in all that TV equipment, were you?"

"No, but it did look impressive, didn't it? I wanted to find out more about the production office."

"Where some of those injector pens are kept," Sam said. "But the one Bailey used came from Joye's dressin' room."

"Yes, but if they were tampered with, the killer had to get hold of the ones he doctored up somehow. He could have taken some of them from the production office, removed the epinephrine, and replaced it with peanut oil, then switched them with the ones in the dressing room."

"By *him*, you mean . . ."

"Reed Hayes had a key to the production office," Phyllis said. "And he had a motive for getting rid of Joye, as well as a possible reason for wanting to frame Bailey."

"Like that lawyer fella would say, that's a good theory. We've got plenty of 'em."

"And no proof for any of them," Phyllis said with a sigh. "I know."

They entered the building. Only a few contests would be held in the hall today, and they wouldn't take place until that afternoon, so the place wasn't very crowded.

The sound of hammering drew Phyllis's attention. It was coming from the side of the hall where the broadcast set was located. Phyllis nodded toward it and said, "Let's go see what's going on over there."

"Sounds like somebody's either buildin' somethin' or tearin' it down," Sam said.

Phyllis remembered what Bailey had said about how the set could be broken down into components and transported from location to location, so she wasn't surprised to see that that was exactly what was happening. Half a dozen workmen were busy disassembling the kitchen, which wasn't nearly as sturdy as it appeared to be on TV. Everything was built of thin plywood so that it wouldn't weigh much.

Another familiar figure stood nearby, watching the activity. Phyllis was a little surprised to see Chet Murdock, although she realized there was no reason for her to feel that way. The fair had security guards on duty around the clock, she was sure, and she didn't know what Chet's schedule was.

"Hey, there, Mrs. Newsom," he greeted her. "I didn't expect to see you back here."

"I know." Phyllis smiled. "I didn't really expect to come back, either. I guess I just wanted to revisit the site of my one brush with fame. Or infamy, rather, as it turned out."

"What happened wasn't your fault," Chet said. "Everybody knows that."

"Not everybody. I'll bet some people who saw the part of

the show that aired will always think of me as the lady who cooked the fatal funnel cake."

"Well, you can't worry about them," Chet told her.

"Has Mr. Hayes been here today?"

"He came by a while ago to check on the carpenters. He may still be around somewhere. I don't know. Do you need to talk to him?"

"No, not really. What about Gloria Kimball?"

"Who? Oh, the local TV lady. Haven't seen her."

Phyllis nodded. She hadn't really expected Gloria to be around. Of the two main suspects in Joye's murder, Phyllis believed that Reed Hayes was much more likely to be the killer. And the fact that he had been here while the set was being disassembled could be taken to mean that he was checking to make sure that all his tracks were covered.

That was a real reach, Phyllis told herself. Supervising the work today would be part of Hayes's job as the producer. She didn't need to start inventing things to point to his guilt.

"I'm sure you'll be sorry to see them go," she said to Chet. "I remember you said you're a big fan of cooking shows."

"Yeah, but this one didn't turn out very well. What a tragedy. And they should've been able to prevent it. I mean, they knew Ms. Jameson had a bad reaction before. Somebody should have double-checked everything so they wouldn't have a repeat of what happened in New Orleans. You'd think they would have learned their lesson."

"I know."

"But I guess the person responsible for checking things is the one they arrested," Chet said with a sigh. "There's a big difference between murder and an accident."

"That's true. What do you think, Chet? Do you believe that Miss Broderick murdered Ms. Jameson?"

"Well, the cops wouldn't have arrested her if they didn't think so, would they? I sure don't know any more than them. As a fan of the show, I just hate to see things end this way. I don't see how they can carry on, though." Chet brightened a little. "But maybe they'll launch a whole new show, get some new blood in there."

"I'm sure they will," Phyllis said. "There's too much money involved just to abandon everything. They'll find someone else to be their star."

"But it won't be Bailey Broderick," Chet said.

"No," Phyllis agreed, "right now it looks like it won't be Bailey Broderick."

Chapter 29

With the broadcast set being taken down, soon there wouldn't be anything left here to see, Phyllis thought as she and Sam said good-bye to Chet Murdock. They were about to walk away when a couple of workers lowered a section of what had been the back wall of the "kitchen" so that it could be carried out and loaded. That allowed Phyllis to look straight through into what had been the backstage region. The partitioned-off area that had served as Joye Jameson's dressing room was plainly visible with the wall down.

Phyllis turned to the security guard again and said, "Do you mind if we go back there, Chet?"

"Want to take one last look around before it all goes away, eh?" Chet shrugged. "Sure, go ahead. There's not much left. The cops already cleared out all of Ms. Jameson's things. I guess they considered them evidence."

"Were you ever back there?"

Chet's eyebrows rose. "You mean in Joye Jameson's dressing room? No, ma'am!"

"I didn't mean anything improper—"

"No, no, I didn't figure you did. It's just that to me, well, she was like a sports hero would be to a lot of guys. You know? That's why I meant it would have been a real honor to visit her in her dressing room."

"I understand," Phyllis said. "Who did go in there while you were around?"

Chet frowned. "Well, Ms. Broderick, of course. And Mr. Hayes. The two of them were in there more than anybody except Ms. Jameson herself. Sometimes Mr. Farrar, the director, but not very often. And that guy Hank, the cameraman. I heard him tell somebody that she liked to go over the way she wanted the show to be shot, which didn't always agree with what Mr. Farrar wanted."

"What about makeup artists, hairstylists, people like that?"

"Eh, not really. I'm pretty sure Ms. Jameson did her own hair and makeup. That was part of the whole lifestyle thing, you know. It wasn't just about cooking, even though that was the show's main focus."

"You really were a fan, weren't you?"

"Yes, ma'am," Chet said. "That's why it's been hard to accept that she's gone."

Phyllis and Sam walked around the stage, staying out of the workers' way, and stepped up to the door of the dressing room. It was open. Nothing was inside except an empty clothes rack where Joye's wardrobe would have been hung up, a couple of metal folding chairs, and a dressing table with a lighted mirror mounted on the wall above it.

Phyllis was sure the police forensics team had swept the room by now, or else it would have been marked off. She said to Sam, "Keep an eye out."

"You gonna do something clandestine?" he asked.

"Maybe."

She walked over to the dressing table and pulled out the drawer underneath it where cosmetics would be kept. That was also the most likely place in the room for Joye's pens to be kept, Phyllis thought. The drawer was empty now.

"Phyllis," Sam said from the doorway.

She looked around quickly. "What is it? Is someone coming?"

"No, but you might want to come take a look at this."

She joined him at the door. He nodded toward the far side of the area where the show had been broadcast. Standing over there, partially concealed by a piece of wall that was still upright, was Reed Hayes. It appeared he was talking to someone, and judging by the grim, intense expression on his face and the way he jerked his hand in a curt gesture, he seemed angry. Phyllis couldn't see whomever he was talking to.

Then Hayes's shoulders slumped slightly, as if he were giving in to the demands of the other person in the conversation. He nodded and said something else, then turned and stalked away.

"Who do you think he was arguin' with?" Sam asked.

"I don't know," Phyllis said, "but maybe we can find out."

She started quickly toward the piece of set wall. By the time she reached it and peeked around the corner, though, no one was there. She spotted Chet Murdock talking to some fair visitors who must have stopped to ask him a question and hurried over to him.

"Chet, did you see Reed Hayes talking to someone just now?" Phyllis asked.

"What?" Chet said as he turned away from the tourists he'd been talking to. "Mr. Hayes? Yeah, maybe. I wasn't really paying attention, but it seems like . . . yeah, he was talking to some woman, over there by the set."

"Gloria Kimball?"

Chet shook his head. "No, I don't think so. Like I said, I didn't look that close, but I think this woman had red hair. I don't recall seeing her around before, but she might have been one of the crew. A makeup lady or something."

"All right, thanks."

Phyllis couldn't help frowning. Hayes might have been upset for any one of a hundred different reasons, but Phyllis was still trying to link him up with Joye's murder. The redhead was a wild card, though. Phyllis had no idea who she was or how she fit into the case.

"Is everything all right, Mrs. Newsom?" Chet asked. "You look worried."

"I'm just trying to fit things together in my head," Phyllis said, "and they don't want to go."

"Like a jigsaw puzzle missing some pieces."

"Exactly."

Chet shrugged. "When that happens, sometimes you just have to put it back in the box and forget about it."

"I know," Phyllis said with a sigh.

The problem with that was that if she put this case back in the box, as Chet phrased it, then there was a good chance Bailey Broderick would be wrongly convicted of murder.

Phyllis's cell phone rang while she and Sam were on their way back to Peggy's house.

"Mrs. Newsom, this is David Miller," the defense attorney said when she answered. "How are you today?"

"All right, I suppose," she told him. "Sam and I have been down to Fair Park to take one more look around. They're taking down the broadcast set in the Creative Arts Building. By this time tomorrow, the rest of the people involved with *The Joye of Cooking* will be on their way back to California."

And with them would go any realistic chance of her figuring out who killed Joye Jameson, she thought.

"I know," Miller said. "There's no reason to hold them here now that an arrest has been made. Did you find out anything?"

"Not really," Phyllis said. She felt an uncomfortable stirring in the back of her brain, as if she had seen or heard something important and just failed to recognize it.

The feeling was a familiar one. She had experienced it a number of times before, when she reached a point where her investigations were at a crossroads, where she faced either success or failure, depending on how she was able to piece everything together. Always before she had succeeded . . . but she had a very real worry that this time that streak might be coming to an end.

"Well, I've found out a few things."

"I'm glad, but I thought you said you wouldn't be able to get any more information out of the district attorney's office until Monday."

"This didn't come from the DA's office," Miller said. "I have contacts in other places, too, contacts that I've carefully cultivated over the years."

Paid off, in other words, Phyllis thought. She couldn't

blame Miller for that. Some of his actions probably stretched the boundaries of the law, but he was fighting for the best interests of his clients.

Miller went on, "This tip came from someone in the forensics lab. That autoinjector Ms. Broderick used *did* contain peanut oil, just like we speculated. Whoever tampered with it really did want to make sure Joye Jameson died. Overkill, so to speak."

"That's a terrible way to put it," Phyllis told him. "Accurate, though."

"Yes, and it's a good thing the killer took that extra step. Good for him, that is, but not for anyone else. The concentration of peanut oil in the funnel cake was small enough that while it was sufficient to trigger an allergic reaction, it probably wouldn't have killed her. If the pen had contained epinephrine like it was supposed to, it definitely would have saved her life."

"So the pen was the actual murder weapon, just like we thought, not the funnel cake."

Sam looked over at Phyllis when she said that. He nodded, as if he had been convinced of that all along. She appreciated his confidence in her.

"That's right," Miller said. "Here's the other thing I found out. There were no fingerprints on the pen except for Bailey's."

"Well, that's no surprise. The killer wiped off the pens he tampered with before he switched them out with the ones in the dressing room. What about the pens that were still in the dressing room? Were they doctored with peanut oil, too?"

"My source didn't know that, but it seems pretty likely under the circumstances. We're dealing with a really cunning killer here. Otherwise he wouldn't have gone to the extra trouble of switching out the cooking oil *and* tampering with the pens. That's pretty obsessive behavior, but like I said, it paid off for him."

Phyllis's eyes narrowed. They weren't far from the exit for Mockingbird Lane now, and that would take them back to Peggy's house. She said, "Mr. Miller, I have to go. Was there anything else you found out?"

"No, and the information doesn't really help us that much. It just confirms what we already suspected. But I wanted to let you know anyway."

"I'll talk to you later, then," Phyllis said. She broke the connection and slipped the phone back in her purse. "Sam, would you mind turning around?"

He took his foot off the gas and said, "No, not at all. Did you think of somewhere else you need to go?"

"I need to go back to the fair."

He looked over at her, and he couldn't keep the excitement out of his voice as he said, "You really have figured it out this time, haven't you?"

"No, but I thought of a different way of looking at it," Phyllis said. "And I hope now I can see all the pieces that will lead us to a killer."

Chapter 30

On the way back to the fairgrounds, Phyllis turned the theory over and over in her head. She thought back to the information she had gleaned from all the websites she had read about Joye Jameson, from the straightforward fan sites to the glitzier, trashier celebrity gossip sites. One thing was conspicuously absent from all of them. By itself that absence didn't mean much, but looking at it in the context of the idea that had come to her, it could be important.

She could tell that Sam was intensely curious about what she had figured out, but he didn't want to ask questions and break her concentration. When she had gone over everything in her mind, she said, "That was Mr. Miller on the phone. He got some information from a source of his in the crime lab."

"Somebody he bribed?"

"That's the impression I got," Phyllis said. "I don't really care about that. What's important is that we have confirmation now about the injector Bailey used to inject Joye Jameson. It had peanut oil in it, instead of epinephrine."

"Well, other than knowin' for sure, I don't see how that helps much," Sam said. "You already had a hunch that must've been what happened."

"Yes, but Mr. Miller made some comment about how it was overkill, switching out the corn oil for peanut oil and then loading that pen with peanut oil, too. He said it was lucky for the murderer—but for no one else—that both methods were used, because there wasn't enough peanut oil in the funnel cake to have killed Joye, especially if the pen hadn't been tampered with."

Sam thought about it for a moment and then shook his head. "I'm still not gettin' it," he said.

"Mr. Miller assumed—and we have been, too—that the person who switched out the cooking oil was the same person who tampered with the pens."

"Yeah," Sam said. "Makes sense, doesn't it?"

"It does," Phyllis said. "But it makes even more sense if *two different people* were responsible for those things."

Sam looked over at her again, his eyes widening with the realization that she was right.

"You should probably watch the road," Phyllis reminded him gently.

"Yeah," he said, putting his eyes back on the freeway and the traffic in front of them. "That changes everything if you've got two would-be murderers instead of one."

"I'm wondering if the person who switched the cooking oil didn't intend to kill Joye. Maybe he just wanted to make her sick."

"Why would anybody do that?"

"Well, think about what happened as soon as Joye had that allergic reaction."

"Bailey jumped in right away with that pen to save her life."

Phyllis nodded. "And unwittingly wound up killing her instead. But if the pen hadn't been tampered with, she would have saved Joye's life. She would have been hailed as a hero. And if Joye had to take some time off because of it, who would step in and take her place on the show?"

"Bailey would have . . . just like Joye took over for Gloria Kimball. And who knows if she ever would've given the job back? It's like Lou Gehrig and Wally Pipp all over again!"

Phyllis shook her head. "Lou Gehrig the baseball player? *The Pride of the Yankees*? What in the world does he have to do with this?"

"Wally Pipp's the guy Gehrig filled in for at first base one day. Twenty-one hundred and some-odd consecutive games later, Gehrig was still playin' first base and everybody had forgotten about poor ol' Wally Pipp, the guy whose place he took. Same thing happened with Joye and Gloria Kimball, and now it might've happened again with Bailey and Joye."

"That's exactly my point, although I probably never would have thought of the baseball analogy."

Sam said, "But wait a minute. It sounds to me like you're makin' a case for Bailey bein' the one who replaced the corn oil with peanut oil. She's the one who stood to gain from it."

"No, I still don't believe that's what happened. She was too shocked when Joye collapsed. She didn't know about the peanut oil. But whoever made the switch could have done it in a misguided attempt to help Bailey become a star."

Sam nodded slowly. "I can think of two fellas who might fit that description."

"So can I. Hank Squires and Reed Hayes. Both of them were around the set all the time, so no one would think it was

odd for them to be there. Both of them were romantically involved with Bailey, so either might have tried to do something
to help her career. Something short of murder, although they
were playing awfully fast and loose with Joye's life. They
couldn't be absolutely sure the peanut oil in the funnel cake
wouldn't cause a severe enough reaction to kill her . . . but
they were counting on Bailey being right there with an injector to save her, either way."

"If the pen had worked," Sam said, "there probably
wouldn't have been any real investigation. The whole thing
would've been written off as an accident that almost had a
tragic result. The cops would never have gotten involved and
tested all the evidence."

"That's the way I see it," Phyllis agreed.

"Would Hayes have done such a thing if he knew that
Bailey was cheatin' on him with Hank?"

"I don't know," Phyllis replied honestly. "He may not have
known about that. He might have set up the business with the
cooking oil just to give Bailey a shot at being a star, and get
back at Joye a little for some of the trouble she had caused him
over the contract negotiations. He could have done it to show
Joye how easy it would be to replace her and to make her come
down on the salary she was demanding. Or if he did know
about Bailey and Hank, he could have come up with the idea
of making Joye sick in an effort to win Bailey back. If he told
her that he was responsible for her chance to take over the
show, he might think she would be grateful enough to him to
end the affair with Hank."

Sam shook his head. "Sounds like sort of a harebrained
scheme to me."

"Unfortunately, once someone comes to the decision to take such drastic action, their plans can turn harebrained in a hurry."

He laughed. "Yeah, we've seen that happen more than once, haven't we? But what about the pen? How in the world did somebody come up with that, and how does it tie in with the rest of what happened?"

"Here's the way I have it figured," Phyllis said. "Whoever tampered with the pen had to know that the cooking oil had been switched. Otherwise there wouldn't have been any way of him knowing that one of the pens was going to be used. He must have seen the switch take place and figured out why someone would want to replace corn oil with peanut oil. Knowing that Joye would take a bite of the funnel cake and have a reaction to the peanut oil, he also knew that Bailey would inject her with the pen. By tampering with the pen, not only did he deny Joye the epinephrine she needed to save her life; he also made sure the reaction she suffered would be severe enough to kill her."

"Who would do a thing like that, and why?" Sam wanted to know.

"I'm not positive yet, although I have a pretty good idea."

"And how could he be sure that Joye would take a bite of the funnel cake?"

"Because she always does," Phyllis said. "Or rather, did. Anytime she and a guest prepared anything, Joye always sampled it."

Sam nodded in understanding. "And anybody connected with the show would know that."

"I don't see how they could help but know it."

"So now we're lookin' for two fellas instead of just one. Who do you think swapped out the cookin' oil, Hank or Hayes?"

"Remember when we saw Hayes arguing with someone earlier today?" Phyllis asked.

"Yeah. Although we don't know for sure he was arguin'. Looked like it, though."

"Yes, it did. I'm convinced he was talking to the person who tampered with the pens."

"My head's startin' to hurt," Sam said. "Now you're sayin' that the two of them are workin' together?"

"Not at all. I think Hayes switched the cooking oil, and the other man saw him and decided to kill Joye by tampering with the pens. But think about it . . . at this point, Hayes doesn't know there was anything wrong with the pens."

"So he thinks what *he* did was responsible for killin' Joye!" Sam nodded emphatically. "So the real killer not only gets away with murder; he turns around and blackmails Hayes over a killin' that he didn't actually commit."

"That's what I believe is going on," Phyllis said. "It fits everything we know and answers all the questions about what happened."

Sam took the exit ramp from North Central onto Interstate 30. Fair Park was only a short distance to the east. They would be at the fairgrounds in a few minutes.

"So does Bailey Broderick really tie into this at all?" Sam asked. "Was the killer tryin' to frame her?"

"I don't think so. She was just a tool he used to get what he wanted."

"Blackmail money."

Phyllis didn't say anything. Sam didn't grasp everything about her theory yet, but she wasn't sure it was correct. There were still a few fuzzy areas. She hoped to find out soon if she was right.

Proving it was something else again. The killer had done a masterful job of manipulating everything, but Phyllis thought she saw one narrow opening she might be able to exploit.

The safest thing to do, she told herself, would be to call Detectives Morgan and Hunt and drop everything in their laps. But to their way of thinking, they had already arrested the killer. They wouldn't be interested in some theory that might well be, as Sam put it, harebrained, especially when there was nothing but some circumstantial evidence to support that theory. They wouldn't follow up on anything she told them. Phyllis was sure of it.

David Miller might be more receptive to her idea. She should have called him back, Phyllis thought.

But it was too late now. Sam took the exit for the fairgrounds, and there it was up ahead, crowded with people out for a pleasant Sunday afternoon in autumn.

And one killer.

Chapter 31

"Are we goin' back to the Creative Arts Building?" Sam asked as they entered Fair Park.

"That's right. I hope we can find the person we need to."

"Scene of our previous triumphs," Sam mused. "You, me, and Carolyn all brought home ribbons from there. Reckon anything like that will ever happen again?"

"It's not likely," Phyllis admitted. "But you never know. Anyway, I'm not sure I should be that proud of my funnel cakes. They played a part in getting a woman killed."

"Maybe, but you weren't to blame for that by any stretch of the imagination. And it doesn't make the funnel cakes any less delicious, either."

"I'm sure I'll be able to look at it like that . . . someday," Phyllis said.

They were walking past the Embarcadero Building and approaching the Creative Arts Building when Sam said, "Hold on. Isn't that Hayes over yonder?"

Phyllis stopped and looked where Sam nodded. Sure enough, Reed Hayes was walking toward the building from a different direction. He strode along rapidly, seemingly distracted by something.

He had every reason to be distracted, Phyllis thought, if it was his scheme that had wound up contributing to Joye Jameson's murder.

Hayes wasn't going into the building, Phyllis realized a moment later. He veered off the path he'd been following and went toward the the big RV that was still parked on the side of the road, the satellite dish on its roof pointed toward the heavens. When the producer reached it, he climbed the steps, unlocked the door, and went inside.

"We gonna go talk to him?" Sam asked.

"Wait," Phyllis said, her voice tense. "Maybe he's meeting the person who's blackmailing him."

"Charlie Farrar, right? He had a reason for wantin' to get rid of Joye, what with all the trouble she'd given him about his directin'. And the blackmail money he'd get from Hayes would help tide him over until he got one of those other jobs he was talkin' about when we were here earlier."

"How do you figure it has to be Farrar?" Phyllis asked. She was genuinely interested. She wanted to know Sam's reasoning so she could compare it with her own.

"Well, the killer's got to be somebody who was around the show a lot, or else he wouldn't have had the opportunity to see Hayes switchin' the cooking oil. And he had to know *why* Hayes was makin' that switch. He had to know that the peanut oil would cause Joye to have a bad allergic reaction. Otherwise there wouldn't have been any point to the whole thing."

"That's right," Phyllis agreed.

"What I don't know," Sam went on, "is just how common the knowledge of Joye's allergy really was. I don't recall hearin' anything about it before all this trouble came up, but then, I didn't even know who Joye Jameson was until not that long ago."

"It wasn't common knowledge," Phyllis told him. "That's one thing that helped me narrow it down. Remember, I did a lot of Internet research on Joye, and not one time did I read anything about her being allergic to peanuts, not on any of the websites. I think Hayes and everyone else involved in the show kept that covered up, probably at Joye's insistence. She probably thought it wouldn't look good for a cooking guru like her to have any sort of food allergy."

"I don't reckon any of her viewers would have held that against her," Sam said with a frown.

"Probably not. But image is everything in show business, and Joye didn't want to do anything to risk damaging hers. We already know that she was something of a control freak. That would fit right in with her making sure the allergy remained a secret."

"Yep, I suppose you're right. Which brings us right back around to the fact that the killer has to be somebody involved with the show, or else he wouldn't have known about it." Sam's frown deepened. "I don't guess it'd have to be Farrar, would it? There are more than a dozen other people who came here from California for these remote broadcasts. Could be any one of 'em. So unless we catch the fella tryin' to blackmail Hayes . . ."

"That's why we're here," Phyllis said. "Earlier, Hayes

looked like he gave in to whoever he was talking to. He's going to meet with the killer again to finalize the deal."

"How do you know that?"

Phyllis nodded toward the Creative Arts Building. "Because here he comes now."

"The killer?" Sam's eyes widened as he searched the crowd. Quite a few people were moving along the walks. "Are you sure? I don't see any members of the crew. But there's that guard fella. Maybe we'd better go get him so he can help us corral the killer."

"That won't work," Phyllis said, "because Chet Murdock *is* the killer."

Sam stared at her in disbelief.

"Watch where he goes," Phyllis went on.

Chet walked straight to the RV, paused at the bottom of the steps, looked around as if to see whether the coast was clear, climbed them, and knocked on the door. A couple of seconds later, it opened. Phyllis caught a glimpse of Reed Hayes. He moved back so the security guard could come in. Hayes closed the door.

"Man, I feel like slappin' my forehead and sayin' 'D'oh!' right about now," Sam said. "I forgot all about how Murdock told us about that mysterious redheaded woman Hayes was talkin' to. There wasn't any redheaded woman, was there?"

Phyllis shook her head. "That was just Chet's way of muddying up the waters. He was the one who approached Hayes with his demands, and he didn't want anybody finding out about that, so he tried to send us off on a false trail. When you stop and think about it, he was around the broadcast all the time this past week, just like the people who work for the show. There's more to it than that, though. Earlier today he mentioned the incident in New Orleans when Joye had an allergic reaction. That means he had to have been there, because that episode never aired. He couldn't have seen it on TV. There was nothing about it on any of the websites, either."

"So he was in the audience that day?"

"According to what Bailey told us, it wasn't even taped, because Joye's reaction happened backstage, just before they were ready to start. The audience wouldn't have known about it."

"So how did Murdock find out about it?"

"He had to be backstage. My hunch is that he was working as a security guard there, too."

Sam's eyes narrowed. "Sounds to me like the boy's a stalker."

"Or a really big fan."

"That's the same thing, sometimes, isn't it?"

Phyllis nodded. "It can be. There's more to it than that, though. If Chet was that big a fan of Joye, would he have killed her? I think he was obsessed with her, all right, but he was *jealous* of her. Of her success. You remember he told us—"

"He wants his own cookin' show. And if this one is canceled, the production company will likely replace it with a new one. If Hayes is the producer, then he could get Murdock a shot at bein' the new host."

"If Hayes believes that he's responsible for Joye's death and Chet is blackmailing him over that, he'll do everything in his power to make sure Chet gets the job. With Hayes's track record at producing successful shows, the executives will probably let him do whatever he wants."

Sam shook his head as if he couldn't wrap his mind around the situation. "All that, just to get on a dang TV show?"

"The lure of fame is strong. That's all some people really want in this world. They devote their lives to achieving it." Phyllis's voice hardened. "Most of them stop short of murder to get what they want, though."

"What do we do now?" Sam asked. "I'm convinced you're right about everything, Phyllis, but how do we prove it?"

"We have to confront Reed Hayes and make him understand that he's not responsible for Joye's death. He can come forward and confess to what he did without risking a murder charge."

"Yeah, but he'd still get in trouble for switchin' that cooking oil," Sam pointed out.

"I'm sure he could make a deal with the district attorney to avoid prosecution if he testified that Chet was blackmailing him. And that would open the door for the police to investigate Chet. I'm sure they'd find that he was in New Orleans at the time of that earlier incident and was in fact working as a guard during those broadcasts. That would create enough doubt to weaken the case against Bailey, and without a sure conviction there, I think Detective Morgan and Detective Hunt would do a more conscientious job of looking into the case. If they could prove somehow that Chet had gotten his hands on some injectors like the one that killed Joye, that might be enough to convince the detectives they arrested the wrong person."

"So we wait for Murdock to leave and then talk to Hayes?"

"I don't see what else we can do," Phyllis said.

They stood there tensely in front of the Embarcadero,

watching the RV. Public restrooms were nearby, and the steady stream of people going in and out of the facilities would make it difficult for Chet or Hayes to spot them, Phyllis hoped.

She felt a little sick inside at the thought of Chet Murdock being a killer. The apparently guileless young man had been friendly to her right from the start. But behind that pleasant exterior lurked a murderer. Phyllis was sure of that. It was the only explanation that answered all the questions and fit all the details of the case.

Another five minutes had gone by when the door of the RV opened. Chet came out first, followed by Hayes. The producer still looked upset and angry, but with a visible effort he controlled his emotions. After Hayes locked the door, the two men started to walk away together.

"Dang it," Sam said. "We need to get Hayes alone. We'll have to follow 'em."

Phyllis recognized someone else in the crowd moving along the path. Without pausing too long to think about what she was doing, she hurried forward, ignoring Sam's surprised exclamation behind her.

"Mr. Hayes," she said as she came toward the two men from the side. "Mr. Hayes, I need to talk to you."

Hayes stopped short, as did Chet Murdock. Alarm leaped into the guard's eyes as he turned to look at her, and Phyllis knew she was right about him. Hayes looked surprised, too, but more confused than worried.

"Mrs. Newsom," he said. "What can I do for you?" He had an undercurrent of impatience in his voice.

"It's a matter of what I can do for you," Phyllis said. "You can stop worrying about killing Joye Jameson. What you did wasn't responsible for her death." She leveled a finger at Chet. "Mr. Murdock here is really the one who murdered her and the one who's going to let Bailey Broderick be convicted for the crime."

Chapter 32

"What!"

The angry bellow came from Hank Squires, whom Phyllis had spotted a moment earlier coming toward them. The sight of Hank had prompted her to go ahead and confront Chet and Hayes now instead of waiting. Hank was only a few yards away, bulling his way through the crowd toward them.

Hayes looked as scared now as Chet did. He said, "I don't know what you're talking—"

"I know you substituted peanut oil for the corn oil," Phyllis rushed on, getting the words out as fast as she could. "But that's not what killed Joye. Chet tampered with the injectors and replaced the epinephrine with more peanut oil. That's what killed her. But you didn't know that, so he was able to blackmail you."

Chet forced a laugh. "I think you've gone crazy, Mrs. Newsom. I wouldn't do a thing like that. I loved Joye's show."

"You loved it so much you were working as a guard while

the show was in New Orleans a couple of years ago when Joye had another allergic reaction. No one knew about that except the people who were there that day, and yet you mentioned it to me just a little while ago."

Chet was still trying to smile, but now the expression was more of a stricken look. He said, "I . . . I . . ."

Hayes turned to look at him. The producer's face darkened with fury. "I knew you looked a little familiar the first time I saw you here in Dallas," he said. "And now I know why!"

Hank had reached them by now. He prodded a blunt finger against Hayes's chest hard enough to make the man take a step backward. "You tried to poison Joye?" he demanded.

"It wasn't poison," Hayes said. "It was just peanut oil. Anyway, he's the one responsible for her death, not me! You just heard Mrs. Newsom say so."

"You just stood by and let Bailey be arrested!" Hank's loud, angry voice was making the fairgoers veer around him now, giving him a wide berth as he confronted Hayes and Chet.

"Well, why wouldn't I?" Hayes said. "She was going to dump me anyway, the cheating bitch."

Hank roared furiously again and started to swing a punch at Hayes's head. Chet acted before the blow could land. He grabbed Hayes's arm and swung the producer against Hank, using him as a club. The two men's legs tangled together, and they fell to the sidewalk.

Chet turned and ran.

Sam pounded past Phyllis, giving chase. Phyllis cried, "Sam, no!" Sam could handle himself in a fight, but he would be no match for the burly security guard.

Sam didn't slow down. People along the sidewalk yelled

and scrambled out of Chet's way as he fled. Sam's long legs carried him swiftly after the killer. Phyllis hurried along behind them, unsure of what she would do if she caught up but unwilling to let Sam face this danger alone.

As it turned out, neither of them had to. Hank Squires had regained his feet and rumbled past Phyllis like a runaway freight train. He passed Sam as they rounded the corner into International Boulevard and the pursuit led toward Big Tex. Phyllis saw Chet throw a frantic glance over his shoulder and speed up, but Hank continued to bear down on him. When the gap had closed enough, the cameraman left his feet in a diving tackle that smashed into Chet's back and drove him off his feet.

Both men crashed to the ground in front of Big Tex, scattering the tourists who had been taking pictures and admiring the towering figure. "Howdy!" the mechanical voice boomed out as Hank and Chet struggled desperately. "Howdy!"

By the time Phyllis and Sam reached them, Hank had gotten the upper hand. He had Chet pinned on the ground facedown with a knee in the small of his back. Hank had pulled both of Chet's arms behind his back and held them so tightly that if Chet struggled too much he ran the risk of dislocating a shoulder.

"Hang on to him," Phyllis said. "I'll call the police."

More of the fair's security personnel came running up to find out what the commotion was, and seeing one of their own pinned on the ground, they started to grab Hank and haul him off.

"Stop!" Sam shouted. "He's a murderer!"

"They're crazy!" Chet cried. "They're all crazy! Help me, guys!"

Phyllis knew that if the other guards freed Chet, he might be able to slip off in the confusion. She said, "Hank, hang on to him, whatever you do."

Hank might not have had a chance to do that against such heavy odds, if a commanding voice hadn't ordered, "Everybody stay right where you are!" Phyllis looked over and saw Detectives Morgan and Hunt hurrying toward them. The officers had their guns drawn. The security guards backed off.

Phyllis was surprised to see Morgan and Hunt but very grateful for their timely arrival, which was explained a moment later when a breathless Reed Hayes came up. "I called them," he said. "I told them I wanted to confess. I just didn't say what I was confessing to."

"Somebody better do some fast explaining," Charlotte Morgan snapped.

Hayes pointed at Chet Murdock and said, "There's your killer right there. He tried to blackmail me, too. I'll tell you everything; just don't let Murdock get away."

Morgan winced. "This is going to be complicated, isn't it? I hate complicated cases." She glanced at Phyllis. "And you! Didn't I tell you to stay out of this?"

"It's a good thing for you that Phyllis is too stubborn to listen," Sam said with a grin. "Otherwise you might've sent an innocent woman to prison."

"I wouldn't have let that happen," Hayes said. "I would have spoken up before it came to that."

Phyllis would have liked to believe that. He was paying for Bailey's defense, after all. Maybe there was still some humanity in him, even if he was a Hollywood producer.

Al Hunt said, "Let's go somewhere quieter and sort this all

out." He put away his gun and cuffed Chet Murdock's hands behind his back. Hank lifted Chet to his feet. The two detectives started herding everyone away.

"Howdy, folks!" Big Tex said behind them.

"We should have gone with you," Carolyn said.

"Yeah, the five of us could've rounded up those bad guys," Peggy added. "We would've been your posse, Phyllis."

Eve said, "Those two police detectives showed up awfully quickly, didn't they?"

The five of them were back in the living room of Peggy's house later that day. Phyllis had explained everything to her friends. Now she answered Eve's question by saying, "Actually, they were already there at Fair Park, inside the Creative Arts Building. They knew everyone from the TV show would be heading back to California tomorrow, so they came out to take one last look around, just to make sure they hadn't overlooked any evidence. I must say, I'm a little surprised they went to that much trouble . . . but I'm glad they did. Chet might have gotten away if they hadn't."

"I'll bet he's lawyered up and not saying a word," Peggy said.

Phyllis shook her head. "Actually, he admitted to everything. He's not really a hardened criminal, just someone who let his ambition get the best of him."

"Sounds like a borderline sociopath to me," Carolyn said. "He wanted to be a star, so whatever he had to do to achieve that goal was all right in his mind."

"You're right about that," Phyllis said.

"So chalk up another murder case solved," Peggy said.

"Carolyn invited me to come visit you folks in Weatherford, but I'm not sure I want to, the way people wind up getting killed around you."

Carolyn made a disgusted sound and shook her head. "I think I can promise you, Peggy, that there won't be any murders if you come to see us."

"Can you? Can you really?"

Carolyn frowned and didn't say anything.

Her silence spoke volumes.

That evening, Phyllis was in the bedroom she was using, taking care of some last-minute packing, when Sam paused in the open doorway and leaned his shoulder against the jamb.

"It'll be good to get home again, won't it?" he said.

Phyllis nodded. "It certainly will. I've had enough of Dallas to last me for a while. A long time, in fact."

"Until next year's state fair, maybe?"

"I'm not sure I'm coming back to the fair."

"You're not gonna defend your funnel cake title? If you don't, that little jackwagon Silva's liable to win it."

"He's welcome to it," Phyllis said. "I just want to stay close to home from now on."

"Speakin' of home . . ." Sam's face grew more solemn. "When we get back, there's somethin' I want to ask you."

Phyllis felt a tingle of apprehension and swallowed hard. "Something important?"

"Well, yeah, I think it's pretty important."

She remembered some of the comments he had made recently that made her think he was contemplating a change in their relationship. She didn't want to face that, didn't want to deal with that sort of upheaval. The way she kept running into murder cases made her life unsettled enough without adding any other sort of emotional turmoil.

And yet she knew she couldn't ignore Sam's feelings. She cared about him too much for that. He had meant too much to her over the past few years, had brought a happiness and contentment back into her life that she had thought she would never feel again.

She took a deep breath and said, "Since you already brought it up, I think we should go ahead and discuss it now."

"It can wait—"

"You said you had a question for me. I might need some time to think about the answer, you know."

He nodded slowly and said, "I guess that's true. It wouldn't be fair for me to just spring it on you and expect you to say yes or no right away. You're right. You deserve a chance to think about it."

He came into the room. Phyllis faced him squarely, lifting her head slightly so that she could look into his eyes. He rested his hands on her shoulders, and as she felt the warmth and strength of his touch, she wondered what she was going to tell him.

Sam breathed in, let it back out, and said, "Phyllis, there's been something missin' for a while, and I think it's time to do somethin' about it. What I'd like to do . . . if it's all right with you . . . what I'd like to do is get a dog."

Recipes

Golden Buttermilk Pie

1 deep-dish pie shell
½ cup (1 stick) butter
1 cup granulated sugar
3 eggs
1 teaspoon vanilla extract
3 tablespoons all-purpose flour
Pinch of salt
1 cup buttermilk
½ teaspoon freshly grated nutmeg

Instructions

Preheat the oven to 400°F. Bake the empty deep-dish pie shell for 5 minutes. To keep the pie crust from bubbling, put a piece of parchment paper or aluminum foil large enough to cover the whole pie and add pie weights, or dried beans, or even clean coins can be used as pie weights. Allow the crust to cool.

Cream the butter and sugar together until light and fluffy. Add the eggs one at a time, beating well after each addition; then add the vanilla.

Sift the flour and salt together and add to the batter, alternating with the buttermilk; beat until smooth.

Pour the buttermilk filling into the lightly baked pie shell and sprinkle the grated nutmeg on top. Nutmeg can be grated on top of the pie if you can judge how much ½ a teaspoon is. Loosely cover the crust with strips of aluminum foil to keep it from burning. Bake for 10 minutes, reduce the heat to 350°F, and bake for 50–60 additional minutes.

The pie should turn a nice golden brown and a knife inserted should come out clean.

Let the pie cool to room temperature before cutting. Hot pies tend to crumble more.

Serves 6–8.

Maple Pecan Funnel Cake

3 eggs

¼ cup granulated sugar

2 cups milk

3⅓ cups all-purpose flour

½ teaspoon salt

2 teaspoons baking powder

1 cup finely chopped pecans

1 teaspoon maple extract

Vegetable oil for frying (Phyllis likes corn oil)

Maple syrup

Instructions

Beat the eggs and sugar together in a large bowl. Add the milk slowly, continuing to beat until incorporated. Add the flour, salt, and baking powder and beat until the batter is creamy. Stir in ½ cup of the pecans and the maple extract.

Pour 2 inches of oil into a large cast-iron pot. Heat to medium hot. Place a funnel cake metal ring in the middle of the pan; you'll use the ring to keep the batter from spreading out all the way to the edges of the pan.

Pour the batter into a funnel, using your finger to plug the hole. Make sure the funnel has a hole wide enough for the batter to go through without clogging. Test the funnel by letting the batter flow back into the bowl to see if it flows. If necessary, you can always use a cup with a spout, or even a plastic bag with a corner cut off.

When the oil is hot, put the filled funnel over the oil and remove your finger so the batter can come out. Move the funnel around to make designs.

Brown the batter until it's a golden color. Use tongs to remove the metal ring and turn the funnel cake. When the cake is brown on both sides, remove and drain well. Let the finished cake sit on a paper towel for a minute to remove even more of the oil, and then transfer it to a plate.

Top with a drizzle of maple syrup and the remaining ½ cup chopped pecans.

> Note: The pecans need to be chopped fine enough to get through the funnel easily. If you want a coarser nut to top the funnel cake, chop them separately.

Makes 6–8 funnel cakes.

Butterscotch Sandies

1 cup (2 sticks) butter, softened
½ cup granulated sugar
2½ cups all-purpose flour
1 teaspoon vanilla extract
½ cup finely chopped cashews
½ cup butterscotch chips

Instructions

Beat the butter and sugar until creamy. Gradually add the flour, beating just until blended. Stir in the vanilla, cashews, and butterscotch chips.

Divide the dough in half, and shape each portion into logs about a foot long. Wrap in parchment paper, cover with plastic wrap, and chill for 1 hour, until firm.

Preheat the oven to 325°F. Line a baking sheet with parchment paper. Cut the logs into ¼-inch-thick rounds and place ½ inch apart on the prepared baking sheet. Bake for 18–20 minutes, until lightly golden. Cool on the baking sheet for 5 minutes. Transfer to wire racks to cool completely.

Makes 7–8 dozen cookies.

Pumpkin Oatmeal Cookies

½ cup (1 stick) butter, softened

1 cup packed light brown sugar

1 cup granulated sugar

½ cup applesauce

1 cup pure pumpkin puree

1 large egg

1 teaspoon vanilla extract

2 cups all-purpose flour

1½ cups old-fashioned oats

1 teaspoon baking soda

2 teaspoons pumpkin pie spice

½ teaspoon salt

1 cup white chocolate chips

1 cup dried cranberries

Instructions

Preheat the oven to 350°F. Spray a half sheet pan with oil.

Beat the butter, brown sugar, and granulated sugar in a large mixing bowl until light and fluffy. Add the applesauce, pumpkin, egg, and vanilla; mix well.

Combine the flour, oats, baking soda, pumpkin pie spice, and salt in a medium bowl. Add the flour mixture to the pumpkin mixture; combine until all ingredients are incorporated. Fold in the white chocolate chips and dried cranberries.

Pour the batter into the half sheet pan.

Sam's Texas-Style Spam Sushi

2 cups sushi rice

2½ cups water

4 tablespoons rice vinegar

3 roasted-seaweed sheets

3 ounces cream cheese

1–2 tablespoons chopped green onion

2 slices bacon

1 (12-ounce) can Spam luncheon meat

1 avocado, sliced

Sliced jalapeño peppers

Instructions

Rinse the rice until the water is clear. Put the rice in a rice cooker. Add the water and stir. Turn on the rice cooker. When the rice cooker switches off (after 15–20 minutes), let the rice sit for at least 10 minutes. Transfer the cooked rice to a nonmetallic bowl. Add the rice vinegar and mix well.

Cut the seaweed sheets in thirds. You'll have a piece left over; put it back in the bag to use later.

Mix the cream cheese and green onion in a small bowl.

Fry the bacon in a large frying pan. Set the cooked bacon aside to use another time. Cut the Spam into 8 rectangular slices approximately ¼ inch thick. In the large frying pan with the bacon grease, fry the Spam slices until brown and slightly crispy. Remove from heat, drain on paper towels, and set aside. The grease will pop while the Spam is frying, so be careful.

Spread the cream cheese mixture evenly on the Spam slices.

Place some water in a small bowl to use as a sealer for the ends of the seaweed wrapper; set aside.

Place a cut sheet of seaweed on a plate. Position a sushi form on top of a sheet of the seaweed so the length of the form is in the middle of the seaweed. The form should be a little bigger than the slice of seaweed. Spread approximately ¼ cup cooked rice across the bottom of the form, on top of the seaweed. Press the rice down with the bottom of a spoon until the rice layer is ¼ inch thick.

Place a slice of Spam on top of the rice, with the cream cheese mixture on top. Layer sliced avocado and jalapeño peppers on top of the cream cheese mixture. Cover with an additional ¼ cup cooked rice; press until the rice layer is ¼ inch thick.

Remove the form by lifting it while pressing down on the layers inside. Fold one end of the seaweed over the rice and Spam layers and press lightly onto the rice. Wet the remaining end of the seaweed slightly with water, and then wrap it over the other piece of seaweed; press down. The seaweed wraps are a little smaller than the Spam and rice layers, so some of the filling will stick out past the seaweed on both sides. Repeat with the other 7 Spam slices. Serve hot.

Makes 8.

Note: You can buy a Spam *musubi* press or cut the bottom of an empty Spam container to make a sushi form. You can also make one out of cardboard cut to the size of a Spam container. It shouldn't have a top or bottom and needs to be just large enough for the Spam slice to fit inside.

Louisiana-Style Muffuletta

16-ounce jar pickled mixed vegetables

1 clove garlic, minced

1 tablespoon olive oil

1 loaf unsliced French bread

6 romaine lettuce leaves

3 ounces thinly sliced salami

3 ounces thinly sliced ham

3 ounces thinly sliced turkey

3 ounces thinly sliced provolone

3 ounces thinly sliced mozzarella

1 or 2 medium tomatoes, thinly sliced

Black pepper (optional)

¼ cup sliced black olives

Instructions

Drain the jar of pickled vegetables, reserving 2 tablespoons of the liquid. Chop the vegetables, removing any stems. In a medium bowl, mix the chopped vegetables, reserved liquid, garlic, and olive oil.

Split the bread horizontally.

Top the bread with the lettuce, meats, cheeses, and tomato; sprinkle with black pepper if desired. Mound the vegetable mixture on top of the tomato, and sprinkle with the black olive slices. Put the top of the bread over the black olives. To serve, cut into 6 portions.

Serves 6.

Note: If you want to give this sandwich a little Tex-Mex zing, add a few jalapeño peppers with the black olives.

Author's Note

The State Fair of Texas, held every fall in Dallas, is one of the oldest and biggest celebrations in Texas. The official website of the State Fair of Texas is www.bigtex.com, and it contains a wealth of information about the fair. I've taken a few minor liberties with the setting for dramatic purposes, but for the most part I've tried to paint an accurate picture of this annual get-together that draws millions of visitors every year.

One of the perils of writing fiction is that occasionally something unexpected happens in real life that affects your story. Just as I was finishing this book, an electrical short inside Big Tex caused this iconic figure to burn down to its metal framework. Following this catastrophe, State Fair of Texas officials immediately assured the public that Big Tex would be rebuilt, bigger and better than ever. I was able to take this into account while making the final revisions on the book, and it's my hope that if any of you decide to visit the fair in the future, Big Tex will be there to welcome you.

Just don't go with Phyllis Newsom and her friends. We all know how dangerous that can be.

Photo by James Reasoner

Livia J. Washburn has been a professional writer for more than twenty years. She received the Private Eye Writers of America Award and the American Mystery Award for her first mystery, *Wild Night*, written under the name L. J. Washburn, and she was nominated for a Spur Award by the Western Writers of America for a novel written with her husband, James Reasoner. Her short story "Panhandle Freight" was nominated for a Peacemaker Award by the Western Fictioneers. She lives with her husband in a small Texas town, where she is constantly experimenting with new recipes. Her two grown daughters are both teachers in her hometown, and she is very proud of them.

Don't miss any of the Fresh-Baked Mysteries

by

Livia J. Washburn

Read on for an excerpt from

Wedding Cake Killer

Available from Obsidian.

Christmas Eve

"Oh, my, look at all the cars," Phyllis said as Sam Fletcher drove his pickup along the block where they lived. "I didn't think people would start showing up this early. They've blocked off the driveway, Sam."

"Yeah, I see that," Sam said. "Tell you what. I'll stop in front of the house and you can get out and go on in. I'll find a place to park down the street and walk back."

"That's not fair. You live here, and these people don't."

"Yeah, but that means they won't be stayin'. They'll all leave when the shower's over. I can bring the pickup back down then."

"Well, I suppose so," Phyllis said. "I just hate to put you to any more trouble after everything that's already happened today."

"You mean that killer we caught?" Sam asked with a smile. "Or that you caught, is more like it. Heck, I'm gettin' used to that. How many times does this make?"

"Don't even think about it," Phyllis told him as a tiny shudder went through her. "I want to put all that behind us. This is Christmas Eve, after all, and it's Eve's bridal shower, too. I think that's plenty to keep us busy the rest of the day, don't you?"

"If you say so." Sam brought the pickup to a smooth stop in front of the big old two-story house he shared with Phyllis, Carolyn Wilbarger, and Eve Turner, two more retired teachers.

They wouldn't be sharing it with Eve for much longer, though. Another week and she and Roy Porter would be married. Eve and Roy planned to come back here to the house after their honeymoon and stay temporarily while they continued looking for a place of their own, but that wouldn't be the same.

But then, nothing ever stayed the same, Phyllis mused as she got out of the pickup. Like it or not, life-altering changes came along every few years. She had become a teacher, gotten married to Kenny, given birth to their son, Mike, continued teaching while they raised him into a fine young man, seen him marry and have a son of his own, retired . . .

And then Kenny had died, leaving her to rattle around alone in that big old house. Dolly Williamson, the former superintendent and a longtime friend, had suggested that Phyllis rent out the extra bedrooms to other retired teachers who were on their own, and once Phyllis had done that, she'd believed that from then on, life would settle down into a serene existence without the upheavals of youth.

Well, *that* hadn't worked out, had it?

People had come and gone in the house. Mattie Harris, one of Phyllis's oldest friends, had passed away. Sam Fletcher had moved in. Now Eve was getting married and moving out. That was inevitable, Phyllis supposed. Although she didn't know the details because Eve hadn't lived in Weatherford at the time, she was aware that her friend had been married several times. Really, Eve had been without a man in her life for longer than Phyllis had expected.

Then there were the murders . . .

But as she'd told Sam, she didn't want to think about that, so she didn't. As she stepped up onto the porch, she didn't allow herself to remember the body she had literally stumbled over there not that long ago. She didn't glance at the house next door, where she had found another body a few years earlier. And as she stepped into the house and saw all the people crowding into the living room, she told herself sternly that nobody was going to try to poison her guests at this get-together.

They'd better not, anyway.

Carolyn Wilbarger spotted Phyllis and quickly came over to her, smiling and nodding to some of the ladies along the way. Still smiling as she reached Phyllis, she said in a tight-lipped whisper, "Oh, my word. I didn't expect this many people."

Smiling as well, Phyllis replied, "Neither did I."

"When you called from the police station and said you didn't know how long you'd be, nobody had shown up yet. But then . . ." Carolyn shook her head. "That other business . . . ?"

"All settled," Phyllis told her. "I'll fill you in on the details later. Right now . . . well, this is Eve's day."

Eve certainly appeared to be enjoying it, too. She sat in the big armchair, beaming at the guests and the pile of presents that surrounded her. There had been some talk about how she shouldn't expect a bridal shower at her age and with numerous marriages in her past, but it was true that she had been living here with Phyllis for several years and didn't really have all the things she would need to set up housekeeping again. From the looks of it, after today she would.

The house was extravagantly decorated for Christmas because it had been part of the annual Jingle Bell Tour of Homes a couple of weeks earlier. Phyllis and Carolyn had added a few things to celebrate the upcoming wedding, including tables for the gifts covered in blue tablecloths with silver trim. They had decided to go with white roses since the cloths were blue and they looked great in the silver vases. Still, the theme remained overwhelmingly Christmasy. In a couple of days, when Christmas was over, they would take down all those decorations and start getting ready for the wedding, which would take place here on New Year's Eve.

Eve, Eve, Eve, Phyllis thought. There was no getting away from it.

"Phyllis!" Eve said, seeming to notice her for the first time. "Come here, dear."

Phyllis kept the smile on her face as she made her way across the crowded room to Eve, who stood up and hugged her.

"Thank you so much for this," Eve said. "I know you've had a lot of other things on your mind, but despite that you've given me the best bridal shower a girl could ever want!"

Phyllis patted her lightly on the back and said, "You're very welcome. I'm glad we were able to do this for you. We're all going to miss you once you've moved out."

"And I'm going to miss you, too," Eve said. She lowered

her voice. "I didn't expect this many people to be here. I put everyone I could think of on the guest list because I thought a lot of them wouldn't be able to come, what with it being Christmas Eve and all. But it looks like practically everyone showed up!"

"Yes," Phyllis said, "it does."

In fact, there were so many ladies in the room that it was starting to seem a little claustrophobic to her, as if they were sucking down all the air and she couldn't breathe. She knew that feeling was all in her head, but that didn't make it seem any less real.

"I think I should go out to the kitchen and check on things," she went on. "You just sit down and have a good time."

"Thank you, dear." Eve leaned closer and added, "I owe you. Big-time."

Phyllis waved that off and headed for the kitchen, motioning with a slight movement of her head for Carolyn to follow her.

When they were in the kitchen by themselves, with the door closed, both of them said, "Whew!" at the same time, then laughed at the identical expression.

"Refresh my memory," Phyllis said quietly. "Did even half of those people out there RSVP to let us know they were coming?"

"They most certainly did not," Carolyn said. "And it certainly would have helped if they had."

"But all too typical these days," Phyllis muttered as she looked at the trays of snacks spread out across the kitchen counters.

There were warm sweet bacon crackers fresh out of the

oven, nutty caramel pretzels, and cheddar garlic palmiers. Phyllis knew from the smell in the air that the stuffed mushrooms were warming in the oven. There was a zesty cheese ball softening on a decorative silver plate with a matching knife. And in the refrigerator, waiting to be brought out, was a tray filled with mini curried turkey croissant sandwiches. Enough food to feed an army, as Sam might say, but that was good because they practically had an army in the living room.

The back door opened, and Sam walked into the kitchen. "Hope it's all right I came around this way," he said. "I didn't particularly want to run the gauntlet out there."

"I don't blame you," Phyllis said. She frowned. "I just remembered . . . Weren't you and Roy supposed to go bowling this afternoon?"

Sam's eyes widened. He slapped himself lightly on the forehead and said, "D'oh! I forgot all about it, what with catchin' killers and all." He took his cell phone out of his pocket. "I'll call him right now and tell him I'm on my way."

"Yes, that would tend to distract a person," Carolyn said.

Sam grinned and waved as he went back out the door with his cell phone held to his ear.

"I'm glad Sam and Roy have become friends," Phyllis said. "I'm sure it's been tough on him, being in a strange town where he doesn't have any friends or family."

"He didn't put a single person on the guest list for the shower or the wedding," Carolyn said.

"I know. But he seems to be all right with it. As long as he's got Eve, I think he's happy."

"He should be. She's a fine woman. He's lucky to have her."

Phyllis smiled. Carolyn and Eve had squabbled quite a bit

over the years, but Phyllis knew that they really cared for each other. Carolyn could be a little on the prickly side sometimes. It had taken her more than a year to get used to the idea of Sam living in the house.

"What still needs to be done?" Phyllis asked, putting her mind back on the matters at hand.

"The chocolate chocolate chip cupcakes are already on the table along with some cookies and the vegetable and fruit tray, and the punch is in the punch bowl. Eve suggested that we spike it, but I vetoed that. The last thing we want in the living room is a bunch of tipsy teachers."

Phyllis laughed. She had to agree with that sentiment.

"Everything seems to be under control," she said. "We'll wait a while before we bring the rest of the food out. Eve wanted to play some games first and then open presents, so it'll be a while before anyone's ready to eat."

Carolyn's eyes narrowed. "I swear, if anyone brought any of those perverted gag gifts—"

"I'm sure everyone will be the soul of decorum," Phyllis said.

Actually, she wasn't sure of that. The retired teachers, the ones from the generation she and Carolyn and Eve belonged to, were all ladies, raised to observe the proprieties. But some of the younger ones, the ones who were still teaching . . . well, you couldn't ever be a hundred percent sure of what they might do.

But even so, the last thing she would have expected to hear as she and Carolyn started along the hall toward the living room was voices raised in anger.